FINDING PERFECT

ELLA MILES

You can get all of the above and more goodies here:
EllaMiles.com/freebooks

1

MILA

Life sucks.

Like really, really sucks. Trust me, I know. I've dealt with my fair share of tragedies. I've had my heart broken, dragged through the mud, and then stomped on. I've woken up hungry and slept under a bridge on the streets. I know what abuse feels like. I've seen, firsthand, how bad addiction can be. Death is a cold friend, instead of a stranger. Loss is all I've ever known.

That's why I have a plan for everything. I stick to a schedule for my day and my life. I know what I'm doing every minute of every day. I know what my next steps in life are. And that keeps me in control.

Chaos is when the worst happens. Tragedy lives in the craziness. I thrive in normal.

In ordinary.

In the expected.

I plan for every mistake, every tragedy, every misstep. That way I'm always prepared. I can handle anything because I've already thought of it first. I know how to bounce back and get my life on track in a second.

So why is today so hard?

Why am I not bouncing back?

Because five years ago today was the worst day of my life. I made the worst mistake, and I've been paying for it every day since.

I'm spiraling. I can feel the anxiety climbing into my chest and tightening until my lungs burn with each breath. My stomach is twisting in knots, and my head is pounding with an unshakable ache.

I need to plan. I need to find a solution and start implementing it.

But for once in my life, I don't want to think about my responsibilities. I want to feel free, if only for a few moments.

I roll the window down of my Subaru, the classic car all Denverites drive. It's cheap and gets the job done. I drive through the mountains, hoping the fresh air filled with aspen and pine trees will soothe my soul. The wind whips through the car too fast to have the window down, but I don't care. I need to feel the wind. It's the only thing keeping me from going into a full blown panic attack.

A man on a motorcycle rides my ass on the single lane road. I'm driving fast, but apparently not fast enough for the dipshit behind me.

The tiny smile I forced onto my lips earlier vanishes. I zoom around a curve faster than I should, and I feel out of control.

I *hate* it.

But Mr. Dangerous isn't driving fast enough. Driving around curves without guardrails isn't enough. He's driving so fast; one mistake could cause his motorcycle and my car to tumble down the side of the mountain. He's risking actual death.

I look for a space to pull off so he can go around me, but there are none. We are in the freaking mountains, on curvy road after curvy road. I'm driving ten miles over the speed limit as it is. I'm not going to let him bully me into driving faster.

I hear the rev of his engine, and the blast of heavy metal music from his motorcycle.

Can he be any more obnoxious?

I don't understand motorcycles. I don't understand the need to make life any more dangerous than it already is. The asshole isn't even wearing a helmet.

I shake my head and try to focus on the road in front of me, instead of the man behind me making me equal parts pissed and anxious. But I drive faster. Too fast. I can't help it. I barely stay in my lane around the next curve.

And I see the bicycler too late.

I slam on the brakes, praying I don't hit the cyclist. I can't slow down enough, and another car is coming toward me in the other lane. I have no choice but to pass the cyclist who is hugging the line of my lane.

I squeeze my eyes closed. *Stupid, I know.* But I can't watch my car scrape the man off the road.

I open my eyes and glance in my rearview mirror. The man is still on the bike as Mr. Dangerous passes him on his motorcycle. I didn't hit the car driving the opposite direction either.

I exhale and try to loosen my death grip on the steering wheel. But I won't be relaxing anytime soon. I see a gravel road leading off the main road, and I take it. I need to get away from the anxiety-inducing motorcycle behind me.

My heart slows as I drive over the bouncy road. I don't know where the road goes, nor do I care. I just need away.

The road winds up a mountain and stops in a parking lot of a trailhead. I pull the car into one of the last remaining stalls and exhale. A loose hair that had fallen onto my face blows up as I exhale.

And then I hear the motorcycle. I glance in my rearview mirror as the dumbass double parks his motorcycle behind mine.

I'm not confrontational. Not unless I need to be to survive. But I'm livid.

I jump out of my car and march over to him.

"What the hell are you doing? You could have gotten us killed earlier! And you can't park behind me. That's illegal."

He raises an eyebrow with a wicked grin on his face as he stares at me like I'm a child. He folds his arms over his chest, revealing his rippling biceps covered in tattoos.

Figures.

"Sorry, sweetheart. If you don't know how to handle a car in the mountains, then you should stick to the main highways. They might be more your speed."

My cheeks puff out as I hold my breath and anger in. I'm sure my face is bright red by now, and my eyes are popping out of their sockets.

"I'm not your *sweetheart.*"

His head cocks lazily to one side as his smile brightens. "You are definitely somebody's sweetheart."

"I'm nobody's anything."

He nods. "Good."

He removes his shirt, and I stare speechlessly at his long legs in running shorts. Damn, his body looks better than any superhero's I've ever seen. He could play Thor easily. His muscles are bigger, his tattoos darker, and his hair is long, like a Greek god.

He smirks and walks closer to me like he knows exactly the effect he has on me.

I can't fucking speak. That never happens. I always have the words for every situation. I can be a smartass when I want. My voice is my best quality.

It's sexy and raspy, and everything men want.

His eyes rake over my body. I'm wearing my scrubs. I just got off my shift, and the loose scrubs do nothing to attract a man. I look like a box instead of a voluptuous woman. Although, even the tightest dress in the universe wouldn't help my cause much. I just don't eat enough to have curves. My scrubs make me look like a dark green blob. Not sexy. The blood stains and mashed potatoes from a patient last night aren't helping either.

He winks at me though, and I think he sees something he likes.

No. He's probably just the type of man who flirts with every woman. He's not interested in me.

He turns a second later and starts jogging toward the trailhead.

"Wait!" I shout, getting my voice back, although the raspiness of my voice makes it sound like my voice just cracked.

The stranger doesn't pause. He keeps jogging but turns his head in my direction flashing me another panty-melting smile. He's too damn good-looking. Some men are handsome in a safe way. The kind who don't threaten everything you've worked for. The kind who smile at you and appreciate you for how beautiful you are.

This man is the kind who glances your way, and you are already signing away your heart, your bank account, and your self-worth for a chance with him.

I usually stay far, far away from men like him. And in about two seconds, I will drive full speed in the opposite direction and never think about him again. But for one moment, I let myself drink him up.

"Your motorcycle is blocking my car!" I shout.

He shrugs. "So? I'm running; you're hiking. I'll be back to move my motorcycle long before you get done with your hike." His eyes tell me he's challenging me. He doesn't think I came up here to hike based on how I'm dressed, but he's daring me to say differently.

I don't.

I don't say anything.

And the sexy stranger disappears onto the trail at full speed.

I stare at the trail and then down at my scrubs and white tennis shoes. I'm not prepared to go for a hike. These shoes have no grip and will turn brown in about five minutes from the dirt on the trail. I didn't even bring a bottle of water with me.

Hiking is not what I need right now. But I don't really have a choice. *Unless I want to back over his motorcycle...*

I grin, liking that idea far too much.

I sigh. I don't have the balls or insurance to destroy his bike like that. I'll hike for an hour, and if Mr. Wrong-for-me-in-all-the-ways isn't back by then, I'll reconsider my running over his motorcycle plan.

———

This is exactly what I don't need, and exactly what I do need.

I'm not a hiker. I don't have time to take out of my day to drive into the mountains and spend hours hiking. Most of the exercise I get is pulling patients in and out of a hospital bed. Occasionally, I'll make time to head down to the gym after classes finish, but that's rare.

The fresh air and wildflowers covering each side of the trail make the hike worth it. I've never seen such bright shades of purple, yellow, and pink. I've never filled my lungs with the scent of pine. Never had my muscles burn as I climb my way up the mountain.

For the most part, I focus on nothing. Just putting one foot in front of the other.

Despite the pretty scenery, my thoughts always go back to planning my life. I'm going to get a job offer from the current hospital I'm doing clinicals at. I've done a great job so far. I only have a semester left of school before I graduate. I've been putting in my time. I'll get the emergency room job I applied for.

I just have to make what little money I have left from my savings last for a couple more months.

I will survive. I always do. I just need to tweak my plan a little.

This year was supposed to be about finding a man. A husband, even. I'm graduating from college. I'm ready to be in a serious relationship. But I might have to postpone that for another year or two. I don't have any time to date. Not when I'm working all the time.

A husband might be a lot of help. Especially if he's rich. Even if he wasn't, two incomes are better than one. My siblings don't offer much support. A wealthy hubby would be perfect right about now.

No, it's not in the plan.

My lungs burn as the oxygen up here is thin. My legs ache and throb. I glance up, and the top doesn't look much further. I can make it. I've made it this far. Just a little further.

Lies.

I climb over the ridge, but it's a false summit. I've heard about these. My life has given me plenty of experience. Just when I think I've gained some traction, everything I've gained gets wiped out, and I have to start all over again.

I'm determined now, though. I won't stop until I've reached the top of this mountain. I don't know how long the trail is, or how high it goes. But nothing will stop me now.

Forcing my legs to keep climbing holds my entire attention now. I can't think about my family problems. I can't think about the jackass who almost ran me over. All I think about is putting one foot in front of the other. Over and over. Until finally, I reach the top.

Breathtakingly, beautiful.

I've never seen anything like it. Gone are the wildflowers, replaced with expansive views. I see the top of dozens of mountains around me. And a small lake sits on top of the mountain. The water's turquoise color is shimmering against the backdrop of the slope in front of me. A small snow patch scatters against the flawless grey rocks.

I smile, really smile, at what I just did. I don't have a clue how high I'm up. 10,000 feet? 12,000? Did I just climb a "14er"? I don't know. But I feel like I'm on top of the world. This was my Everest. And I beat it.

I sit down on a rock on the edge of the water, wishing I had a water bottle and snack to enjoy along with the view. Several other hikers are relaxing around the lake, enjoying the fruits of their efforts. But I don't see the man who caused me to be hiking in the first place.

Good, I might get to run over his bike after all.

After resting my legs for a while, I decide it's time to head back down. Should be much easier and faster than my way up.

I'm so wrong. The rocks that were so enjoyable to hike up are now death traps. My shoes have no traction as I climb down their slick surfaces. The streams of water I walked over before now race with enough water to soak my feet as I step through them, drenching my shoes and socks. And the slick dirt causes my feet to slide with each step, making each movement exhausting.

My thighs tremble. I used too much energy climbing, and have almost nothing left to climb down. I consider just rolling down the mountain, but with my luck, I'd probably roll off the path and plunge to my death.

And don't even get me started on my knees. I've never been in so much pain in my life. Each step stabs into my knees, making me grit my teeth with each step.

I thought I understood the beauty of why people spend their free time hiking. Now I think it's just because they like torturing themselves with pain and fear.

I try to make my legs move faster. The faster I run, the faster I will be off this treacherous cliff.

Faster is good. My momentum is carrying me down. I can do this.

One more step and then another and then...

"Fuck."

I'm not one to curse. I've probably sworn less than a dozen times in the last year. But the sharp pain I feel in my ankle, knee, and hip as I hit the ground is enough to warrant it. My ankle is hurt the worst; my hands grip it as I writhe in pain.

"You should be careful. The rocks are slippery," a boy, who looks to be about seven, says as he jumps over me wearing flip-flops.

I frown. I'm sure his parents are with him, but right now I want to throw the kid off the cliff for his snide remarks.

He disappears, and I do in fact see his father chase after him a second later. He doesn't stop to see if I need help. This trail isn't heavily trafficked, so apparently, I'm on my own at the top of Everest. I'll probably die up here. Does it snow up here in the summertime? Will frostbite get me? Will a bear or mountain lion be my end? Or will I die slowly from starvation?

Dammit! Why the hell did I decide to climb this mountain?!

Oh yea, because of a cocky, arrogant smile with dimples, tattoos, and muscles. If I survive this, I'm getting my eyes carved out. I don't need them. They get in my way and cause me to make bad decisions.

"You okay, sweetheart?" a deep voice asks.

I keep my eyes closed shut because I know the source of the voice. It would be my luck he is the one to find me and offer to help me.

"Perfectly fine. Just enjoying a nice relaxing nap in the middle of the trail."

He chuckles and touches my leg.

I jump. My eyes fly open at the jolt shooting through my leg. I don't know if it's because of my injury or the electricity of his touch.

"That hurts," I pout, as he examines my right knee after pushing my ripped scrubs up.

He ignores me and places my leg down before picking up my left ankle.

I wince and bite my lip to keep from cursing him as he touches me.

"It doesn't look broken. Probably just a sprain."

I know his words are meant to be encouraging, but I don't like hearing 'just' anything. Whatever it is, it hurts. Sprain or broken makes no difference.

"Thanks, doctor, but I got it from here. I know all about RICE."

"Rice?" he asks, cocking his head to look at me like I'm crazy.

I roll my eyes. "Rest, ice, compression, elevation. I know how to take care of a sprain. I'm a nurse." *Well, not technically. But I will be a nurse in a few short months.*

He nods, looking at my scrubs again like he's just now realizing why I'm wearing such a thing on a hike.

He holds out his hand to me, but I'm too stubborn to take it. I don't need his help.

He looks amused as I try to push myself off the dirt. It takes a couple tries to get my shaky legs under me, but I'm finally able to get up.

"Need any help?" he asks, smiling at me like I'm the funniest thing in the world.

"No."

I take a step, and my ankle gives out. Luckily, there is a tree nearby I can grab to keep from falling again.

"Seems like you could use some help." His hands grab my

hips trying to steady me. And I swear I feel his erection on my ass. "I could always kiss it and see if that helps."

I swat his hand away as I turn glaring. "I don't need help from a man who almost got me killed and just wants to hit on me."

I start stomping down the mountain ignoring the pain of each step, and the man slowly walking behind me. It takes everything in me not to turn around and check him out again. Sweat drips down his chest from his run, but when he approached me earlier, he barely seemed out of breath.

I will not look at him.

I will not ogle him.

I will not think about him.

I will not ask him for help.

Ten steps later, tears are filling my eyes. I can tolerate pain just fine. I have a high pain tolerance. But knowing it's going to take thousands of more steps to get down the mountain is melting my morale.

I stop, unable to continue on my own.

The man behind me stops as well. If he ran down, he'd probably already be down by now.

I sigh and turn slowly to him. "I guess you are my only option."

"Oh? I didn't think you wanted my help."

"I don't." I exhale into a frown. "But I want to live more than I don't want your help."

He smiles smugly but doesn't move to help me. In fact, he crosses his arms like he's not going to touch me now, even if I asked.

"What are you doing? I need your help. You've been following me this whole time because you intend to help me. So help."

He shakes his head.

"What?"

I'm so impatient with this man.

"I think you owe me something first."

My mouth gapes. He can't be serious. His eyes say he is dead serious. I see the lust there.

"I'm not going to blow you or fuc..." He raises an eyebrow as he realizes I hate using foul language. "Or have sex with you. I'm not that desperate."

He steps toward me, filling my personal space with his strong presence. It consumes all my thoughts, my smells, and my space.

"I think you are that desperate," he breathes onto my neck.

I freeze. *I'm not. I'm not. I'm not.*

But I am. He's not my type. Not at all. I like men who are good for me. Good-looking but not too good-looking so they think they can do better than me. Smart, caring, cautious, sturdy.

This man is none of those things. He's dangerous, threatening, and mysterious. He lives by a different moral code.

My lip trembles, considering what I should say or do. *Should I kiss him?* He might carry me down if I did. Make him think I'd have sex with him later, only to disappear before he has a chance.

He laughs, seeing the conflict in my eyes.

"But I'm not asking you to be that desperate. When I fuck you, it will be with your full permission and willingness. Not because I saved you."

"You are so not saving me. Let's not be dramatic. You are helping me walk down a mountain, not saving me from a burning building."

I snap my mouth shut when he stares at me. Damn me and my snarky mouth.

"What do you want then?"

"An apology."

I frown. "I don't owe you an apology."

He shrugs and starts walking down the trail past me.

Dammit!

"Fine!" I shout as I watch the only help I might get walk away from me.

He pauses and turns. I hate apologizing. Especially to his smug ass when I have nothing to apologize for. But he's right; I'm desperate for the help.

"I'm sorry..."

"Ace Knight."

I roll my eyes at his last name. I'm sure it's not his real name. He's no knight in shining armor.

"I'm sorry, my knight in shining armor, for saying I don't need your help when I clearly do. Will you please help me down the mountain?"

"No," he says deadpan.

Shit. Now what? Does he expect me to suck his dick? Because I so won't...okay, I totally would. That's why this man is dangerous for me, and I need to stay far, far away.

He grins. "Kidding."

He approaches me. "Climb on."

"No."

"Get the fuck on my back, sweetheart. I can carry you down in twenty minutes, or you can hobble along with me by your side and take five times as long."

He's got a point. I climb onto his glistening, muscular, tattooed back. My thighs wrap around his waist as he carefully grabs my legs to help keep me up. He feels thick, hard, and strong between my legs. I can only imagine what another part of his body would feel like between my legs.

Not going to happen, I remind myself.

"Hold on, sweetheart."

"My name is not sweetheart."

"Then what is it?"

I scrunch my nose. I don't want to tell him. If I do, he could find me after this.

He bounces us roughly as he jumps over a stream, and I groan as his back rubs against me turning me on more than I want him to know.

"Sorry, sugar tits."

"My name is most definitely not sugar tits."

I can feel his grin even though I can't see it.

"Sweet cheeks?"

"No."

"Hot stuff?"

"No."

"Fuckable mouth?"

"No."

"Pussycakes?"

"No."

"Cocksucker?"

Ugh, this is getting ridiculous. I know he's just trying to goad me to get me to tell him what my name is, but I'm tired of the curse words. They make me flinch every time he says them.

"Mila Burns. My name is Mila Burns."

Shit. I didn't mean to tell him my full name, but it just slipped out.

"Mila Burns," he repeats cautiously, his voice slightly higher than it was before. "So what are you doing out here, Mila Burns?"

I keep my mouth locked tight. If I don't speak, then I can't say anything stupid. I can't agree to go on a date. I won't drool all over his back. I won't say anything rude. Mouth tightly shut is good.

He laughs, shaking his head. Then, pulls out his phone and

presses a button before loud heavy metal music starts blaring, just like when he was on the motorcycle.

Obnoxious prick.

I sigh, resting my head on his shoulder as he jogs down the hill singing along to the music, while I do everything to not fall in love with him. Because he's wrong for me.

So, so, so wrong.

He's all the things I'm not. He would be a complication. He probably spends all his free time smoking joints and getting more tattoos. Not what I need right now.

I don't know how the time flies so fast, but we are down the mountain in record time. He should compete professionally at something he's that good.

"Thanks," I mumble as he gently lets me down next to my car.

"Do you need me to drive you to a hospital?"

"No."

"How about dinner?"

Nope, nope, nope. He doesn't get to hit on me. I can't handle it.

I don't respond. I don't look at him. I pretend this is all a dream. I slip into my car, not paying attention to what he's doing, and back out before I even get my seatbelt on.

And then I speed down the gravel road. I only look in the rearview mirror when I'm far enough away I know I won't turn around and go back and say yes no matter how charming he is.

Shit.

His motorcycle is in tatters. *I ran over his fucking motorcycle! How did I not notice when the metal started crunching as I backed out?*

I expect him to chase after me. Demand to see my insurance or exchange numbers so I will pay for the damage I caused.

Instead, he's standing there with a broad grin and determined eyes. I'm afraid I may have started a war.

2

MILA

"No Ren, I can't babysit this weekend," I say into my cell phone, as I stare at my watch. I have exactly one minute left of my break, and I don't have time to argue with my sister.

"Why not? I thought you said you had Saturday off?"

I sigh and close my eyes trying to keep my heart rate calm. I should start practicing yoga or meditation or something with the amount of stress I deal with.

"I have Saturday off, but I work a twenty-four-hour shift on Friday. I will spend my Saturday sleeping. There is no way I can babysit."

"Fine, fine. I get it. The kids just haven't seen you in forever. You should stop by Sunday at the very least to have dinner with us."

I roll my eyes. What my sister really wants is to check up on me and make sure I haven't lost my mind again. She tried to get me to come over on the anniversary, but I couldn't. I love my sister, but she has everything I want. A wealthy husband who loves her. Two children: a boy and a girl. Her own private practice as a pediatrician. Her life is perfect.

I can't handle seeing her when I feel like my life is falling apart. It's not really, but every year, on the anniversary of when my life as I knew it ended, I feel how easily I could lose everything again. But I won't let it. I'm in control. I can make my life anything I want.

"Okay, I'll stop by on Sunday," I relent. "But only for dinner! I'm not going to play board games or any of the family time afterward."

"Great! I'll see you on Sunday!" Ren says, ignoring my conditions.

I pocket my phone in the front of my blue scrub pants and then head toward the nurse's station as my twenty-minute break ends. I didn't even have time to pee; Ren took up all my time talking on the phone. But I need to sit down and rest my ankle. It's better now that I've iced it, taken some pain medications, and wrapped it.

"Any new patients?" I ask Felicity, my clinical supervisor. She's been manning the desk while I've been on break.

She frowns. I think she permanently has a frown on her face, or she hates me. I bite my lip. Felicity is grumpy, that's just the way her face is. I shouldn't take it personally. I've been doing a great job. It's just too bad Felicity is the one who will determine whether I pass or fail.

Felicity rolls her eyes like she can't believe I asked the question.

I ignore her and force a smile on my face. She can be grumpy all she wants, I'm happy. I'm positive. I'm in line for getting a job offer here. Just keep working hard, and this will all be worth it.

Felicity huffs as I sit down in the chair next to her.

"What?" I ask.

She nods her head in the direction of the waiting room.

"You shouldn't have your boyfriend showing up at work. Get rid of him," she says.

"I don't have a boyfriend..."

She eyes me again. "Oh, sorry, lover, hookup, one night stand, whatever he is, he needs to be gone. I can't have him hogging my waiting room."

"I don't have a boyfriend or any kind of guy friend."

Felicity ignores me, typing on the computer.

I bite my lip again as I try to think who could be in the waiting room. I won't know until I walk over to see. So I force myself up even though I just want a moment to sit. I'm toward the end of a twenty-four-hour shift, and I just want to relax and rest.

Instead, I'm storming to the waiting room, sure whoever is there isn't for me.

"Henry," I say when I open the door and see my brother pacing like he's waiting to find out if I made it through surgery or something.

"What are you doing here?" I ask as I make a mental note of telling Felicity later he's my brother, not my boyfriend.

He frowns. *Why does everyone do that? Do I have one of those faces that need to be frowned at?*

"You know why I'm here. I left you a message yesterday on your cell phone."

I shake my head as I grab his arm and lead him out of the waiting room. If he's going to scold me, I'd rather him not do it in front of dozens of patients' families I may have to talk to later.

"I didn't get any message."

He runs his hand through his hair in disbelief. "You are such a child. You can't even be bothered to check your voicemail and call your brother back."

I steer Henry away from the nurses' station, down a hallway I hope is empty.

"Why are you here, Henry?" I ask, already tired of his scolding.

"I want to make sure you are okay. Today's the anniversary of—"

I give him a dirty look.

"Well, you know what it's the anniversary of. And you get a little crazy. I want to make sure you don't do anything stupid this year."

"The anniversary was yesterday. Not today. And I didn't do anything crazy." Unless you count climbing a mountain for the first time, rolling my ankle, and having to get carried down by a hot stranger, before running over said stranger's motorcycle. *Nope, definitely not crazy.*

"Whatever. It's still around that time, and I'm not leaving until I'm sure you are fine."

I put my hand on my hips, staring my brother down. "No, you mean until you ensure I won't do anything that will put the Burns back in the papers again and ruin your business." I didn't do anything that bad last year. I just got drunk, and I didn't have any money for an Uber home, so I slept under an underpass. The cop that found me wasn't happy with my decision, even though I thought it was the right one.

He shrugs. "I'm here to make sure you don't fuck up again."

I shake my head. Everyone in my life has a perfect life, except me. Even though my mistake was years ago, it still haunts me. I still have the guilt and nightmares, even if I can't remember the details of that day. My family will never forgive me for what I did. No matter how much I've changed. No matter how much I try to be exactly like them. Maybe when I have a husband and kids, they will feel differently, but until then, they think of me as the screwup who they have to fix every year.

I hear the sirens, and I know we have another patient coming in.

"I have to go," I say, running down the hallway to meet the ambulance. My pager goes off, and Felicity starts giving me the info. Two male patients. Both critical. Not sure what happened, but they need all teams on hand.

"Mila! I'll be waiting until the end of your shift to talk to you," Henry says.

I keep racing down the hallway, ignoring my brother, who thinks I need a babysitter. I don't. But he won't leave until I prove to him I'm okay. Last year was just a fluke. It wasn't my fault. This year, I'm better.

I run to emergency bay one and start collecting all the supplies we could need to take care of the incoming patients. Two other nurses enter as well. When I turn around a man is being pushed in on a gurney. We transfer him quickly to the bed.

"What happened?" I ask the nearest paramedic.

"Not sure exactly. It was a car accident. He was riding in the passenger seat. His heart stopped once during transport, and he's struggling to breathe. Blood pressure is low. He's been unconscious almost the entire time and is now. Bleeding from a wound in his chest and leg." He doesn't have to say more about the car accident. I can see in his eyes he suspects a drunk driver.

I start cutting off his clothes, while the rest of the staff begins jumping on their jobs. IVs, tending to wounds, checking blood pressure, oxygen. We work in unison, a perfect dance, moving and speaking with each other in synced rhythm with each other. We all know exactly what needs to happen to keep this man alive.

The fabric I cut from his clothes is expensive. It takes a lot of energy to cut the suit from his body due to the thickness. He wears a Rolex on his wrist, which I remove as well. And then I grab gauze to press to the lesion on his head. It doesn't appear horrendous, compared with the wound on his chest. Another nurse is addressing that gash.

I flick his hair up so I can continue covering his laceration. Despite his condition, I can't help but think how beautiful he is.

Gorgeous man. His body is fit. His hair is thick and brown. His eyes are blue and sparkling.

His eyes!

Are open.

"Sir, can you hear me? You are at the hospital. We are going to take good care of you."

He doesn't speak, but his eyes tell me he understands what I'm saying.

"Relax. Do you remember what happened?"

"No," he says carefully.

I smile, happy to hear his voice.

"The paramedics said you were in a car accident. We are assessing your injuries now and determining if you need surgery or not."

He smiles back at me. Patients in this much pain usually don't smile back at me.

"How much pain are you in on a scale of 1-10?"

"0."

I frown and look down at Felicity who administered his IV. The drugs shouldn't have taken effect that quickly. She looks back at me just as concerned. He's probably in shock.

"0? Are you sure? You don't feel any pain in your head or chest or leg?"

"No."

Concern covers my face. He may be worse off than I thought. I look at the doctor who shares the same worry.

"I'm not in any pain because I'm staring at a beautiful angel who I would have never met had I not gotten injured. So the pain I feel is masked by how lucky I feel to have found you."

I blush and shake my head. I've been hit on plenty as a

nursing student. But never so blatantly by a man in such a serious condition before.

The doctor in the room laughs. "I think you are going to be just fine if you can joke at a time like this."

"I'm not joking. Before I leave, I will have your number. And we will start an epic love story."

I blush more and laugh nervously. If he asks, I will give him my number in a heartbeat. He seems like exactly the kind of man I'm looking for.

"Okay, Romeo. Just relax and focus on getting better, then we can talk about dating," I say.

———

Cole Traver's the one.

Blue eyes, prince charming, and I saved his life.

He's exactly what I'm looking for. I haven't been able to stop thinking about him all day. He's the last one on my rounds to check on. I have one more patient first.

And then I get to have my fairy tale come true. I get to go out with a man who is charm itself. It will be better than the fairy tales. They could make a movie out of our love story. "Love in the Emergency Room" they could call it.

I scrunch my nose. Obviously, the movie people would think of a better name than that. But our story will be epic. I can't wait to shove it in my brother's face later. And tell Ren about it on Sunday. She's going to freak when I tell her I fell in love so quickly. Okay, maybe it's not love yet, but it will be. I can tell from his tailored suit, dreamy eyes, and smile, he's the one for me.

I knock on the door and then enter, hardly waiting for a response from the patient before entering.

"I'm Mila; I'm here to give you more pain medication and

check to see how you're feeling," I say, as I head to the computer to look up the patient's information.

"I know who you are, Mila."

No. Fucking. Way.

I was too much in my own fairyland to even get a good look at the patient when I entered. Usually, I would have looked up my patient on the computer before entering their room to ensure I was prepared. I didn't this time. I'm too blissful and wrapped up in my prince charming in the next room to worry about this one.

I narrow my eyes as I look at him. Ace Knight. This can't be happening.

"Are you stalking me now?"

He chuckles and then lifts the cast on his arm. It's then that I see the gash on his head. The broken leg and the IVs coming out of his body. Whatever happened was serious.

"No, they typically don't give you a say in which hospital you go to when you're unconscious."

I flip my head back to my computer ignoring him. I need to get this done as quickly as possible. I scan the computer looking for my orders from the physician. Check his vitals and administer his next dose of antibiotics and painkillers. Easy enough.

"I need to check your blood pressure and oxygen levels."

I grab the blood pressure cuff and tighten it around his bulging bicep. His arm is so big the cuff barely fits, after a few rough jerks from me to get it to fasten.

"Jesus, woman! I didn't do anything to you," he says at my aggressiveness.

I narrow my eyes. "You called me *sweetheart.*" He called me a lot worse, but I won't be repeating those words.

He grins, and it only pisses me off more.

"You ran over my motorcycle. I think we're even."

I glare. "We are most definitely not even."

"You're right. You owe me twenty grand to fix my bike."

Shit. Are motorcycles really that expensive? That's more than my car costs. I can't afford that.

"Your blood pressure is fine." I put the blood oxygen monitor on his finger, and it reads above ninety. Great, he's breathing just fine, while I'm sure if I tested my oxygen levels right now, it'd be below fifty, and my blood pressure would be sky high.

I don't bother listening to his heart. I don't want to be that close to him. Instead, I fetch his medications and walk over to his IV to administer them.

"So what do you think, sugartits? Am I going to live?"

I push in the antibiotics, but toss the painkiller in the trash without administering it. I shouldn't do it, but I'm pissed. I'm tired of dealing with his crap.

He grins. He won't be grinning in an hour when he's writhing in pain. I'll be off my shift by then, so it will be some other nurse's responsibility to give him pain medicine. He won't be in agony for more than an hour.

I purposefully drag my hand over his IV, tugging on it.

He growls. It's a deep, menacing, sexy sound that comes from deep in his belly.

"Oops."

"You aren't much of a *sweetheart,* are you? I'll have to think of another name to call you."

"You won't be calling me anything. I won't see you again after my shift is over." I'm too angry to suppress the raspiness in my voice. I'm used to talking in a high pitched, bubbly voice to hide my natural sultry sound. But now, it slips out.

Knight cocks his head, and his eyes darken into tight slits. If he thought I was a prize before, now he thinks he's hit the jackpot. I'm the ultimate possession he wants to claim.

He's never going to have me. He's the absolute wrong man for me. And I'm the wrong woman for him. Knight is looking for a woman to have fun. A one night stand. Or a string of nights. Nothing serious. It's clear from his tattooed covered body and tattered clothes that he doesn't take life seriously. I would just be his next conquest.

I've been down that road before. It leaves me in tears. My heart, broken. And my family telling me, "I told you so." I'm done with bad boys. I want a good man with a steady job, and his priorities straight. It may be a bit boring, but it's what will keep me safe.

"I think I will see a lot of you. You owe me for my bike."

I glare at him. "No, I don't owe you anything. I probably saved your life."

He cocks an eyebrow like he doesn't follow. "How do you figure that?"

"You were in a car accident, right?"

He doesn't answer, but his silence tells me I guessed right. I could check his chart, but I've seen enough patients to know the exact cause. And a man in his twenties is usually brought in for only a few reasons: brawl, being an idiot showoff, overdose, or car accident. His severe wounds lead me to guess car accident. Drunk driver or reckless driving most likely.

"If you had been riding your motorcycle, especially without a helmet, you probably would have been killed."

Knight pauses, drinking in every word falling from my lips like I'm playing an orchestra just for him. I need to focus on not sounding like a harlot around him. I don't know what it is, but my sultry voice comes out near him.

He leans forward, and I find myself doing the same until we are inches apart. Eye to eye, nose to nose, mouth to mouth. I lean in further, thinking he's going to kiss me. And despite how angry I am, I'm desperate to taste his lips.

"You owe me, sweetheart."

Stunned. That's how I feel.

He chuckles like he knows just how much control he has over me.

My body may respond to his like any other warm-blooded woman's would react to a sexy man. It doesn't mean I'm going to act on my feelings. I have self-control.

And I have the perfect man waiting for me in the next room.

I won't let Ace think he has any hold on me. Men like him won't ever let me go if he thinks he has any power over my body.

I tug on his IV again, this time not being sneaky at all about it. It's clear it's not an accident.

"Stop calling me sweetheart or I'll—"

I don't finish.

His rough hand finds the nape of my neck, and he closes the distance between our lips. I gasp, my mouth opens as he swallows me.

I hate him, I think.

I hate him. I hate him. I hate him. I repeat the mantra in my head. Trying to convince myself to not fall into his trap.

Too late.

I've fallen. I'm lost in his kiss. The kiss is as rough as I expected a kiss from him would be, but also softer. Sweeter. Gentler.

The way his thumb presses at the base of my jaw is less controlling than I expected the gesture to feel. It's tender like he knows how his touch is radiating down my neck and into my core, persuading me to keep kissing him instead of pulling away like my head is telling me.

"You're fired."

I blink several times, not registering the words I just heard.

The kiss ends. I don't know if Knight or I was the one to end it, but it ends. And I've never felt sadder to face an end.

I lean back, my eyes focused on Knight's. His dark brown eyes aren't on mine though. They are behind me.

How could he think about anything but me at this moment?

His eyes slowly drift back to mine, and that's when I see it. The sadness. It matches mine. I don't understand why he's sad or where it's coming from. But it's there. Same as mine.

"Mila? Did you hear me?" Felicity asks.

Felicity!

I turn toward the shrill woman.

"I'm sorry. No, I didn't hear you."

"I said, you're fired. Go to your desk. I'll have security meet you to take your badge and change your computer logins."

"Wait? Fired? I'm not an employee here." *Stupid.* It doesn't matter if I'm an employee here or not. I'm no longer finishing my clinical rotation here. I might not even be graduating this winter at all.

She smiles like she has been waiting for years for a reason to fire me and the moment has finally come, even though she's only dealt with me for four weeks. "It's against the rules to kiss patients. I'm failing you. You'll be lucky if another hospital takes you after the report I write."

She walks over to the bed. "I'm so sorry, Mr. Knight. That was highly inappropriate for her to behave that way. I assure you the rest of our staff will behave with the utmost professionalism toward you the rest of your stay. We will ensure you get the best care while you are here. And as I said, she will be let go for her indiscretion."

Knight glances my way. But his eyes barely focus on me before he glances at Felicity. His eyes focus in on her cleavage.

Asshole, I think as I walk out of the room, my lips still tingling from his kiss.

I feel tears welling, my heart clenching. This can't be happening. I did everything I was supposed to do. I planned. I'm a few months away from graduating. From being forgiven by my family. I did everything I was supposed to.

And now...

Now, I'm going to end up with nothing. Living on my sister's couch. I'll be a nanny for the rest of my life. Trapped and unable to leave the sanctuary of my family.

I will never be on my own. Never live up to my potential.

I'll never graduate college now. I know that. I know, without even talking to the administrators, I'll be expelled. *Who kisses a patient and then gets to become a nurse still? No one.*

I watch as a tear falls and lands on the linoleum floor. I did everything right, and I still fucked up.

I look up and see Henry staring at me. The disappointment plain on his face. He doesn't know what happened. He doesn't have to. He knows me too well. It's why he's here.

I always fuck up. I ruin everyone's lives. But this time, I just ruined mine.

I won't ask my brother for money. I won't live on my sister's couch. I'll live on the streets under an underpass before I ask for their help again. Not after everything I've put them through.

I walk past the door of Cole Traver's room. I consider bursting through the door and telling him to save me. He probably could. He has enough money to more than take care of someone like me.

I'm tired of being saved. It's underrated. Being rescued doesn't make anything better. It just puts me in their debt and makes it that much harder the next time I fail again.

"I could have loved you. We could have had an epic love story," I whisper under my breath, staring at the tiny crack of light peering around the edge of the solid door.

I sniffle, trying to keep the tears away.

"What happened now, Mila?" Henry asks. His voice isn't angry. But he doesn't try to hide the disappointment. That's all I am: one big disappointment.

"I was born, and then tragedy attached itself to me. I'm

tragic, a dark storm cloud, a thorn that when pulled free from the skin finds another place to jab into and cause pain."

Henry rolls his eyes. "Stop being so dramatic, kiddo."

I wince at the nickname. That's all I am to him. A kid. A burden he can never get free of.

It ends today.

"I need to be alone." When I'm alone, I can't hurt anyone but myself. No matter how much I fuck up, I'm the only one I'll break.

3

—————

KNIGHT

"WHAT ARE YOU DOING HERE?" I ask as I stand in the doorway of my office.

My best friend, Cole, sits in the chair with his feet up on my desk.

He raises an eyebrow. "I could ask you the same question."

I roll my eyes and shut the door behind me, before walking over to the mini bar and pouring two fingers of bourbon.

"I'm working."

Cole eyes the glass in my hand. "It looks like you are drinking your problems away. Didn't the doctor tell you not to mix pain medications with alcohol?"

I sip the liquor down in one shot.

Cole smirks. "I guess not."

"What do you want, Traver?"

I pour more amber liquid into my glass.

"What happened?" Cole says, removing his black loafers from my desk and sitting up straight in my oversized leather chair. I know what he's asking. The police finished their investigation and determined it was an accident. No one's fault. But it's hard to understand how someone could lose control of a car on a sunny day, with little traffic, and no texting, alcohol, or distractions.

I shrug and slowly sip the liquor.

"I lost control of the car. The road was slippery. Another car slammed into us," I say, trying not to relive the night. It happened weeks ago, but it still feels like it was yesterday. At least my body healed quickly. The only signs I was in a car accident are the scars on my body and pain whenever I move.

"You fucking lost control? That's the story you are going with?" Cole stands up, and I know he's going to punch me for what happened. I deserve it. He could have died. As it is, he's never going to walk right again. He'll always have a slight limp. Scars will mar his body. Nightmares will invade his sleep. *Because of me.*

I take another drink of the liquor, wishing it would take away the pain. And I'm not talking about the physical pain I'm in. Although that would be nice too; my ribs burn every time I fucking breathe. But that's not why I drink. I drink to get rid of the undeniable pain embedded in my heart.

"You were fucking drinking? Weren't you? Barely under the legal limit, huh?"

I don't answer. He wouldn't believe me anyway.

Cole drops his head. He's not going to punch me, even though I wish he would.

He walks over to the bar, pours himself a drink, and returns to my chair to perch his feet on my desk. He doesn't look at me as he nurses it. We both sip our drinks in complete silence. It's not normal, even for high powered men like us to be drinking this much alcohol on a Monday morning, but then our lives have never been normal. Most people don't become millionaires before their twenty-fifth birthdays either.

"You owe me," Cole says, breaking the silence as he studies the picture of Abri and me on my desk. He takes a seat again.

"Although, I did meet this attractive nurse. Young, hot, long brown hair. Sharp eyes, perky boobs, and her voice. My god, I could listen to her all day."

His lips curl up a little in a smile as he pictures the woman in his head. A woman I know all too well.

"I thought she would come back to my room, but she didn't. Probably got off shift early. I'm sure she'd be interested in giving me a checkup." He chuckles to himself at his crude joke.

"Mila Burns?" I ask.

Cole stops laughing. "She was your nurse too?"

I nod.

His eyes light up. "We haven't competed for a woman in a long time. Not since high school. This could be fun."

"You already lost. I kissed her." *And got her fired. Most likely, ended her college career.* But I don't tell him that.

He smiles like I just said the greatest thing in the world. "I don't believe you."

I walk over to the expansive window and look out at the city below. So many people are walking, going through their regular, ordinary days. Hoping they make enough money to make it through the next day. I would give anything to be them.

"It doesn't matter if you believe me, it's true."

Cole studies me closely. "Are you saying she's off limits then?"

"No, I don't care. Fuck her. I got what I wanted from her."

He shakes his head, muttering under his breath.

"But I do want to pay you back," I say.

"There is nothing you can do to pay me back."

"I could sell you my company."

He sighs. "I don't have enough money to buy your company even if I wanted to, which I don't. How is that paying me back?"

I down the rest of my drink. Not because I need encouragement to say my next words, but because I need the alcohol just to breathe.

"The favor is I'm selling it to you for twenty dollars."

Cole laughs hysterically. Like it's the most absurd, ridiculous thing he's ever heard. It probably is.

"You're not serious."

"I am."

"I don't want your boring company. I'm into much more risky endeavors."

"Liar."

Cole takes his feet off my desk for the second time since I've entered the office. He looks at me like I'm insane and he's considering having me admitted. He studies me, but I don't give anything away. I don't have any emotions to feel.

Cole curses under his breath. He knows me too well. He knows what I'm doing.

"I'm not helping you hide your money from Abri."

"That's not what I'm doing."

"You fucking asshole. It's exactly what you are doing. You'd rather sell your company and get nothing, then let her have a penny of it."

I shrug. He's not wrong. My bitch of an ex-wife doesn't deserve any of my money. *Well, almost ex-wife.*

"Abri would take both of our asses to court if I bought your company for so little and cut her out."

"She won't."

"She will. And it will be deserved. She deserves to have half of the company. Or half of the money when you sell it."

"Fine, I'll give her ten bucks when I sell it to you."

Cole shakes his head. "What happened to you, man? You were so in love. Abri was your partner in crime. She gave up everything for your company. For you."

I don't answer.

"Fine, I get it. You were way too young when you got married. You grew apart. Love didn't last. Just sign the divorce papers and give her half of everything she helped you build, then go your separate ways. Move on."

I've tried moving on. But he has no idea what I've been through. No idea how badly I need to cut her out of my life permanently. Giving her half of my money won't stop her. Giving her all of my money won't slow her down.

If I told him the truth, he wouldn't believe me. If he did, he'd try to talk me out of my plan. It's my burden to bare.

Cole studies me. He's my best friend. He's been with me through everything. My highest and lowest. He's like a brother. He would do anything for me. And the look in his eyes tells me as much.

He stands up and walks to me until he's inches in front of me.

"I'll buy your company for twenty dollars. If that's what you really want. I'll help you make sure Abri doesn't get anything from you."

I sigh in relief.

"But you have to do something first."

I narrow my eyes, not liking the tone of his voice. I don't like making deals.

"Prove to me you've moved on. Prove to me you will get past Abri. That you will date again. Prove to me that selling your company isn't just about Abri, that it's about starting over."

Mila pops into my head. Beautiful, sexy, flawless Mila. Her voice so sultry I could listen to her ramble about nothing for hours. Such a stark contrast to her sweet, innocent personality.

Damn her lips. Her red, fuckable lips. All I've thought about since she spoke when she got out of her car is her lips. How it would feel to have her wet, plump lips wrapped around my cock. Her innocent eyes, big with desire. I expected innocence when she spoke when she couldn't even swear. She wouldn't let herself curse. But then, she spoke, and I was captivated. She was all I thought about as I ran up the mountain. The last image I had as the headlights came crashing toward us and there was nothing I could do to stop the impact.

The car crash almost killed us. It should have been the single worst moment in my life. For most people, it would be.

Not mine.

Abri changed my life. For better and worse.

But Mila, she's like a comet headed straight for me. We've been on a collision course for years now. It would be easy for me to step aside. Avoid the impact, but I can't force my legs to move. Even though I know how this ends.

I know we won't ever be together.

I know if we were, we'd end up like Abri and me, devastated and alone. I won't put another person through what Abri and I have been through.

But Mila is the solution to getting free.

"Do we have a deal?" Cole asks, extending his hand.

Mila can help me convince Cole I've moved on. She can help me get rid of Abri once and for all. Then we can both start a new life, alone.

But that damn kiss. I can't get the kiss out of my head. Just thinking about it makes my cock ache. A feeling I haven't had in years.

Mila is going to hate me for that one. I got her fired. I ended her college career. Never has one kiss been so destructive. But it was necessary. Or at least I thought it was. It didn't end in exactly the way I thought it would.

Mila will come around though. She doesn't have a choice now that's she broke, and possibly homeless.

I brush passed Cole's hand and take a seat at my desk.

"Deal."

4

MILA

Sweat is disgusting. It's sticky and wet, and there is no hiding it. I don't care how much deodorant I wear; I can still smell the sweat dripping off my forehead, armpits, and ass. *Why does my ass sweat so much?*

Because my life is on the line right now, that's why. The sweat gives me a gross distraction. The smell infiltrates my nostrils, and every time I move, I feel the slimy liquid. My clothes cling to my skin like they are attached with glue.

Focus. I've spent the last couple of weeks reading everything I could about how I can continue with school. How to convince people you are innocent and deserving. Be confident, but not too confident. That means don't let them know you're sweating. Look them in the eyes when you talk. Smile, but not too brightly. Be firm in your words, don't use um, or like, or uh. But don't get defensive when you speak. Dress professionally, but show enough skin that you don't look like a young teenager instead of an adult. Admit your faults, but highlight your strengths.

I got this.

"Miss Burns, we have heard Felicity's account of what happened. We have a written statement from the patient in question. Can you tell us in your own words what happened?" Mr. Warren, the dean of the college, says, staring at me with serious eyes.

This is it. This is my chance to finally explain.

I open my mouth, and the dryness prevents me from speaking. It's like a desert in my mouth. Dry, and no words form.

"Miss Burns?"

"I'm sorry, um…" *Shit, don't use um.* "It was a misunderstanding. The patient, Mr. Knight, I had met previously on a hike. He helped me with a minor leg injury. When I went to take care of him, he thought I wanted more. He was on a lot of pain medication and was delirious. He kissed me before I could tell him it wasn't appropriate."

"Did you report to your supervisor that you knew the patient and it would be inappropriate for you to take care of him?"

"Well…um…no, but as I said, I didn't know him. I met him for like five minutes on a hike." And he carried you down on his glistening back. But unlike the sweat pooling in the armpits of my white, I'm-so-innocent blouse, his sweat was sexy. I wanted to lick it off his pristine body.

"Mr. Knight kissed you?"

I nod.

"I've kissed many people, Miss Burns. They were always aware when I was about to kiss them. They gave me permission before I kissed them. They could stop the kiss at any time and could prevent it from happening in the first place. Why did you let Mr. Knight kiss you? Was it because you wanted it to happen?"

"What? No! I didn't want him to kiss me. I wasn't expecting it. We were arguing before he decided to kiss me. I had no idea what he was about to do." I sound defensive.

"What were you arguing about?"

"Um..." *Why did I say we were arguing?* "Just about how he treated me when he helped me on the hike."

Silence. The ten people in the room all stare at me, waiting for me to continue. I stare down at my hands which I have carefully folded on the wood table in front of me. It's supposed to show how confident I am. Confidence equals innocent.

"Mr. Knight called me some words I would rather not repeat here."

"Is that all that happened?"

I suck in a breathe. *No, but I'm not going to tell you.* But the words spill out of me. For some reason, the look on his face prevents me from holding anything back. "And I might have accidentally hit his motorcycle when I was backing my car out of the parking lot."

"I see." He writes something down on his notepad.

I scan the room, and everyone is either writing notes or scowling at me like a five-year-old who spilled milk on her mother's favorite shoes.

This is hopeless.

"Thank you for meeting with us, Miss Burns. We will discuss your case and have a ruling for you by the end of the day. But I think I can safely say I don't think you are fit to be a nurse. I think you should seriously consider a new career. One where you aren't dealing with vulnerable patients."

He looks at me like he thinks I might rape a patient in their sleep.

"Yes, sir," I say because there's nothing left to say. I stand, listening to the high pitched scrape of my chair against the fake wood floors.

I wince and then scurry out of the room. My legs can't move me fast enough. I find the bathroom down the hall, vomit in the nearest stall, and then wash my face. I can't believe that just happened. I can't believe I'm a semester away from graduating, and I'm going to let it all slip away.

I walk back out of the bathroom.

"Miss Burns," I hear the dean's voice.

I turn and stare at him with big eyes.

"I wanted to let you know our ruling. You'll get a formal letter with our decision in the mail, but we decided to suspend you."

"Suspend? What does that mean?"

"It means you will not be allowed on campus for any reason for the semester. You will not be allowed to take any classes or live in the dorms. Your scholarship will be revoked. And in the spring you can reapply. We will reconsider your case then, although as I said, I might recommend you finish your degree in business or something more cutthroat. It would match your personality better."

Tears sting my eyes. "I can reapply in the spring?"

He nods. "Know the only reason we didn't expel you completely without a chance to reconsider is because of Mr. Knight's testimony."

I frown. *This wasn't a murder case. Testimony? I know he wrote a statement, but did he do more than that?* Whatever Mr. Knight said I'm sure it didn't help my case. He's the reason I'm in this mess in the first place.

"Thank you, Mr. Warren. I'll consider reapplying in the spring."

I walk away before the tears fall. I've been embarrassed enough. I head back to the dorm room I share with Lana. I don't look anyone in the eye. I know the other students see my tears, but it doesn't matter. I don't look around at the campus. At the tall buildings I love. I don't think about any of it. I focus on my goal. Getting to my dorm room.

Lana is lying on her bed with a textbook resting on her lap while she paints her nails.

"How'd it go?" she asks.

I crouch down and reach under my bed until I find the bottle of contraband. This alone could have gotten me kicked out of the dorm rooms. I unscrew the bottle of tequila and take a long swig.

"That bad, huh?"

I don't respond. I don't even feel the burn as it sets my throat on fire. I just keep gulping.

Lana gets up and slowly takes the bottle from me, before she wraps her arms around me.

I sob into her bony shoulder.

"Shh, it's going to be okay."

"No, it's not. I have to move out. I have nowhere to go. No money. I think I have a twenty dollar bill in my pocket. I can't even afford a tank of gas, let alone food or a place to stay."

"Stay here. How will they know?"

A knock on the door. *Ugh.*

I walk to the door and throw it open as the RA stands there frowning at me. "I'm here to ensure you move out today. I will need your keys."

I glance back at Lana in an I-told-you-so sort of way.

"Thanks, Aurora, for being so sensitive in Mila's time of need."

"It's not my fault she kissed a patient and got expelled."

"Suspended. I can come back in the spring. It's just for a semester."

"Well, you can't be here now."

"I know. I'm going to need some time to pack."

She folds her arms across her chest like she's going to stand in my doorway and watch me pack the entire time.

"Leave," Lana says walking to the door.

"I'm supposed to collect her key."

Lana rolls her eyes. "I'll make sure she drops it off by noon. In the meantime, this is still my dorm room, and I can still kick you out whenever I want."

Aurora sighs, but leaves.

"Bitch," we both mutter after she leaves.

Lana smiles. "Swearing again, are we?"

I nod. "Only when people deserve it."

She hugs me again. "It's good to see the old you back."

I frown. I hate the old me. The old me is what gets me into trouble. Although, the new me also seems to get me in trouble. But the old me has to come back if I'm going to survive.

"Are you going to go live with your sister?"

"No."

"Where are you going to go then?"

I shrug. "I'll live in my car until I find a job and figure something out. It will be fine. I'll wait tables, bartend, babysit Ren's kids some. I'll make enough to survive, and then I'll come back next semester. It's not a big deal."

Lana knows I'm lying. It is a big deal. And I'm not even sure if I can come back yet. But she doesn't call me out on the lie.

She digs into her pocket and pulls about a ten and a five dollar bill. "It's not much, but take it."

I shake my head. "I can't."

"I'm not asking."

"No, I'll be fine. I'm not taking your money, Lana." She's broke, same as me. She doesn't have family helping her. And she deserves the money more than I do. She isn't the one with a constant stream of fuck-ups.

Damn, the cuss words just keep coming back. I haven't even thought a curse word in years. Now they are staining my every thought and spilling out of me far too fast.

She sighs and puts the money back in her pocket.

"You can help me pack though."

"I'd rather just give you the money," she moans.

I chuckle and toss her my backpack to start filling up. I have a backpack and a duffel bag with a broken zipper. That's all I have to pack my possessions in. Good thing I don't have many possessions because there is no way I can even afford boxes right now to pack.

It takes us all of ten minutes to pack up everything I own. Some of my textbooks don't fit so I'll have to carry them, but otherwise, everything fits in the two bags.

Lana hugs me one last time. "Call me every day."

I nod. "I'll keep in touch. You can't get rid of me this easily."

"I'll make sure our bitchy face RA gets your key."

"Thanks," I say putting my backpack on, draping my duffel bag over my shoulder, and picking up the textbooks I plan on selling. I won't get much, but twenty dollars might mean the difference between eating or starving.

I glance one more time at the dorm room that had become my sanctuary. I had a full scholarship that covered everything. My classes, books, dorm room. All I had to cover was food. Something an occasional bartending job could cover. I took extra classes so I could graduate early. Now it's all gone.

I will not cry. *Not again,* I repeat to myself as I walk out of the dorm and into the sun. The sun always shines in Colorado. Over three hundred days of sunshine a year. I usually love that about Colorado, but not today.

"Can't I get some rain? Some clouds? Anything but your cheeriness?" I mumble under my breath, but of course, the sun still shines, making me feel like I'm the only person in the world dealing with a shitty day.

My arms grow tired as I walk across campus to my car. At least I only have to make one trip. That's a positive. Although, I have no idea what I'm going to do when I get to my car. Start applying to jobs I guess.

No, I need a new plan, that's all. When I have a plan, my life is good.

I will apply to the bar on the 16th street mall that just opened. It's in a touristy part of town, and I would make great tips. I will sleep in my car until I get my first paycheck. Or I'll ask for an advance. Then, I'll find a roommate who has a cheap room to rent out. A closet-sized room is about all I'll be able to afford. I heard there are some cheap apartments near north Denver. I'll—

"Umf," I grunt as I run into a brick wall.

My books tumble to the ground, and my duffle bag falls off my shoulder, clothes tumbling out of the bag.

"Shit," I say when a scarf gets caught in the wind and starts blowing away.

"I got it," a man says.

I look up as he catches the scarf. I didn't run into a brick wall. I ran into Cole, the perfect specimen of a man from the hospital. He looks like he's healed well in the weeks since I last saw him. His face is still bruised, and he will always have a scar on his forehead, but it will fade over time. He seems to be walking well, although I see a tiny limp as he brings the scarf back to me. Most people wouldn't notice the limp, and it shouldn't have a significant impact on him unless he were an athlete or something before the accident. Very possible considering how built he is.

He grins, and I melt.

"I didn't think I was going to get to see my favorite nurse again."

Swallow, breathe, stop drooling.

He chuckles at my speechlessness. "Didn't mean to make

you speechless. I think your voice might be my favorite thing about you."

"I'm sorry for running into you."

He shakes his head. "Entirely, my fault."

We both bend down and start picking up the rest of my clothes before they blow away. Cole holds up my red lace thong, the only sexy item of clothing I own.

He raises an eyebrow before I snatch it out of his hand. I know I'm blushing and won't be able to look him in the eye again.

He puts a finger under my chin, so I have to look up at him.

"Don't do that. You have nothing to be embarrassed about. I've had dreams about you in similar underwear. Now my dreams are about to get a whole heck of a lot dirtier."

I blush more.

"Um...thanks." *Great word choice*, I think to myself. *God, can I embarrass myself any more?*

Cole stacks my books up. "Let me help carry these to your car."

"Thanks," I mumble because I don't trust my voice to say anything more.

"Can I ask where you are going? A last-minute trip before school starts again? Or are you ditching classes?"

I should keep my mouth shut. But the alcohol has now loosened my tongue, and I'm beyond exacerbated at this point. "I got expelled. Well, not expelled, suspended. They're kicking me out, and I will probably spend the rest of my life alternating between sleeping on my sister's or brother's couch and sleeping in my car, while I wait tables and get hit on by drunk guys who like to grab my ass and listen to my voice and think that because I can't help but speak sultrily it gives them permission to fuck me."

Cole's eyes go big, but he doesn't speak. He probably thinks

I'm insane after witnessing my mini-meltdown. He's probably trying to figure out how to get away from me as fast as possible.

We make it to my car, and I pop the trunk, not even caring to move the McDonalds wrappers in the back. I put my bags in, and Cole places the books next to the bags.

He opens his mouth, and I know words come out, but I can't hear them over the engine of a motorcycle speeding into the parking lot. My gaze focuses on the motorcycle.

No fucking way.

Knight parks the motorcycle in a no parking zone and then spots me.

Shit. This is not happening. He can't see me like this. I'll kill him.

I turn to the still bumbling Cole. He can save me from Knight. Knight won't come over if he thinks Cole is my boyfriend.

I move up on my tiptoes, barely grab Cole's cheeks, and kiss him. Our eyes both take a second to close as I've taken us both by surprise, but it happens. I push my tongue into his mouth, needing to take this kiss with me when I go. It might be a while until I get to kiss a man like this. *Unless I decide to whore myself out to survive.*

Cole wraps his arms around me caressing my face as he does. His tongue is gentle in my mouth, exploring but not as frantic as my tongue. He moans softly, showing me he enjoys the kiss, but nothing more.

No sparks fly.

No electricity lights.

No emotions form.

Nothing. The kiss is nice, but nice isn't enough. Not when the fucker who got me fired's kiss did all of that and more. I've been getting myself off every night to the memory of that kiss. A kiss that should be my worst nightmare has become my fantasy.

We both pull away and smile at each other like we've just

been having a friendly conversation. *Nice.* Cole Tracker is the hottest man I've ever kissed, and all I felt was nice. He's tall, dark, and handsome. He's wearing an expensive suit. It's clear his life is together. I should fall for a man like him, but instead, I want the bad boy who is barreling toward us.

Cole doesn't turn around, but I can see in his eyes he feels the danger approaching. "This is going to hurt," he mumbles so quietly I'm not sure I hear him correctly.

I see the blood before I realize what happened. I expect them to get into a brawl. I expect Cole to whip around and punch Knight in the face like he deserves. I grab my phone ready to call in reinforcements to break them up if I need to.

Nothing happens though. Cole laughs as blood drips from his nose. His eye is already swollen and turning different colors with every second that passes. Red, purple, and blue.

Knight glares at me and then walks back to his motorcycle. He looks good. His tattoos hides the scars on his arms; I only find a faint one on his cheek. His hair is cut shorter, but still longer than most men's. And his eyes see through to my soul. The engine roars, and he's gone as quickly as he came.

"What just happened?" I ask, my mouth gaping. "Do you know him?"

"You don't want to know."

I stare in the direction of Knight's exit. I really do want to know, but I don't push Cole. Instead, I watch as the dust settles back on the asphalt by the curb.

"I might have a job for you," Cole says.

I stare at him, dumbfounded.

"What?" I have no idea what he just said.

He strokes my cheek. It's not a loving gesture, more like a goodbye.

When he finishes, I'm left with nothing. No chills, no goosebumps, no reaction. Knight had a stronger reaction to me, and he didn't even touch me or speak to me.

Cole reaches into his back pocket and pulls out a business card. He hands it to me.

"What's this?"

"A way for you to do more than just survive."

I blink, not believing my luck might have changed. That Cole might not be able to get my panties wet, but he is obviously successful. He might be able to get me a job. Which, right now, I need more than a boyfriend.

"What's the job?" I ask.

He smirks. "Meet me at the address tonight at eight. And wear your nicest outfit. I'll make sure you have a job by tonight."

He turns to leave.

"Thanks!" I say, suddenly getting my voice back.

He nods solemnly. "And stop kissing strange boys, it keeps getting you in trouble."

I blush and smile at his words. He has no idea how much kissing men has gotten me in trouble. He said boys though, not men. I watch Cole walk away, while Knight's body flickers in my head. Neither of which I would call a boy. They might be closer to my age than I realized at first appearance, but they are successful. They have built a life. They know how to charm me. Only a man could do that.

5

KNIGHT

I sit down next to my asshole of a friend. I don't know why I'm even here except for a chance to pummel his face again for what he did.

"No ice? You didn't even bring me a drink?"

I roll my eyes. "You don't need me to bring you anything. You have women to do that for you."

Cole shrugs and then eyes one of the waiters who smiles at him. She comes over immediately.

"Can you get me ice for my face? And two double Maker's Marks, neat."

"Blanton's for me."

Cole rolls his eyes as if he thinks he ordered the better bourbon. He didn't.

Neither of us talks as we sit in the corner of the bar in our usual booth. Cole watches the ass of our waiter as she prances away, while I spend my time glaring at him. But we both know better than to speak until we have alcohol in us.

The waiter returns quickly. Chrissy is her name, I think. She usually waits on us when we are here. Although, I'm too much of a dick to remember her name or anyone else's in this club.

She sets our drinks down and then makes a show of pressing the ice pack to Cole's face, showing him her boobs in the process.

"Thank you, Chrissy," I say, needing to get this conversation over with. I have better things I need to be doing.

She smiles. "I'm surprised you know my name."

"I don't. It was a lucky guess."

She huffs but leaves us alone after a glance from Cole encouraging her to go, with a promise he'll make it worth her while later.

"What the fuck was that about?"

"I was flirting with the waitress. What's so wrong with that? I enjoy mixing business with pleasure." Cole winces as he presses the ice to his eye.

"I'm not talking about Chrissy. I don't care what you do with her. I'm talking about Mila."

"Mila? I'm not sure I know who you are talking about."

"The woman whose tongue you had in your mouth this afternoon."

"Oh, her." Cole puts the ice down and rests his arms on the back of the booth. *Jackass.* He knows exactly who I'm talking about. I don't understand what game he's playing.

"Explain yourself, now. Before I beat the hell out of you and make you wish you never touched a woman again."

"I thought you didn't care about Mila."

"I don't."

"Please. The only reason I found her, or tasted her luscious lips, is because I know you have a thing for her."

"I do not."

Cole ignores me. "I knew you wouldn't ask her out on your own, so I decided an intervention was needed."

"I was headed to find her five minutes after you left. That's why I saw the two of you swapping spit."

"How was I supposed to know?"

I growl.

"Fine, I knew you'd go after the girl."

"Mila."

"Mila. I knew you'd go after her, but I knew she wouldn't go for you."

"Why the hell not?"

"For one, your game isn't what it used to be. You've been out of practice for the last five years."

I shoot daggers with my eyes. But I pick up my drink to sip and let him finish.

"Two, you got her suspended from college with your kiss, so she hates your guts."

I drink. I can't argue with that one. I royally fucked that up.

"And three, she's still totally hung up on me."

I slam my drink down and about climb over the table to get to him.

"Whoa, chill. She's not into me anymore."

I sit back. "How do you know?"

"The kiss."

I growl again. "Don't remind me."

"She kissed me to avoid having to talk to you, but I know she's secretly wanted to do it since she saved my life."

"She didn't save your life; I did when I pulled you out of the burning car. Although I don't know why I did that now, you butthead."

He smiles. "Butthead is tame."

"Well, you're my only friend. I don't want to piss you off too much."

"How do you know she's not into you anymore?"

"The kiss."

I groan, *again with the damn kiss.*

"There was no spark. Chicks care a lot about if there is a spark on the first kiss."

I narrow my eyes. "Chicks always find a spark with you, although I have no idea why."

He shrugs. "There wasn't one. I even gave her my best kiss to piss you off thoroughly. Nothing happened though."

We both sip our drinks in silence as I process what Cole said.

"Nothing happened?" I repeat.

"Well, I offered her a job because she is desperate now that you've made her destitute."

"What kind of job?" I growl, hoping the job is in his legal department or something.

He glances behind me. "Mila's here, right on time for her job interview."

"What?" I snap my head around and find Mila. She seems both out of place and precisely in the right place. She's wearing a skirt and suit jacket two sizes too big for her frail body. Her shoes are dark pumps that also appear too big. Her hair is up in a high ponytail, and she's wearing red, fuck-me lipstick. I don't know whether she is looking for a job in a law office, or if this is part of her act when she goes on stage and strips.

"No, she's not fucking working here. She's not becoming a stripper, or escort, or whore. Not even a waitress here."

Cole smirks as he relaxes into the booth.

"I'm going to kill you. I'll give you another shiner to match the one you already have."

"No, you won't. Now, I can offer her a job, or you can. The choice is yours."

I grab my drink and down it, hating that he's calling my bluff and forcing my hand.

This is what I wanted though. A chance to make Mila mine. An opportunity for her to agree to my plan.

She spots me the second I stand. I'm not hard to spot. I don't exactly fit in at this club. I'm not a suit with a hard-on for young girls.

I see her eyes, and I know what she's thinking. She should turn and walk out the door. But Cole's right. She's desperate. I could probably convince her to spread her legs for half the men in this club if it paid well. I don't know what's happened to her, but I hate seeing her this way.

"Mila, I didn't expect to see you in a fine establishment like this."

"I didn't expect to see you again, at all."

My cock is instantly straining against the zipper of my jeans when she speaks. I've never heard a voice like hers.

Thankfully, she doesn't notice. *Or maybe, unfortunately.*

"Here for a job?" I ask.

"No."

"Oh, then I guess you're here to watch the women dance. You could have told me you were into women; I would have left you alone."

She glares. "I'm not into women."

I circle behind her as she stares ahead, trying to pretend like the naked women in front of her don't bother her.

"I know."

She shivers.

I touch the nape of her neck. "Your body responds to my words, my touch, my presence."

"Don't flatter yourself. I don't want to talk to the asshole who kisses me, gets me fired, and gets me kicked out of college. How could you?"

I see the pain in her eyes when I move back in front of her.

"I'm sorry."

Her mouth drops. She wasn't expecting me to apologize.

"I thought I was helping you."

"How could kissing me be helping me?"

"Your supervisor walked in when you purposely tugged on my IV. And I think she saw you throw my pain medication in the trash, although I can't be sure. I thought if she saw me kiss you, she'd realize I'm a bastard that had been sexually harassing you, and she wouldn't punish you for what you had done previously."

Her mouth forms the perfect 'O.' And I can't help but wonder if that is her same look when she orgasms. I don't say that though. I'm already in the doghouse with her. And as much as she hates me, I need her help.

"Well, that backfired badly."

"I know, I'm sorry. I talked to the dean, but he had already made up his mind. Although, I think I can help you."

"I don't need your help."

I cock my head. "You sure about that, pretty girl?"

She rolls her eyes. "I'm sure."

"It seems I owe you a job after what I did."

"You own this place?" she gasps.

I shrug.

"Of course, you do. Only sick bastards like you would own a strip club."

"It's not just a strip club. It's also an escort service and every man or woman's fantasy. It's a club for the elite, and can become whatever they need."

She scans the crowd, realizing everyone here is in an expensive suit. Well, everyone but her and me.

"Do you want to talk about the job or not?"

I see the beads of sweat dripping down her neck. She licks her lips trying to moisten her dry mouth. I can hear her heart beating wildly against her cheap suit jacket.

She's considering what she will do or not do for money. No, not for money, to survive. It's obvious she's been through enough to be a survivor. She will do what she has to.

I admire that about her, but it won't protect her. She will still end up hurt in the end if she agrees to my plan, no matter how I try to protect her.

"I'm listening."

I don't know whether to smile or frown. As soon as I tell her my proposal, she will say yes. I still don't know entirely what I'm proposing, but I know it won't be good for her. It might even destroy her.

I turn and walk toward one of the private rooms. I stop Chrissy to get her to bring us drinks. I don't turn to see if Mila is following me, I know she is.

I've seen desperation. I've felt it. It's how I'm living. I will do anything to fix my current predicament. So in that regard, we are the same.

I hold the door open for her to the private room, and she steps inside cautiously, like a lamb walking into a lion's den. She takes a seat on the chair while I spread out on the couch.

I don't speak until Chrissy has brought us drinks.

I take them both from her. "Tequila or vodka?"

"Vodka," she answers.

"Good," I say handing her the vodka drink.

"That doesn't look like tequila."

I sip my whiskey. "It's not."

"Then, why did you offer me a tequila drink?"

"I knew you'd want one or the other. I guessed, but if you'd asked for tequila, I would have gotten that for you."

"Why do you think I would prefer vodka?"

"Because tequila represents your wild, carefree, fuck it side. Vodka is just as strong, but you feel more in control when you drink it, which is what you think you need around me."

She doesn't answer, which means I guessed correctly.

"I think you dressed incorrectly for the job, though. I don't think you're capable of what I need in that."

She frowns and sets her drink down.

"You don't think I'm capable of stripping in front of a bunch of horny men?"

"No."

She stands up suddenly, pulling her shitty phone with a shattered screen from a pocket in her skirt. She presses a button and music begins playing. These rooms are soundproof. They have to be to ensure the utmost privacy.

Slowly, Mila begins moving her hips to the music. I'm mesmerized. I can't move or think. All I can do is watch.

She slowly moves her hands over her body, until it gets to the button on her suit jacket. She undoes the button and lets the jacket gape open. She's not wearing a shirt underneath, just a red, lacey bra.

Fuck me.

Her boobs spill out of the bra, even though her body could use more meat on her bones.

She sways again, as her hands move to her back. She begins unzipping her skirt, and then it's a puddle on the floor.

I know I'm drooling; I have to be as I watch her. And my cock has never been this hard.

She's wearing nothing but a lacey, red thong and bra with her black pumps. She takes a step toward me, then another and another until she's right in front of me.

She hesitates for just a second, and then she's on my lap. Her body is gyrating over my crouch. *Why the fuck did I wear jeans? Sweatpants, always wear sweatpants.*

She reaches up and pulls the hair tie from her hair. Her hair cascades around me in long, thick strands.

"Fucking, beautiful," I curse.

She pauses, not expecting my words.

"Still think I can't strip in front of a room full of men?" she asks, as she caresses my neck and moves her lips inches from mine.

"No." I grin.

She glares. She immediately rolls off me and starts dressing again. "I just stripped in front of you."

"Stripping in front of *me* is different than stripping in a room full of men. And you didn't fully strip anyway."

Another scowl.

"Close enough," she whispers.

I grab her wrist and pull her back onto my lap. "No, not close enough. But that's not why you can't strip in front of a room full of men." Our faces are inches apart, and I want nothing more than to kiss her again.

"Why?" she breathes.

"Because I can't stand to watch you strip in front of anyone but me."

She gasps.

It takes her a while, but she finally finds her words. "I'm not sleeping with you to make money. I'm not a whore."

I frown. "You are definitely not a whore. And I'm not going to fuck you."

She narrows her eyes. "Then what do you want with me, Knight?"

I love the way she uses my last name as my first. I know it's supposed to be her way of teasing me, as I do by picking out random nicknames for her. She doesn't realize I've never gone by Ace though. I've only been Ace to one person. Knight is who I am. And it's sexy as hell for her to figure it out on her own and call me that.

"I want you to do whatever I say, no questions asked."

6
____

MILA

Knight wants me to fuck him. That's what he means when he says he wants me to "do whatever I say."

I can see it in his eyes, his voice is dripping with it, and even though he's wearing jeans, I can feel his erection press against me. Hard as a rock, begging to be inside me.

Right now, I don't know whether to regret that I'm straddling his lap almost entirely naked or to be thankful. *How did I get myself into this mess?*

My cheeks blush as his eyes rake up and down my body. I felt bold when I stripped for him even though he didn't ask me to.

I thought it would give me the upper hand.

I thought he'd be distracted by my body.

I thought he'd be speechless.

I thought he'd realize I'm capable of *anything*.

Instead, I'm horny and embarrassed, and can't do a damn thing about either.

I consider trying to move off his lap again, but his hands are firmly gripping my waist. I'm not going anywhere until we finish this conversation, no matter how uncomfortable it makes us.

This conversation is going to happen eye to eye, lips inches apart, with all of our lust on full display. Both of us completely vulnerable to each other.

Except, I feel a lot more vulnerable than he seems. Because I'm practically naked.

I grab the hem of his shirt.

He raises an eyebrow but doesn't protest as I lift the shirt over his head. I immediately regret it. I forgot how insanely hot he is. He's all abs, tattoos, and muscle. Even the few scars and bruises now covering his body do nothing to make him any less attractive.

"Are you trying to get me to fuck you?" he asks.

"No, just want to level the playing field."

"So, will you do anything I want?" His lips curl up as if he knows I'll do anything he wants for free, and more than that for money.

"No, I'd rather strip for strangers than give you whatever you want."

He shakes his head. "Stripping won't pay the bills." And the darkness in his eyes says he won't let me anyway. Even though I don't need his permission. We aren't dating. We aren't anything except two strangers who have kissed and are clinging to each other while shirtless.

"What does *anything* mean?"

He narrows his eyes but doesn't speak.

"If this isn't about sex, then what? You want me to pretend to date you?"

"I don't want you to *pretend* to do anything."

I gasp. I wasn't expecting that. I wasn't expecting any honesty in whatever it is we are doing.

"Why?"

"Because nothing I do will ever be pretend. I will always be honest with you, with my actions and words."

I believe him; I do. He will be candid with me when he speaks, but that won't stop him from hiding things from me. He is hiding the truth.

"I have a delicate situation I need your help with," Knight says.

I study him, but he gives nothing away until he's ready to. And I have a feeling I could work for him for years and never know what he's hiding.

His hand tucks a strand of hair behind my ear, and I shiver. Our eyes lock, and I want nothing more than to fuck him. I don't care if I have enough money to feed myself. I don't care if I have a place to live. I'll live off the high and afterglow from the orgasms he will give me.

Knight notices my reaction and removes his hands, placing them gently on the couch. My eyes are glued to his rough hands, capable of playing me like a guitar. And then I spot the tan line where a wedding ring used to be.

"You're married?"

"Separated. Soon to be divorced."

I lean back. "That's what you want my help with. Making your ex jealous?"

He chuckles, leaning back on the couch. I like his smile. I like everything about him almost as much as I hate him.

I fold my arms across my chest. "Why was that funny?"

"Because you don't know my ex. She doesn't get jealous. She has no reason to. When we were married, I loved her with everything I had. I didn't notice other women. I wouldn't let myself. It was her and me against everything."

"But not now?"

"No. Now I just want this over."

His voice changes when he says *over*. It's dark, deep, and broken. It's final.

"Messy divorce?"

He doesn't answer, which means yes.

"What do you want me to do then, if not make her jealous?"

"Anything I tell you."

My cheeks blush as his cock twitches beneath me, making his words dirtier than they should be. I look away and try to compose myself. I gently blow air out of my pursed lips, and I expect him to make a dirty comment about how we should fuck, he knows it's what I want.

But when I look at him again, he's serious. His lips thinned, his cheeks plain, his eyes focused.

"What does *anything* mean? Can you give me some examples?"

"You will come to my office every day. Your formal title will be my assistant. I will then have you do *anything* I need. Bring me coffee, retrieve my dry cleaning, attend events with me."

"Dry cleaning?" I eye his jeans and T-shirt. I doubt he even owns a suit.

He ignores my snarky remark.

"That's it? I just get your coffee and go to a few events with you, and you will pay me—"

"I'll pay you $250,000 over the next five months."

My mouth gapes. I've never had that kind of money before. I knew he had money. He said millions.

"I never realized the strip club business was that lucrative," I say when I get my voice back.

He chuckles and leans in like he's going to kiss me but stops short. "It's not."

I suck in a breath. Never have I been so breathless. I need to go to the hospital when this is finished and get hooked up to some oxygen until I can breathe again.

"I will also guarantee you can continue your nursing degree in the spring."

My eyes widen. "You can't guarantee something like that."

"I can with the donation I will be making to the school."

Holy shit! He is rich, and he must really want me to work for him if he's willing to donate money to the college.

"Shouldn't you be doing that part for free since you're the reason I got suspended in the first place?" Is what my smart mouth says instead of thanking him.

"No, *you* ran over my motorcycle. You denied me pain medications. I think if anything, you owe me."

He's right, but I'll never tell him that.

"Why me?"

"You don't think you are capable of getting me coffee?"

"I can get you coffee, but that is not what this job really entails. It's not about getting you coffee. It's about doing what you ask without question. And I'm sure most of the time I will just be getting you coffee, until…"

"Until?"

"Until the real reason you want to hire me. Until you ask me to do something illegal, dangerous, or sexual."

"I would never ask you to do anything illegal."

We stare at each other, neither of us blinking. *But he would ask me to do something dangerous or sexual?*

"Why me?"

"Because you are perfect for the job."

"That's not an answer."

"That's the only answer I'm giving you."

"What happened to honesty?"

"I'm being honest. The job pays well, and you will hate me by the end of this, but you will have your life back."

I frown. I don't want his honesty anymore. This is a bad idea. The last time I dated a bad boy, it almost destroyed my entire family and me. I know he's not asking me to date him, but he's asking for me to be vulnerable, for me to trust him.

I'm not sure I can trust him, not when he isn't honest with

me. His words are the truth, but he's hiding something. Something he isn't saying. The real reasons he wants me to work for him. Something to do with his soon to be ex-wife.

"You're young to have a wife."

"I'm young to have millions sitting in my bank account too."

I nod. "You're not secretly a fifty-year-old man or something?"

"I'm twenty-four."

I study him. He's only two years older than I am, but somehow life has taken us on very different paths. I'm broke and about to do anything for money. He's rich but desperate to get out of a bad situation. Money doesn't fix anything; it just makes life more complicated. I should know.

"I'll agree on one condition."

He perks up, his eyes open more fully, and his lips purse like he's going to kiss me if I say yes.

"You already said you'd never ask me to do anything illegal."

He nods.

"And I can live with a little danger." *I already have enough danger in my life.* "But no sex."

"No sex?" he asks slowly.

"Yes, no sex. I won't fuck you for money."

He smiles when I say fuck.

"I'm not asking you to fuck me for money. I don't pay for sex. I'm not going to pretend with you, Mila. Everything that happens between us will be real. I won't fuck you if you don't want me to."

I will just break your heart. He doesn't say the words, but they are implied. If I do this, I will end up broken.

It's not possible to be more broken than I've been. He doesn't know about my past.

"Last condition."

He chuckles. "You said that last time."

"Whatever." I roll my eyes. "I need an honest answer."

He leans back, waiting for me to continue.

"What do you want?"

"I want you to work for me."

"No." I shake my head. "I mean, what do you want from life?" I can't work for a broken man who is just out for revenge. He doesn't have to be a saint, but I need to know his life is more than making his ex's life a living hell.

Knight looks away, and I don't think he's going to answer me. It's a personal question, and I need a truthful answer to agree to do this.

He's not going to be honest. He's going to let me go. I'm not going to get this job.

"I want freedom."

Our eyes meet, and I realize the truth. It's what we both want.

Freedom from our pasts.

Freedom to be ourselves.

Freedom to be happy.

Freedom to have a future.

"I accept your job offer." I hold out my hand, even though I'm not wearing a shirt or pants.

Even though he's shirtless.

Even though we've kissed.

He smiles and shakes my hand. "Miss Burns, I think we are going to make a perfect team."

7

———

KNIGHT

"NOW WHAT?" Mila asks, her eyes big with fear about what's coming, but also a tiny bit turned on. I know if I reached between her legs right now I'd find her wet. I haven't let my eyes glimpse her cunt that's wrapped in sexy lace. If I did, I wouldn't be able to keep my promise of not fucking her without her permission. I'd turn into an animal who wouldn't be able to stop.

"When does my job start? What hours do I work?"

"Immediately, and any hour I want you."

She shivers on my lap, which doesn't help my hard on. It's been too long since I've wanted a woman this badly.

I want to tell Mila to give me a lap dance. To see how far she will take her new job responsibilities. I want to torture her, but I'm not sure who I would be torturing more.

"What does my bad boss want me to do now?" she teases in her sultry voice.

"Get dressed."

Her eyes widen further into big green orbs.

"And never talk dirty again. It doesn't suit you. Your voice is more than enough."

"I wasn't trying to—"

I give her a look, and she stops. She was teasing me, trying to get under my skin. I know she thinks I'm nothing but a bad boy. She probably thinks I stole the money I've earned. Or earned it off of young women who dance for me. She doesn't know I've barely earned a penny from this club.

Mila climbs off of me slowly, like she's deliberately trying to drive me crazy as she rubs her body against mine. But I know it's not deliberate. She just doesn't realize how sexy she is.

She pulls her skirt on and buttons the jacket over her bra. She picks up the hair tie and ties her hair up high on her head into a ponytail again. And I'm left wondering if she was sexier in her lingerie or now fully dressed. I don't have an answer.

She stares at me, and I smile smugly as she eats me up.

"Are you going to get dressed?"

"Huh?" *Oh, I forgot I wasn't wearing a shirt.* I grab my T-shirt and throw it over my head.

"Have you eaten dinner yet?" I ask even though I know the answer. *No.* And if she did eat, she needs to eat a second dinner; she's far too skinny for what is healthy.

"Eat dinner here, at the club?"

"No."

"Okay."

"Okay?"

Mila frowns not understanding my words.

"I think a more appropriate answer when your boss gives you an order would be yes, sir."

She laughs. "Not happening, Knight."

I pout, and she laughs harder almost knocking herself off balance on her heels. I stand up and grab her hand, just before she crashes to the floor and I have to take her to the hospital. As much as I enjoyed our first kiss at the hospital, I don't want to have to go back to the hospital with her anytime soon.

"You sure, Mila? I could make you."

She stares down at my arm where I'm holding her. "You could, but you won't. You may be an asshole, but you won't force me."

"How do you know?"

She frowns and shakes her head. "I don't know how I know. I just do."

I nod, understanding completely.

I take her hand and walk her back out to the world of dangerous men, sex, and money. A world I want her far away from.

I lead her quickly out of the club, and then to my motorcycle that is waiting for us.

"Do you always park your motorcycle illegally?"

"No, it's the club manager's job to know when a client wants to leave."

"I don't care how expensive this motorcycle is; I'm not getting on it."

I let go of her hand and collect two helmets and hold one out to her.

"No." She stubbornly crosses her arms.

I sigh. "The agreement was that you do whatever I tell you to do. Without argument."

"I don't think that was the agreement."

"Read the fine print."

"There is no fine print. We didn't sign anything."

"Exactly. Your job is to do what I say without question or our deal is off. I won't pay you. I won't ensure you have a diploma waiting for you in May." *It's not true. I've already donated the money, and she's already enrolled next semester. She would be re-enrolled this semester if I didn't need her help first. And I won't let her starve or live in her car, which is what she'd do without my money.*

Mila huffs but then takes a step forward. "I will ride on this motorcycle tonight, but if we are to travel together in the future, I kindly ask you consider a different form of transportation. I'll even ride the bus."

"Why? What do you have against motorcycles?"

"They are dangerous."

I grin. "All the more reason you should ride them."

She snatches the helmet out of my hands and then straddles the bike behind me. I don't give her time to grab my waist before I jolt us forward. I love the squeal that escapes her as her hands squeeze around my waist.

I whiz around a corner, and she screams louder. I don't want to push her too far in one night, so after having a few moments of fun, I slow down.

"Faster," she whispers in my ear.

My mouth gapes. She can't be seriously asking me to speed up. So I test her. I rev the engine and step on the gas after the next stoplight.

"That isn't fast." She breathes on my neck.

Fuck.

I pick up speed, pushing both of our limits this time as I round another corner.

"Yes, Knight!" she cries out like she just came from the excitement of having black shiny rumbling metal between her legs. *Damn, why did I think this was a good idea? Now I want to be between her legs, spreading her, giving her a real reason to be screaming my name.*

I zoom through the city, the stars sparkling overhead somehow shining through the fog of the night. I zip between cars, not caring that what I'm doing is illegal and dangerous, as I hug the middle line to speed between two cars. One guy flips me off as I drive by.

I always drive fast, but I haven't felt this good on my motorcycle. I like teasing women on my bike, but this is different. More than I expected.

We reach our destination too fast, and I slow down, parking it on the side of the road in an actual parking slot this time.

Mila lets go of my waist, and I hear her removing her helmet as I do the same. Then, I turn and stare at her with disbelief.

"What was that?"

"Huh?"

"I thought you said you hated motorcycles."

"No, I said I shouldn't ride them because they are dangerous for me."

"Meaning?"

"I like them too much. The only dangerous things are those that we love. Even if motorcycles weren't inherently dangerous, it wouldn't matter, because I love them. Loving something is the only danger."

I nod, agreeing with her completely. "So you want me to pick you up in this again tomorrow?"

"I'm pleading the fifth." She smiles and tucks a loose strand of hair behind her ear. *That's a hell yes.*

"Where are we going to eat?" She searches the restaurants around us. "Ooh, are we going to that one?" She points at a restaurant on the third floor overlooking much of the city across the way.

"No."

"Where are we going then?"

I point in the opposite direction. A tiny little place that looks like a hole in the wall.

"Ramen? I'm going out with a millionaire, and he's taking me to get the only food I can afford on my own."

I laugh.

"Come on; it's one of my favorite restaurants in town."

"I doubt that."

I take her hand and start leading her across the street to the restaurant.

"What are you doing?" She stops dead in her tracks and stares down at our hands like she's holding onto a spider instead of my hand.

"Holding your hand. Since I've already seen you basically naked, I didn't think you would have a problem with me holding your hand."

"I have a problem."

"Noted."

I release her hand and place my hand instead on the small of her back. She shivers. "I don't need you to guide me to the restaurant. I know where we are going."

I nod. "Just trying to get you more comfortable with me."

"Why?"

I shrug. "Because I want you to like me."

She shakes her head. "That will never happen."

"We'll see."

"Knight, we weren't expecting you," the male host, Joni, says.

"That's okay; we don't mind waiting." I drop my hand from Mila's back and immediately notice her squirm. She can pretend all she wants that she doesn't want me to touch her, but I know better. I know she wants me to touch her, hold her, even kiss her again.

Mila glances around at all the people waiting for a table.

"It must be at least an hour wait."

"Two hours, actually, but we will move you to the front of the line. Just don't tell anyone," Joni smiles at Mila and winks. If I were on a normal date, I would pull her to me in a protective manner. I would let this asshole know that Mila's mine. It takes everything in me to resist the urge to touch her.

She shivers again and looks up at me with her big eyes.

"You need something?" I raise an eyebrow, but my lips frown. *I can't stand this.*

"Nope."

"Right this way," Joni says, leading us to a small table toward the back.

We both take a seat, and I make sure to keep my hands to myself. I don't even pull her chair out for her.

Mila looks around the room suspiciously.

"What are you thinking?"

"That I don't know what I'm doing here."

"I told you. I need dinner, and I hate eating dinner alone. I want us to at least be civil toward each other."

"No, you want to butter me up and make me fall for you, so when you are finally ready to ask me to do the one thing you actually hired me to do, I'll say yes, instead of calling you a bastard."

I sit back in my chair. "So sure you have me figured out, huh?"

She nods.

I don't disagree with her. She has me figured out more than she realizes. But in other ways, she doesn't have a clue.

We both order a stiff drink, and I know I won't be driving my motorcycle home after this.

"I think I know why you like this place. They treat you like a god here, and nicer restaurants have much higher clientele they need to take care of than a place like this. You don't have to dress in a suit to go to dinner here. There is a dispensary next door for you to grab a joint from on your way home. And you don't have to spend much money on your 'dates' you bring here."

I stare at her as I take a drink, not letting her know how close or far away she is from the truth. She needs me to be a bad boy, so I will be.

"And the food is delicious; you are forgetting that part."

She rolls her eyes, not believing me.

"Tell me about yourself."

She frowns, downs her drink, flags the waiter for a second one, then responds. "No."

"You need to find a different word; you aren't allowed to tell me no."

"I will tell you *no* as often as I want."

"I will dock a thousand dollars from your pay every time you tell me no."

"Asshole."

"Somehow, you don't seem to have a problem using curse words anymore."

"You bring out the best in me. Am I not allowed to call you an asshole either, without you docking my pay?"

"No, call me whatever you want."

She rolls her eyes. "I have two siblings, both older. My sister is a pediatrician in Aspen. My brother is a lawyer in Cincinnati. My parents died when I was in high school, a freak accident."

"I'm sorry." *She doesn't know how sorry I am, but no words will make the pain go away, so I keep silent.*

She stares into space like she is reliving something, something dark I can't see. She quickly comes back to reality though.

"I bounced around to various community colleges and jobs until I got a full scholarship to CU Denver. I'm not as smart as either of my siblings, so I thought I would go for a less challenging degree, nursing. I was supposed to graduate this winter, until you happened. And now here I am, what about you?"

I stare.

"You seriously aren't going to answer after you demanded I answer? I don't think that's fair."

"Get used to things not being fair."

She glares at me, and I don't know whether to keep holding

back to keep getting that adorable glare or start talking to get her to pout again.

"I don't have any siblings. My parents are very much alive last I checked, although I haven't talked to them since I was five. I lived with my uncle until I turned eighteen, and then he kicked me out of the house."

"I'm sorry."

"Don't be. I was a terror or a 'bad boy' as you would say. I was always in trouble. I spent high school drinking, smoking, and fucking."

Her lips twitch as I speak. *Jealousy perhaps?*

"I got accepted into Harvard. I was going to go. Get a law degree and stick it to my parents, but then I met Abri."

Her auburn hair and brown eyes float through my head. I hate thinking about her.

"We decided to take a year off before starting college. Go travel the world. We ended up eloping and started a million dollar company instead."

Her mouth drops. "You never went to college?"

"Nope."

"You got married at eighteen?"

"Nineteen."

"And you are a millionaire?"

I nod. "You already knew that."

She swallows. "I guess I did, but I'm still not sure I believe it."

"You will when the money hits your bank account."

"I'll know that you have $250,000 to spare, not that you are a millionaire."

Two bowls are placed in front of us.

She stares wide-eyed at the glorious bowls that look nothing like the ramen you get out of the little packets.

"Wait a second." I pull out my phone and get ready to take a picture.

"What are you doing?"

"Proving you wrong. Take a bite."

She gently takes the spoon in her hand and dips it into some of the broth, slowly lifting it to her lips like she thinks this might be a trap. She drinks the liquid and then smiles contently as she moans.

I snap a picture of her face. *Blissful.*

I hold out the phone to her.

She blushes.

"Fuck you, Knight."

I cock my head, not sure why she's cursing at me.

A tiny smile forms and she tries to hold it back. "This is the most delicious thing I've ever tasted."

I grin. "I know."

She looks to either side of her bowl. "How do I eat the noodles? There's no fork."

I grab two sets of chopsticks from the container at the end of the table and hold one out to her.

She eyes them like it's a snake about to bite her but hesitantly takes them.

"Do you know how to use chopsticks?"

She carefully breaks them apart and then attempts to position them in her hand, but instead of holding them correctly she holds it like a knife. She tries to stab the noodles with them.

I laugh.

"Fine, I have no idea how to use chopsticks. I have never been to a restaurant that uses them."

I position them in my hand. "Like this."

She studies my hand, trying to mimic the position of my hand. She dips her chopsticks into the ramen bowl, scoops up some noodles, and they immediately fall back into the bowl.

She growls.

I laugh before lifting some of my noodles into my mouth.

She stares at me with a gaping mouth, watching me slowly slurp the delicious noodles. I purr quietly, reminding her of just how good the food is.

"You're an ass."

I shrug and keep eating.

She licks her lips and then scoops more of the broth into her mouth. If she keeps doing that she won't have any left to eat her noodles with.

"Fine." She slams her spoon down.

"Yes, princess?"

She glares. "Will you please help me?"

"Of course, pretty girl."

I reach across the table touching her hand lightly so that I can see the goosebumps on her arms. And then, I move her top chopstick slightly in her hand.

"That's it?"

I nod. "Try now."

She clasps a noodle and brings it to her mouth. She chews the noodle slowly with her eyes closed. When she swallows, she opens her eyes.

"I've changed my mind. Knight, you have just become my favorite person in the world."

I chuckle. "I'm sure you'll change your mind again soon enough. But I'll take the compliment for now."

We both eat more of the ramen, slowly enjoying the best food in Denver.

"Tell me something no one else knows," Mila begs suddenly.

I think for a moment, trying to come up with something good.

"I pretend to hate my parents for leaving me, but I secretly wish they would come back every damn day. Even though I'm a grown man now, I still wish they would come back and be my parents."

Noodles fall out of her gaping mouth.

"I also have only ever loved one woman. Only had one serious girlfriend who turned into my wife. One love and now I think love is overrated."

She drops her chopsticks. She's going to regret that because she's not going to remember how to hold them correctly when she picks them back up again.

"Oh, and I've never been to a concert before."

"You've never been to a concert before?"

"Nope, I've listened to bands play in bars, but never bought a ticket and gone to an actual concert before."

"Why not?"

"Because I'm afraid I'll leave disappointed when I realize the band isn't as good as they are on the radio. That they are just normal guys playing instruments, and the only reason their voice sounds like that is autotune."

She frowns. "I'm taking you to a concert."

"What about you? Tell me something no one knows about you."

Her eyes sear into mine. "My favorite movie is 10 Things I Hate About You, my favorite musician is Taylor Swift, and my favorite food is tacos."

"Really? I poured my soul out, and you tell me your favorite food is tacos? That's not telling me something no one else knows."

She wipes her mouth on a napkin, her eyes not meeting mine. "Yes, it is."

I tilt her chin to look at me. "No, it's not."

She sighs. "I don't have many friends. My roommate is all I have, and we don't have time to talk about our favorite anythings because we are always working and trying to scrape by with enough money to even feed ourselves. And my family..."

"What?"

"Well, they hate me."

I narrow my eyes not understanding. "Your family can't hate you."

"They do. They put up with me, but they don't like me. They only care about making sure I don't put our name back in the newspaper again. They don't care what I like."

Our waiter returns, and I hold out my credit card, unable to take my eyes off Mila. I don't know what happened to her. I don't know what pain she's felt, but from the look in her eyes, it rivals my own.

She thinks we are polar opposites, but I think we are exactly the same.

I hold up my bowl and motion for her to do the same. Both bowls contain a few remnants of broth. We clink our bowls together and then drink until it's gone.

We both smile at each other when we are finished. I no longer hear the music playing in the background, I no longer feel the heat of the other people in the room, I no longer smell the soup. All my senses feel is her.

The connection I feel to her is instant. And I regret saying I won't fuck her. Because right now it's all I can think about.

I hold my hand out to her, sure she's going to brush me off and say she can walk without holding my hand, but to my surprise, she takes it.

I pull her to her feet and lead her out through the restaurant. The cool evening air hits us as we both reach outside, and I breathe in sharply like I haven't taken a breath in hours.

She leans into my chest as I jerk her closer, needing to feel her body against mine until our lips are inches apart.

Her eyes are doe-eyed, her mouth parted, and her tongue traces around her lips. Kiss me, she begs with her body.

I step back. *I can't. I will ruin her and any chance of her helping me.*

"Ever smoked a joint before, pretty girl?"

"No."

"Good, I want to be your first."

She gasps at the words I whispered in her ears.

I grin. *Damn, I'm not going to be able to resist her.* I thought I could, at least until I got what I needed from her. But my smart-mouthed girl won't open up easily. I need more time with her. Time without fucking her. But my dick disagrees.

Maybe my plan can work if I fuck her once? Maybe my plan can work even if she hates me?

8

———

MILA

I HOLD his hand in the backseat of an Uber like we are sixteen and being driven by our parents. Neither of us makes a move, but I know it's only because we have an audience. I know the second we are in his apartment we will be humping each other against a wall.

Knight is a bad boy, just like I always knew, but he's also incredibly broken. More than I realized. He thinks he's opening up to me, and being honest about his past, but he's not. It shows me that he's hiding more.

I know because I'm hiding plenty, even from myself.

The Uber stops, and Knight kisses my hand. *Yep, we are definitely fucking if I agree to go up. And I'm definitely staying at his place because I don't have any other place to stay unless you count sleeping in my car. That's the only reason I'm going up,* I tell myself the lie over and over. *Not because I want to fuck him.*

We step out into the night and walk into his building holding hands. We enter the elevator our fingers still intertwined. I expect him to kiss me. I expect fire and his hands to grab my hips and push me against the wall. I expect to be panting and begging to come within seconds of entering the lift.

81

Instead, nothing happens. Sure, the electricity continues to pass back and forth between us where our hands touch. And yes, I have butterflies swarming in my stomach. And my panties are wet from the dirty looks he keeps giving me. But other than holding my hand, Knight doesn't touch me.

The doors open and he pulls me into his apartment.

"Of course you have an apartment on the top floor. Can you be any more predictable?" I tease.

He shrugs. "Would you prefer I have a loft on the second floor?"

He opens the door, holding it open for me as I step inside. *No, I want him to have this apartment and let me have my own room here. Because damn.*

"That's what I thought," he smugly whispers behind me.

I don't even care. I'm afraid to step further inside for fear I will break something, and I know I can't afford to fix a lamp let alone replace any of the furniture if I accidentally spilled a drop of wine.

He places his hand on my lower back and leads me around. To the living room, dining room, kitchen, piano room, five bathrooms, and four bedrooms. *He has room for a fucking piano! That's crazy!*

"Do you play?" I ask, suddenly wanting to hear him play me something.

"No."

"Then, why do you have it?"

He shrugs. "Doesn't every fancy apartment have a room just for a piano? What else would I put in here?"

"A bar, a pool table, a man cave, I don't know. Normal guy stuff that you would actually use."

He blinks but doesn't say anything.

"Oh...sorry." I realize my mistake when I see the pink throw pillows on the couch next to the piano. This is the place him and Abri shared. I suddenly like it a lot less.

"Why haven't you re-decorated, if you hate her so much?"

He shrugs.

I'm getting tired of his shrugs.

"Knight?" I press again.

"I don't know. It doesn't bother me. I'm used to it the way it is. I'll change it when the divorce is final."

I frown. *Does he think there is a chance that they will work things out and she'll come back?*

I don't want to know the answer to that question.

"So that's it," he says leading me back to the kitchen where he starts pouring us drinks. Except he hasn't shown me the whole apartment. He never showed me his bedroom. I consider asking him to show me, but maybe he thinks we'll end up there in a few minutes anyway.

Knight pours himself a whiskey and me a vodka with a splash of lime.

"Let's go out on the patio."

I nod and follow him outside onto the patio. He takes a seat in the single chair while I sit on the couch. He hands me my drink, and I make sure to let our fingers brush together as I take the glass from him.

Knight frowns, seemingly displeased with the touch. *Maybe because he wants more? But why would he sit by himself instead of the couch if that is what he wanted?*

He pulls out the joint he bought before coming home and lights it. He takes a hit and passes it to me.

I take it from him looking at it curiously. Trying my best to seem like this is my first time smoking a joint. I try to fumble with it and cough as I take the hit, but it's like home in my mouth.

He eyes me suspiciously. "You've smoked before."

"What? No, I uh—"

"You've smoked a joint before."

I blush. "Yes, how did you know?"

"I didn't, you just confirmed. After watching you with the chopsticks, I can tell when you are trying something new and when you aren't."

I avert my eyes, trying to think of what to say. I don't want to tell him about my past. That's not what tonight is about.

He doesn't ask though. Instead, he takes another puff before passing it back to me. We continue like this, alternating between smoking and drinking.

I spent my high school years smoking, drinking, and fucking, his words play in my head. We've done two of the three. Now it's time for the last one.

Knight doesn't realize everything he is doing is turning me on more and more. I may know a good guy in a suit with a fancy job is better for me, but deep down I only like fucking bad boys like him. And I'm growing impatient and more attracted to him by the second.

I set my drink down on the glass table slowly, careful not to break the table or the glass.

Knight chuckles.

"What?"

He shakes his head, still smiling at me.

I don't know what he's laughing at. I'm not too drunk; I'm just being careful. Then I spot the joint. *Oh yea, the weed. I'm being paranoid.*

I stand up and remove my jacket revealing my lace bra again. I should have worn a shirt underneath the jacket, but I didn't have a nice shirt to wear, and I couldn't afford to buy anything. *It makes the outfit sexier*, I remind myself.

I step between Knight's legs, pushing them apart to fit my slim frame.

He eyes me, still holding his glass in his hand as he stares. He doesn't have to say anything. I know from his low growl, from his intense eyes, from his thinned lips that he wants me.

I grab the hem of his shirt again, pulling it off carefully so as not to spill his drink. Revealing the abs, scars, and tattoos again. I haven't had time to study the ones on his chest, so I take my time doing that now. I kneel in front of him and begin kissing his stomach.

His eyes burn into me, but still, no words leave his mouth. I kiss the first ripple, then the next, then the next. I make it to his chest and kiss the Chinese words, the dragon, the bottle of whiskey, the swirling lines, and then I stop.

The letters A-B-R-I are across his heart.

My eyes swell looking up at him. He loved her. He still loves her. *What the hell am I doing?*

He grabs my wrist and pulls me up.

"Stop."

I bite my lip. I don't have to ask what he means. *Stop thinking that he still loves her.*

He puts his drink down and pulls me to his lap until I'm straddling him. Our breaths come hard and fast, and our eyes lock together in a dance, trying to decide who is going to make the first move.

We both kiss at the same time. I moan as he nibbles on my bottom lip. Then he sweeps his tongue into my mouth. I open, letting him in. I might never let him into my heart, but I will let him into my body anytime.

This kiss is hard, full of a passion and desperation that wasn't there the first time we kissed. This kiss is rough, primal, exactly what I would expect from a bad boy who knows his way around a bedroom.

I grasp at his chest as he grabs my waist, not letting the kiss end. One kiss rolls into the next, then the next, then the next.

Our moans bounce off each other in one endless sound. Our tongues find the innermost part of each of our mouths.

I've never been kissed like this. Not like I'm wanted. Not like I'm the only person in his universe.

"Just one taste," he mumbles under his breath.

"Wha—" I gasp as he pushes my bra aside freeing one of my breasts so he can take my nipple in his mouth. He nips at it gently before lapping his tongue over it. Teasing and taunting the hardened point.

"Yes, Knight."

He doesn't stop. He gives me more than a taste of what his tongue is capable of. *Yes, yes, yes.* It's been forever since I've had a man that knows what he's doing with a woman's body.

He grabs my legs and lifts me up as he attacks my other breast. My head falls back as he carries me inside.

I attack his mouth, his rough stubble brushing against my cheek with each kiss. *More, more, more.*

I grab his thick hair, keeping his mouth on me even as we ascend stairs.

Wait...stairs? I don't remember climbing stairs on our previous tour of the house.

He smirks against my lips. "I have my own, private staircase to my bedroom."

"Oh."

He pulls on my bottom lip, sucking it into his mouth and nipping roughly.

I growl, it only makes him suck more forcefully.

Knight pushes the door open, and I want to scan the room. I want to know everything about him. What makes him tick. What secret he's hiding. Maybe there is some clue in his most personal of spaces.

But I can't let go of him. I can't stop kissing him. I can't stop staring into his deep eyes or smelling his manly cologne long enough to care what his room looks like. It could be covered in dirty clothes, the sheets unwashed, with an odor of a pig and I wouldn't care. I want Knight too much to let anything stop this from happening.

Knight's eyes leave mine long enough to spot his bed behind me. *Yes, bed!*

He tosses me onto the warm sheets that have clearly been washed; the fresh linen smell trickling up to my nose. I hold onto his neck as he tumbles on top of me.

"Umpf," he moans.

I laugh. "Not expecting that, huh?" I like it rough when I'm not in a relationship and whatever Knight and I are doing is not a relationship.

How can we have a relationship when all we've done is lie and hide things from each other? We can't. But we can have hot sex while we 'work' together. That is something we should do a lot of from the way his thick length is pushing into my stomach. I can already tell how impressive he is and he hasn't even undressed yet.

Knight grabs my wrists and pushes them to the bed over my head. He wants rough too. There won't be anything sweet about this.

His eyes scan mine, searching to see if I want this. I purr and let my eyes turn to red-hot slits, begging to be fucked.

"I want this," I whisper.

He closes my eyes with a hand, and I can't help but get the feeling that he's shutting me out.

"Go to sleep, Mila." He used my name. He only does that when he's being serious and not teasing.

"What?" I try to sit up, but he continues to hold me down, his body pressing over mine.

"You heard me. Sleep, Mila. I'm not going to fuck you tonight."

My eyes are wide open now.

"We have work in the morning. You need to be well rested." He slowly lets me go and stands up.

My fingers automatically go to my lips, where seconds before he was kissing, gnawing and tearing his way into me with promises of what he was going to do to my body. Now, he's telling me to sleep. *How can I sleep with him in the bed next to me?*

But he's not walking to climb in the bed. He's walking toward the door. He won't even be sleeping in the bed with me.

"It's because you still love Abri?"

Knight's eyes darken, and his body stiffens. "No. This has nothing to do with Abri."

"Then, why? Why won't you fuck me? Why won't you even sleep in the bed next to me? Your bed, by the way."

"I only fuck sober women who want me and aren't using me to deal with their own problems."

I feel like he slapped me. He was the one who started us down this path, not me. I hate him. I won't ever fuck him.

Knight walks to the door, lingering in the doorway. "Sleep Mila, or tomorrow you'll hate me even more."

9

MILA

Buzz, buzz, buzz—

What the hell?

My eyes shoot open as the most annoying sound in the world hits my head. It feels like someone is repeatedly pounding on my head.

I roll over, find the obnoxious alarm clock and hit it off. *Sleep, I need sleep.*

I roll over, closing my eyes only for the alarm to sound again.

I slam it off again, and that's when I notice the note lying on the nightstand.

Be ready to leave at seven. Your day will usually start earlier, but I let you sleep in today because I'm nice. I'll meet you at the office. My driver will be downstairs waiting.

—Knight

Seven is sleeping in? What kind of crazy man thinks that? I sit up before I realize the room is spinning. And my stomach...

I run to the bathroom as the contents of my stomach come up. I spend the next five minutes heaving over Knight's toilet.

What would he think if I called in sick on my first day? I don't even have his number to call in sick though. I'm sure his driver would though.

I wash my face in his sink surrounded by granite counter tops and a mirror five people could easily use to get ready at the same time. And then I walk to the bedroom and find my phone to read the time. Five 'til seven.

Shit.

I race through the room, searching for any clothes I can change into. I find nothing but men's suits. He kept the pictures of Abri but got rid of her clothes, terrific.

I pull open a drawer and smile when I see women's jeans, but when I pull them out I know I would never fit into them. They are tiny. And I don't even know what I'm supposed to wear to this job. All I know is Knight owns a strip club, and I'll be his assistant. I assume it doesn't matter what I wear.

But I don't have time to stop by my car I parked just off campus to change my clothes, and there is nothing here for me to wear other than my clothes from last night. I pull on the jacket and skirt and stare at the wrinkles in the mirror. I look like I was just fucked. And I was, only not in the way I wanted.

I run my fingers through my hair and then tie my hair up in a high ponytail before slipping my heels on and racing downstairs.

I walk out into the crisp morning air. "Hello, Miss Burns."

I stare up at a man in a suit standing outside of a blacked out Audi sedan.

Knight really meant driver, not Uber.

"I picked up a coffee and a bagel for you. It's in the back, but if you'd prefer tea or—"

"Coffee is great. Thank you..."

"Gallagher."

"Thank you, Gallagher."

I climb into the back seat of the luxurious car and spot the coffee and bagel. I sip the coffee, and although I'm going to have to suffer through my massive headache all day, the coffee helps.

Gallagher begins driving in the front seat, singing along quietly to the music.

"Where are we headed? Are we going to the strip club again?"

Gallagher chuckles, raising an eyebrow.

"Oh sorry, I meant gentleman's club."

He shakes his head. "Why would we go there?"

"Because Knight owns it. He said I would be his assistant for the next couple of months. Does he have separate offices away from the club?"

Gallagher smiles gently. "Something like that."

That's rather vague.

"Tell me about Knight. Is he a good boss?"

He nods. "He compensates me very well."

Vague again.

"Did you ever drive him and Abri?"

Gallagher stills, but nods.

Does he still love her? Is that what he's hiding from me? I don't ask my questions though. It's clear Gallagher won't answer me anyway.

I eat my bagel, trying to anticipate what is going to happen when I arrive, but I have no idea what to expect. If I weren't desperate for the money, I would have quit after last night. I need to talk to him about a payment schedule or getting an advance so I can find a place to live instead of sleeping in his bedroom or in my car. I need to formulate a plan like I always do for the rest of my life.

Gallagher stops the car in front of a high rise. Before I can open the door, he has it opened for me. No one has ever opened a door for me. Not even past boyfriends.

"Thank you."

He smiles and holds out his hand to help me out. I grip his hand as I stumble out, still clutching my coffee in my other hand. I'm going to need more when I get inside.

"Here's your security badge, Miss Burns. Mr. Knight's offices are on the top floor. He's waiting for you."

I nod and take a step forward, feeling like Bambi learning to walk for the first time.

"Would you like me to accompany you up, Miss Burns?"

I smile and take a deep breath to compose myself. "No, I got it. Thank you though."

"Of course, Miss Burns."

"Gallagher, will you be driving me every morning?"

He nods. "Most likely. I usually drive Mr. Knight, but he has made you my assignment for the foreseeable future."

"Then please call me Mila."

"Mila, I would suggest you hurry inside. Knight isn't a patient man."

He drops the mister from in front of Knight's name as well, and I start to think the 'mister and miss' was just an act Knight requested him to do, and not how he usually behaves.

I know I should hurry inside, but after what Knight pulled last night I don't care. He's an ass. I don't care how much money he is paying me. He can wait.

I walk inside, flashing my card to the security guard. I wait at the elevators with a dozen other people all sipping their coffees in their expensive suits and heels.

I glance down at my wrinkled mess of clothes. I thought I looked okay for going to a strip club, where I expected it to be mostly empty. This place isn't empty. It's full of sharp looking business people.

I swallow hard and stare at the doors, begging them to open so I can get this hell of a day over with. The doors open, and we all cram inside. I can't even see the buttons to tell if my floor is pressed or not. It takes forever to climb the more than twenty stories as the elevators stop on almost every level to let people on and off. But finally, it's just a woman left and me.

"First day?" she asks.

I nod.

The doors open, and she smiles knowingly. "Good luck, working for Knight is a tough job. You're going to need a tough skin to survive here."

I blink, not understanding. *How did she know I was working for Knight?*

"Good morning, Mila," Cole says when I step off.

I smile. "I didn't expect to see you here. Do you work with Knight?"

"Something like that."

Ugh, again with the vagueness.

"I thought I'd show you to your office and get you set up. Knight is currently in a meeting."

Cole's eyes rake up and down my body. "I'm glad you and Knight seem to be getting along."

I frown, realizing now why Knight ensured I would show up in this outfit. To make Cole think Knight fucked me. *Bastard.* Knight wants to claim me without really claiming me.

"I still can't believe you and Knight get along well enough to work together."

"We get along better than that. We are best friends."

I stop, not believing him. "What?" I snap.

"I've known him since high school. He's my best friend. I would die for him."

I doubt that. I follow Cole and watch as he limps. Scars still cover his arms and face. Knight has healed faster than Cole.

"Here's your office," Cole says holding a door open to a small room.

A door! I've never had an office before. Most people here don't have an office; they have cubicles.

"Why do I get an office? I figured I'd be stuck in a cubicle somewhere. I'm only Knight's assistant."

Cole bites his lip like he wants to say more, but can't.

I step inside and run my hand over the bookshelf covered with books. Over the white desk that looks like it was designed for a woman. I look out the large windows that have a view of the mountains. I could work here forever. I'm not even sure I want to be a nurse again if the pay is this good and I get a view like this.

"So what is the name of this company? What does it do?"

Cole eyes me like he can't believe Knight hasn't told me already. *We were a little busy not fucking.*

I sit behind the desk and drink the last drop of coffee. Cole walks over to where a coffee maker sits in the corner of my office. He pours me a fresh cup and hands it to me. "You have your own coffee maker so you can make coffee at any time, but there is also a coffee shop two floors down that your employee card will get you access to for free coffee."

I sip the coffee that tastes even better than the cup Gallagher got me. I don't think I'll ever need to leave this office.

"The company is called Perfect Match. We help match people up."

"Doesn't that already exist? Tinder, Match, Ok Cupid?"

Cole frowns. "Yes, those exist, but that isn't the goal of Perfect Match. We're not just a dating site, although some of the users are on the app to find dates. Most people are looking for more than dates. They are looking for companionship. They are looking for people to go to baseball games, people to share a room, people to start a company, travel the world or work on saving elephants. You get the idea. The app has you answer questions about your life, and then it matches you to people it thinks you need in your life. You may not even realize you care about saving the elephants, but the app will realize you do and match you with a similar person who also cares about elephants so you can go save the world."

"Huh, I've never heard of it."

"Not surprising since it looks like your phone barely functions as is." He glances at the phone on my desk.

I grab it and throw it in the top drawer of my desk.

"So what does Knight do here?"

Cole's lips curl up. "Knight—"

"Needs you in his office," Knight says standing in the doorway.

I stand nervously looking Knight up and down. He's wearing a suit that fits like a second skin to his muscles and is far more expensive than the suit Cole is wearing from the look of it. Knight's suit is tailored to fit him, while Cole's is nice, but doesn't fit quite as well.

"I'll let you two talk. It appears you have a lot to talk about," Cole says turning to walk out. "If I could be a fly on the wall," he mumbles and then disappears.

"My office. Now."

I jump to my feet at his harsh words and then chase him the two feet to his neighboring office.

He takes a seat at his sizable black desk.

"Shut the door."

I jump again but shut the door behind me. I'm taken aback by his voice and his outfit. I'm baffled. If I were to look at him now, I'd say he is the opposite of a bad boy.

"I need you to move my nine o'clock meeting with Jacob to ten. I don't care what he says, make sure it's ten. I need you to schedule a meeting with Catherine Scully for one this afternoon. Check over the rest of my schedule and confirm with my driver we can travel to the one o'clock meeting in time. I need you to drop off my dry cleaning at the building on Anaheim and have it picked up by seven tonight. Order lunch to be delivered from Tony's at one sharp."

"I thought you had a meeting at one."

Knight smirks. "You are listening. It didn't appear that you were since you aren't writing anything I'm saying down."

I blink. "I have a perfect memory."

"I doubt that."

I sigh. "Nine o'clock with Jacob move to ten, no matter what. Meeting with Catherine Scully for one this afternoon. Confirm schedule with Gallagher. Drop off dry cleaning on Anaheim and make sure it's ready by seven. Lunch from Tony's at one although you have a meeting then so I'm not sure if it's a lunch meeting or a mistake."

He smiles. "I knew I chose well."

I nod. "I didn't realize you were serious in needing an assistant. Who was your assistant before?"

He doesn't answer. *Another secret.*

"The lunch order isn't a mistake. I will eat while he talks."

I nod.

"Shall I continue?"

I sigh as he continues spouting about meetings, emails, and errands he needs me to run. I'm barely listening. He frowns the whole time, assuming I'm not listening. But if I hear it, I won't forget it. It's a blessing and a curse. Every time he thinks I'm not listening to him, I repeat the last few sentences, and he growls before continuing.

That's when I spot it. His nameplate. Ace Knight, Founder and CEO.

Holy shit!

"Wait, you own Perfect Match?"

Knight stands up and walks around to the front of his desk. "Yes."

My mouth gapes open. "Do you own the strip club?"

"No, Cole does. I'm a minor investor, mainly because I'm his friend, nothing more."

"You own Perfect Match, not a strip club?"

He nods again.

I cock my head to the side like I'm seeing him for the first time. *Maybe I am? How could I have gotten the men so wrong?*

"You're still an asshole." I cross my arms and stomp my foot to accent my point.

"You still have a smart mouth."

I glare. "When do I get paid? I don't have any money to afford rent. Can I get an advance?"

"Add meeting with HR to your agenda today. I'll cover your living expenses while you are working here, and I'll make sure you get an advance on your paycheck. You will get your checks in regular increments until you are finished, with a bonus in the end." *When he asks me to do the thing that will cause me to hate him, and possibly myself.*

I nod.

"You're dismissed, Mila."

I bite my lip to hold my tongue. I want him to use a nickname. I don't like him calling me Mila. It's like he's scolding a child.

I turn and walk out of his office and return to mine. I won't think about Knight. He's a dick. I don't think about figuring out whatever task he really hired me for either. I have a job that is going to pay me six figures in less than six months. I have a job that will keep my mind occupied and ensure I never have to worry about money again when I get back to finishing my nursing degree.

Just as I open the shiny laptop on my desk, the phone on my desk rings.

I hesitantly pick up, "Hello?"

"That's not how you answer your phone. You are the voice of Perfect Match. The first voice anyone hears when they call our offices. Try again," Knight snaps.

I sigh. "Hello, you've reached Perfect Match, Mila Burns speaking. How can I help you?"

"Better, but don't speak like you are having phone sex."

"I don't talk like—"

"I have more tasks for you."

Shit. I listen as he rambles a dozen more tasks. I don't know what my hours are, but there is no way I will get all of this finished by seven when I'm supposed to pick up his dry cleaning and when I assumed our day would be done. I'll be lucky to get everything done in time to sleep at all tonight.

———

I hate Knight more than I thought was possible.

He's yelled at me more today than I've ever been yelled at before. And my siblings like to chastise me, a lot.

I got yelled at when his lunch was two minutes late. I got yelled at when Jacob didn't show up for his meeting. I got yelled at when I took a pee break and missed Odette's call. I'm beginning to think whoever had my job before me didn't last long. I don't care how much it pays; if I weren't desperate, I would have quit already.

And more than anything, I've realized Knight has a split personality. I think I prefer when he wears the tattoos and biker outfit. That version of him isn't dangerous. He's nice, kind even, compared to the jerk in a suit sitting in his office.

"How are you holding up?" Cole flashes me a knowing grin

as he steps into my office without knocking.

I smile, happy he's not Knight. I'm not sure I can handle another demand from him. If he asks me to do one more thing for him, I'm likely to quit.

I bite my lip when Cole approaches me. It's hard not to show my appreciation for the man that looks like dessert in a suit. Although I no longer want Cole, I can still appreciate his charming smile, his tight ass, and the warmth he brings with him when he enters a room.

My phone rings and I pick it up and slam it back down without answering, already knowing it's Knight. If he wants to talk to me, he can get off his ass and come to my office to have the conversation face to face. I won't deal with his scolding over the phone.

"That bad, huh?"

The phone rings again, and I again pick it up and slam it down.

I shrug. "It could be worse I guess. I could be working as a stripper in your club."

Cole walks behind my desk, and I turn in my comfy executive chair to face him. Cole's eyes drop to me, and he turns me toward the desk as he steps behind me and starts massaging my shoulders.

"Mmm."

"If you worked at my club, you would be treated like royalty, not like a dog who constantly disobeys."

I close my eyes and lean into his hands. I didn't realize how tense I was until Cole's hands touched me. If I'm going to survive five months at this job, I'm going to need to hire a masseuse to make it through.

"I didn't realize Knight could be more of an ass than he already was."

Cole chuckles. "He's been going easy on you. It's going to get worse from here."

I sit up, and Cole drops his hands. "What? How can it get worse?"

Cole rubs his neck like he's trying to decide what to tell me and what to keep private. "Knight is intense. He cares a lot about this business as much as he pretends not to. His first assistant was amazing. She had the same level of passion he did. He didn't have to ask her to work crazy, ridiculous hours, she just did. She was the other half of his brain. They were able to communicate without speaking. They were a perfect team."

"Why did she leave then if she was so perfect?"

Cole looks out the window instead of looking at me. "She fell in love."

I nod, realizing who he is talking about. Abri. Knight's first assistant became his wife. Then his ex. There is no way I'll be able to live up to whatever he had with her. I can't fuck him in his office when he's upset like she could.

I sigh and kick my feet up on my desk. I have five minutes until I need to leave to pick up Knight's dry cleaning.

"It will get easier. Knight will realize what he has with you. He'll realize that you are different than Abri. In a way, you are exactly what he needs right now."

"Knight told me the same thing. That I'm perfect for him. I'm exactly what he needs, but I don't understand. I'm anything but perfect, and I haven't met this Abri yet, but she sounds like his perfect match. I'm just here because Knight thinks I can help him hurt her."

Cole frowns and tugs my hand, forcing me to my feet. I sigh, silently cursing my heels as I stand up. *Tomorrow, I will not be wearing heels.*

"You're not perfect for Knight because you can help him hurt Abri, although I have no doubt that is why you are here. You are perfect for Knight because you challenge everything in his life.

Abri made his life easier; you will make it harder. She fell into his lap, but he will fight for you."

I blink several times, not understanding, but then his wet lips press against mine, and I'm even more confused. I thought he was done kissing me after the last time. And as much as I might like Cole, I'm not sure I can trust him after he kisses me.

I push him off me as I hear a familiar creak in the door. Cole's hands are wrapped around my waist despite me attempting to push him off me, and Knight is standing in the doorway to my office.

Knight looks at me like he hates me. And I thought he was supposed to be making me hate him, not the other way around.

I have nothing to apologize for. I didn't kiss Cole. He kissed me. If anything, I could file sexual harassment charges against Cole. And Knight and I are nothing more than boss and employee. He made that clear last night.

"The deal is off," Knight says as he turns to leave. I'm not sure if he's talking about his deal with me or if he has a deal with Cole.

Cole chuckles. "No, it's not."

Apparently, Cole thinks Knight is talking about him. Knight stops walking and then storms back into my office, punching Cole in the face on the same spot that he punched him before. Then, he turns to me.

"Don't talk to Cole again, or you're fired."

He's gone in an instant while I'm left gasping for air.

Finally, I regain my breath and glare at Cole. "What was that for?"

"Don't worry; I didn't kiss you because I like you, although you are hot as hell. I kissed you to help you both."

I narrow my eyes not understanding.

"How the hell does kissing me and almost getting me fired help me?"

"Because it reminds you how much Knight wants you. I've never seen him punch anyone. I've kissed countless of his girlfriends and dates before. He never cared that I kissed them. He just ended the relationship. He wants you, even though he will never admit it because he has an ulterior motive. And he thinks fucking you will get in the way of that."

"Why are you telling me this?"

"Because I think him fucking you is exactly what you both need. He needs to forget about his past and find his future."

Cole adjusts his tie and touches the side of his cheek where a bruise is forming. I don't know whether to thank Cole or punch him.

So I slap him across the cheek.

"Jesus, woman. What was that for?"

I storm toward my door. "For kissing me. Don't do it again. Ever. Or I'll do a lot more than slap you."

"Fine, no more kissing."

I pause in the doorway. "And for the record, I can fight my own battles. I can decide if I want Knight to fuck me or not. Knight might need to get laid, but it's not what I need. I need the money. I need to finish my degree. Graduate and get a real job where I take care of myself. I don't need a man to help me with that."

I leave my office. My body shakes to my core. I'm furious. And turned on. Not because of Cole's lackluster kiss, but because of the look in Knight's eyes when he saw what happened. I'm a fucking mess, and all I've done is kiss Knight.

I meant everything I said to Cole. I can't fuck Knight. I'm here to get paid and then move on with my life. That's the plan I'm sticking to. No matter how charming, or good-looking he is. No matter what naughty words are whispered in my ear. I won't give in. I've let one bad boy ruin my life before. I won't do it again.

10

———

KNIGHT

WHY DOES *Mila keep fucking kissing Cole?*

He's not that good-looking, he has the personality of a sloth, and he's the ringleader of bad boys. The opposite of everything Mila claims to want.

I stare at my computer screen, angrily scrolling through my various emails and appointments for today. I can't work, not when I can't get the image of Mila and Cole kissing out of my head.

My door opens without a knock. I don't look up. I don't care if it's Cole or Mila coming to beg for my forgiveness. I don't want to see either of them right now.

"I updated your schedule so you can fit in the Thompson meeting tomorrow at nine between your eight-thirty and ten o'clock meetings," Mila says.

I don't look up. I'm sure my devil eyes would scare her off if she saw what was going through my head right now.

"I also want to assure you that I'm a professional. I will keep my private life private from now on. It was unacceptable what happened, and it won't happen again."

I shake my head but keep my mouth shut.

"Knight?"

I can't take it anymore. I look up and see her standing across the desk from me glowing. I haven't called her into my office for the last three hours because every time she leaves it, clearing her body from my mind takes twice as long as her voice to leave my head when I talk to her on the phone. I can't have my productivity hampered that much.

"I'm on my way to pick up your dry cleaning. Is there anything else you need before I go and then head out for the night? I talked with HR, and they said you would write me a check for my advance so I can get an apartment."

"Yes," I hiss. "There are some things I need you to do for me before you are done for the night."

She sucks in a breath but otherwise doesn't flinch.

"I need you to generate July's P&L, prepare an update for our investors, read the ten articles that were submitted to be included in the company newsletter, give me summaries of the spreadsheets Daniel sent me, find a place to host the fall party and finish answering my emails."

Her eyes get big, but she doesn't argue. She was expecting me to add more to her plate. I want to threaten her job if she so much as looks at Cole again, but I don't want to bring up my bastard of a best friend again.

"Done." Her eyes narrow and her lips thin. "My advance?"

I smirk. "I don't think you have earned your advance yet."

She raises an eyebrow. "I've worked my ass off for you today."

"Liar. You did the minimum needed. And then you kissed and would have most likely fucked, my best friend in your office. That doesn't sound like someone who is a hard worker."

She frowns.

"You're really not going to give me an advance?"

"No, but don't worry. My bedroom is yours until you get paid at the end of the month. Although, I have a strict no men allowed rule that I doubt you will be able to follow."

"Fuck you."

"I'm letting you stay in my condo for free. I think you should be thanking me."

"Thank you, Knight, for ensuring that any feelings I had developed during our drunken and high night together have completely vanished. I will work hard and earn my money. And then I'll be out of your life, forever."

"Good, you've finally learned."

She leaves without another word. *It's for the best*, I remind myself. I'd rather destroy her now than later.

"I'm leaving for the day," Cole says sticking his head into my office.

I growl. "Get the fuck out, Cole."

Cole doesn't leave. He steps inside with his smug ass expression.

"Dammit Cole!" I slam my computer down, and it breaks. "I thought you kissed her the first time to mess with me."

"I did."

"Then, what the hell was that?"

"You are holding back. You aren't going to pursue her beyond whatever stupid thing you hired her to do. I was helping."

"I don't need your fucking help, Cole. I need you to get out of my life."

"Don't worry. I'm done meddling. It's clear I'm not helping anyway."

"You were wrong. Mila likes you."

Cole laughs. "That's what you think? Mila slapped me. It stung worse than your weak ass punch too."

Mila slapped him. *Shit*. And I pushed her away even further.

"Mila wants you. Although, I'm sure you were an ass to her and now you'll be lucky if she keeps working for you."

I was, but he doesn't need to know that.

"I meant what I said about our deal. I'm selling my company to someone else. You don't deserve it."

Cole shrugs. "I have more than enough money. What are you going to do about Mila?"

"Nothing." *Not a damn thing.* I shouldn't have even hired her. She can't help me. No one can. It was a gut reaction. I thought she could help, but she can't.

Cole shakes his head. "Tell Mila now that you broke your computer and she needs to get you a new one, rather than waiting until later when the Apple store has closed." And then he's gone.

I need to lock my damn door. I get up to do just that when Abri steps inside.

"You talking to me yet, Ace?" Abri asks with a smile on her face. She brushes her hand over my chest, and it takes everything in me not to grab her wrist and throw her out of my office. But that's precisely what she wants.

"No, not after what you did."

She cocks her head to one side and twirls her auburn hair. Anyone else would think she looks like an innocent teenager, not a dangerous twenty-four-year-old.

"What did I do?" Her smile grows larger, and she bats her eyelashes like she couldn't have possibly done anything wrong.

"Nevermind," I mumble under my breath. I step back and watch as her hand falls into the space between us. I want to retreat behind my desk again, but it would be a victory for Abri. I'm not going to let her win. Even for a second.

Abri knows me too well though. She skips over to my desk and takes a seat like this is as much her office as it is mine. It was once. It's one of the many reasons I want to sell this company and start over.

"I heard you hired a new me and gave her my old office."

I clench my teeth together to keep from growling. I hate her behind my desk, and I don't want her to notice Mila. I should have never brought Mila here. I keep my expression blank and indifferent. Abri doesn't need to know Mila is a weakness.

"I did. You weren't exactly cutting it as my assistant anymore."

Abri rolls her eyes. "Partner, if I recall. My title was partner."

I shrug. "You seemed like an assistant to me."

"If the new girl isn't up to the job, all you have to do is ask me nicely, and I'll take my job back. I'll even let you call me your assistant."

I snicker. "You haven't had a hard day's work in months. I doubt you even remember how to work hard."

She tucks her hair behind her ear revealing the curve of her neck, my favorite place to kiss her. She knows it. It's why she always exposes that spot of soft skin around me. To distract me and remind me what I can never have again.

She doesn't realize the spot no longer attracts me to her. My cock no longer responds to her advances. You couldn't pay me enough money to touch her or even kiss her.

"We could try to keep it professional this time. You know I'm the best assistant you've ever had. The others haven't even lasted longer than a week."

I narrow my eyes. The others haven't lasted because of Abri, not me. She's tortured them. I'm not the best boss. I work all of my assistants hard, easily working them a hundred hours or more a week. But I pay them well, really well. When I hire them, they understand what is expected, and I know that no one will stay at a job for more than a year, two max. But none survive even a year; the money isn't enough to deal with Abri.

"Miss Burns will last longer than a week." I hate calling Mila, Miss Burns. It sounds too formal, not at all like Mila truly is.

Abri pouts and then pulls out a tube of red lipstick from her purse applying it slowly to her lips like that is going to make me want to kiss her or something.

"Are you finished? Some people have work to do."

She slowly puts the tube back into her purse. "You should get the A/C checked. It's scorching in here, Ace."

She slowly removes her jacket and hangs it on the back of my chair. My chair will smell like her Chanel No. 5 perfume the rest of the day.

Dammit.

I know she's pushing her boobs up in her lace tank top, but I don't notice. I'm tired of her damn games. She started this, but I'm going to finish it.

"I think I'm going to check in with your new assistant tomorrow. Miss Burns, is it? Show her some pointers to ensure she lasts."

"I don't care what you do as long as you get out of my damn office."

Abri licks her lips. Her last move at trying to seduce me. She forgets I'm more than aware she's a manipulative bitch.

Abri runs her hand through my hair. "I miss your long locks, Ace. You look too grown up with this haircut."

I grab her wrist this time. I can't help myself. "I'm not a teenager you can play games with anymore without consequences, Abri. If you play with fire, you are going to get burned."

"Maybe, but so far I think I'm winning. And you haven't even seen what I have planned for my grand finale yet. It's good, Ace. I would surrender now while you still have something left you love. Otherwise, I'm taking everything. You don't get to fuck with me and get away with it."

I drop her wrist. "Out."

Abri leaves without another word, but she makes sure to sway her hips in hopes I will watch her go. I watch her leave, not because she looks sexy, but because I need to make sure she's actually leaving.

I walk over to my desk, grab the jacket, and toss it in the trash. Then I text Mila to have a cleaning crew clean out my office ASAP. I don't want it smelling like Abri tomorrow. I won't get any work done.

I want to tell Abri to stay the hell away from Mila, but I can't. It will make it worse on Mila. Mila wants to fight her own battles, here's her chance. Mila can hate me all she wants, but I'm not the devil. Abri is.

11

______

MILA

I STORM UPSTAIRS to my bedroom in Knight's apartment. He isn't home yet, but the driver gave me a key to his apartment. Well, apparently *our* apartment until I get paid. I kick my heels off revealing the blisters on my toes and then fall onto his large bed.

I've never been this exhausted before. I love working hard. I've pulled twenty-four shifts at the hospital. I thought nothing could top that, but working for Knight does. Not just physically, but emotionally and mentally. I can't keep doing this every day. No matter how much money he is paying me.

I need a bath and a change of clothes. I stand up and walk to his closet again to try and find some sweatpants or something of his I can force to fit me after my bath.

I gasp when I open the closet. My clothes are hanging neatly next to his. My duffel bag, backpack, and books that were in my car line the bottom row. *How did he find my car? Did he break into it?*

And there are more clothes in my size next to mine. Mostly work clothes it seems. Heels I will never wear line the bottom of the closet.

Who did this? It sure wasn't Knight. I've had to do everything from getting his coffee to answering his phone. I'm surprised he didn't want me to wipe his ass when he takes a shit. There is no way he did this. *How many other assistants does he have? And why does it seem he dumped the most work on me?*

Questions for later. Right now, I need a bath. I grab my sweatpants and a T-shirt and carry them to the bathroom where a large tub sits in the corner. The tub could easily fit four people, and I'm going to have it all to myself.

I turn the water on as hot as it will go and add soap so that bubbles form. Then I strip and step into the tub, and everything else disappears. I close my eyes and doze in the tub. When I'm finished, I'll order some pizza or something and then collapse in the bed. I don't have time to argue with Knight tonight. Not if I have to do this again tomorrow.

Everything melts away. The hate. The pain. The aches. The lust. All of it. I don't think about Knight. I'm lost in my own world until I take a deep breath. My stomach growls as flavors of Mexican food drift up to the bathroom.

I'm starving. I haven't eaten since breakfast, and it's almost midnight now. I couldn't afford anything in the cafe downstairs, and I didn't want to ask Knight to pay for my lunch.

Please let Knight still be at work or already in whatever bedroom he's sleeping in now. Please don't let him be downstairs.

I get dressed quickly and creep downstairs, careful of what I'm going to find.

"You like tacos, right?" Knight says smiling, pleased with himself as he sits at the bar where he has two plates of food. One sitting in front of him, the other in front of an empty chair for me.

"Good job, you remembered I like tacos," I say sarcastically as I approach the bar slowly like it's a trap.

Knight hasn't changed out of his suit. He's removed his jacket and tie, and his sleeves are rolled up. Otherwise, he still looks all business.

He pulls the chair out for me, and I take a seat. I stare down at the glorious tacos, my mouth watering.

"Eat," Knight commands.

I sigh. He likes bossing people around. We are going to have to work on that.

But I'm too hungry to fight him right now. I take a bite, and it's like heaven exploded in my mouth.

"Oh my god! This is the most delicious thing," I say with my mouth still full. I take another bite and then another.

"Did you order these from somewhere or did your cook make them?"

He raises an eyebrow. "I didn't order them, and I don't have a cook."

"Then who cooked these?"

"Me."

My mouth gapes as I stare at Knight. There is no way he made these. The tortillas are homemade, along with the green chile sauce, and the pork tastes like it's been stewing all day.

"Liar. I thought you would always be honest with me. There is no way you had time to make these. I bet you can't even cook toast without burning it."

"I don't lie. At least not to you."

I blink rapidly, not understanding. But when I examine his kitchen, I notice the dirty pots and pans stacked in his sink. I notice the spilled sauce on the counters, and when I look at his shirt, I spot the drops of grease on his shirt. He cooked this.

"Thank you."

He smirks. "Don't thank me. I would have cooked something whether you were here or not. It's my time to destress."

"You don't go to the gym for that?"

I blush when he realizes I'm talking about his hot body.

"I do, but cooking helps me wind down before I sleep."

I nod and eat more of my tacos.

"I still hate you, you know."

He stills, then nods. "I know."

"It's what you wanted though, isn't it? You want us both to hate each other."

Again, he nods.

"Well, mission accomplished. We hate each other. You don't have to worry about us developing feelings for each other."

"Good."

I wipe my mouth on the napkin next to my plate. He even remembered to give me a napkin. No other guy I've dated before would cook for me or even remember something simple like a napkin.

"But if you want me to keep working for you, which I know you do, I have some demands. I've already heard most of your assistants don't last the week."

He nods slowly.

"Then you have to treat me nicer."

"Nicer? Are you serious?"

"Yes, you can be a bit of an ass."

"I've heard." He smiles like he's proud of it.

I sigh. "Yes, if you want me to keep working for you it wouldn't hurt to say please and thank you. Or to give me all of my tasks at the beginning of the day, as opposed to throwing random tasks at me throughout the day so that I can plan. I'm a bit of a control freak and like to have my day planned in advance."

He turns and stares at me, and suddenly my heart is fluttering. "That's not what you want. You want me to go easy on you. Give you less work."

"No, I like work. I will earn the money you are paying me. Just say please and thank you."

"Fine."

"Fine?"

"I will say please and thank you."

That was too easy. Something is up with him.

"And I would like my own place."

"Then get your own place."

"I can't afford it without my first paycheck."

"I don't see how that's my problem."

I sigh. *Just take the first win for today and move on.*

We finish eating in silence although if he saw what was going on inside my body, he wouldn't be silent. Because every time he takes a bite it draws my attention to his lips, and then I want to kiss him. I shouldn't want to kiss him. He treated me like a slave today. He lectured me for a kiss that wasn't even my fault. I should hate him, but hate isn't that far away from love. They are both strong emotions that make people do stupid things.

I will not kiss him. I excuse myself quickly when I eat the last bite of my tacos and then race upstairs. I fall into his cushy bed that smells like him. Rough, manly, and bad boy.

I want to leave, but I also want to stay. His bed is incredible, better than anything I can afford. That's the only reason I want to stay, I tell myself. *That and the cooking. His scent. And the way he stares at me like I'm the most important thing in his world.*

Maybe I am? Why else would he make me my favorite food for dinner?

Because he was trying to apologize for being an ass without having to say I'm sorry. That's all. Tomorrow it will go right back to how it was before. The more we work together, the more I will hate him. Then I won't want to kiss him anymore.

I take another deep breath and get a whiff of his shampoo from his pillow. I'm just going to steal this pillow when I leave.

My phone buzzes. A message from Lana.

Lana: Are you living on the streets yet?

Me: No, I'm living like a princess in the highest tower.

Lana: Explain, NOW.

Me: Too tired. I'll call you tomorrow before work at six AM.

Lana: That's too early! Tell me now.

Me: Sleeping...

———

I glance at my watch that says a quarter 'til seven. Knight usually gets here by seven, sometimes earlier, which is why I got here at five. He thinks I don't want to work hard. He believes I haven't earned my advance yet, but today I will prove him wrong.

The elevator doors open, and Knight steps out in a dark grey suit and piercing blue tie. I step out of my office to greet him before he enters his.

"Good morning, Knight."

He narrows his eyes at me. "Morning," he mumbles.

He opens his office door, and I follow him inside. Sitting at his desk is a large coffee and the oatmeal breakfast he requested. He takes a seat behind the desk.

"I already made sure to confirm your schedule for today, I've answered all of your emails, and made summaries of your emails and voice messages. I also wrote out some thoughts about the meeting with Gerard. He left a detailed email, and I don't think you should merge with Wayfinder. Their business is floundering and will take your company down with them."

"Thanks for your advice," he says snarkily.

"I know you are new to this, but that's not how you thank someone."

I wait for him to say something but he doesn't. So I take matters into my own hands.

"Thank you, Mila, for getting here early, making sure my coffee and breakfast were sitting here waiting for me, and going above and beyond in your work," I say in a deep voice mimicking his.

Knight doesn't even look up from his breakfast.

"You're welcome. If you have more tasks for me to complete today, please compile them and call me into your office or send me a detailed email, instead of calling me every five minutes," I say in a higher pitched voice.

I deepen my voice. "Of course, Mila. Oh, and here's your advance."

Nothing. No response.

I sigh, running my hand through my hair before shifting my weight in my heels. I wasn't going to wear heels, but I couldn't resist these sparkly Gucci heels that were in the closet. They match so perfectly with this light grey and blue dress. I've lined all of the outfits up for the next week in the order of my favorites so I ensure I can wear them all. It seems Knight and I decided to match today.

Something catches my eye, and I turn my head toward the trashcan in the corner where a woman's jacket lies on top.

What is a woman's jacket doing in the trash?

It hits me quickly. That is why Knight wanted his office

cleaned last night. He fucked someone in his office and didn't want it to smell like sex this morning.

I turn to leave but stop.

"And please give me a heads up today if you are going to bring a woman into your office to fuck. My office is right next to yours. I don't want to interrupt or overhear anything accidentally."

Knight's head shoots up, and he stares at me for the first time this morning.

"What makes you think that I would fuck someone in my office?"

"Because you did last night."

He licks his lips and glances at the evidence in the trash. "I didn't fuck anyone last night."

"Liar."

He rolls his eyes. "I thought we've been through this. I won't lie to you."

"Why is there a woman's jacket in the trash? Why did I have to hire an emergency cleaning crew to come in last night?"

Knight takes a second and then slowly stands up and walks to me, but at the last second instead of touching me, he leans against his desk.

"Abri left her jacket here. She has the strongest perfume in the world. I hate it. I knew I wouldn't be able to stand to work in here this morning if the room wasn't clean."

"Oh."

"And make sure you fire the cleaning crew. They should have taken the trash out along with cleaning."

I frown and walk over to the trash can to throw out the trash. I snatch the bag containing the jacket up and begin to storm out, but Knight blocks my path.

He steals my breath with just a look. And I hate myself for letting him affect me so.

"And just so you know, Mila. I don't plan on fucking anyone in my office. Not unless you are offering. Why would I want anyone but my hot, sexy assistant?"

"I'm not fucking you."

"I've already got you sleeping in my bed. You'll be begging me to fuck you by the end of the week."

"I hate you."

"I know."

He's right. If I keep letting him get to me like this, then I will do more than beg him to fuck me. I will jump him and let him fuck me here on his desk, no matter who hears.

He moves out of my way, and I storm back to my office, determined to start thinking of him as nothing more than my asshole of a boss.

My watch turns to seven in the evening. I've finished every task Knight has given me. I might get to do something fun this evening. Something to distract me from Knight. I should text Lana and see if she wants to go to a movie or get drinks with me tonight. I have a twenty dollar bill I can blow since Knight is providing me with food and a place to live.

A knock on my door startles me.

"Dammit, Knight. I finished everything you asked me to do; I'm going out."

The door opens. "Sorry, I'm not Knight. Well, I am but not the Knight you are thinking of. I promise not to put you to work." A gorgeous woman says as she pokes her head into my office.

I open my mouth, but no words come out.

"I'm Abri Knight. I'm a partner here at Perfect Match. I

thought I should introduce myself and give you some tips, so you don't get fired on your first week."

She steps inside and closes the door behind her. She's tall, slim, perfect. Her dress is tight, but not too tight for people to think of her as anything but professional. Her hair hangs in loose curls, and her makeup highlights her face instead of overwhelming it like it does when I wear makeup.

"I'm Mila Burns. I'm uh...Mr. Knight's newest assistant."

We shake hands cautiously, and it feels more like she's sizing me up rather than being friendly.

She takes a seat across from my desk without being invited to do so. I take a seat behind my desk.

"How has your first couple days been?"

"Um..."

"That bad, huh?" She smiles. "Don't worry; I wanted to quit my first week too. Ace can be intense, but he seems to like you. So maybe he'll go easy on you and keep you around."

I shake my head. "Knight... I mean, Mr. Knight doesn't like me. He just thinks I will be good at this job."

She studies me carefully. "Anyway, I know it's only your second day here, so I'm sure you still have lots of work to finish, but I wanted to see if you wanted to take a break."

"Actually, I've finished for the day unless Mr. Knight adds any more tasks."

"You are the best assistant he's hired, then. Well, since me." She smiles. "You want to go work out with me then?"

"Um...I was going to go meet a friend for a drink."

"We can do that afterward. Earn our drinks." Damn Abri and her perfect fit body and tight ass. My rail-thin frame with no muscles can't compete with hers. I'm a stick; she's a goddess.

"I don't think—"

"I won't take no for an answer. Besides you may need me to defend you to Ace for leaving early on your second day whether you finished the work or not." She winks at me like we are best friends.

"I don't think Mr. Knight would mind."

She walks over to me and hooks her arm in mine. "He would. Trust me; you don't want to get on his bad side."

She yanks me up. Her body is much stronger than mine.

"You can call him Ace you know. He hates being called mister."

I nod. "I know, but I prefer to call him Knight. Sometimes, asshole."

She smiles at that as she drags me out of my office.

Knight's door opens like he was coming to talk to me, but stops when he sees us together.

"Oh Ace, you won't mind if I steal your assistant away. She finished all her work for the day."

Knight's face tenses, his jaw thins, and I know he wants to tell her no.

"It's up to Mila, what she wants to do."

I look at him, but he isn't looking at me, he's looking at Abri. I can't find any sign if he wants me to get close to Abri or not. I don't want to go with Abri, but if I go with her, I might be able to learn more about Knight. Why they broke up and what he has planned for me to do to help him.

"Do you have anything else you need from me? If not, I'd like to go with Abri."

Knight's jaw twinges.

"Yay, I'm so excited to have a new friend," Abri exclaims, not giving Knight a chance to answer as she drags me toward the elevators. I don't look back at Knight. I know that scowl on his face and the pain in his eyes. He doesn't want me to go. But I need to figure out why.

I regret my decision immediately. "I thought you said we were going to the gym, Abri."

"No, I said we were going to work out. What fun is going to the gym?"

"Um, it's safe and air-conditioned."

"Where is your sense of adventure? Nothing fun will ever happen to you running on a treadmill."

She opens the back of her jeep, one of the last cars this well-dressed woman should be driving. She changed into a sports bra and leggings, while I'm wearing a T-shirt with the arms cut out and shorts. I'm not prepared for this.

"Grab the ropes," Abri says swinging a bag over her shoulder.

I grab the ropes and stare up at the massive mountain we are climbing. *I can't do this, but I'm not backing down.*

Abri starts setting up the equipment. And every time she opens her mouth, I think I've heard it before. I'm missing something. She's familiar, but not too familiar. I may have met her before, but only in passing. And after the entire twenty minutes I've known her, I don't know whether I like her or hate her.

"Have you climbed before?"

I frown. "No." This feels like a competition. Like I should be able to do anything she can do. Which is silly. We aren't competing for Knight. He's her ex, and I'm his assistant. We can be friends.

"No worries, this one is an easy climb. We will do it together, and Jamal and Blake will spot us."

Two men arrive as Abri says their names. Both attractive men are going to watch me fall on my face. Abri gives me a very quick tutorial about the equipment and then we are strapped in and slowly climbing up with the men spotting us from the ground.

"So how did you and Knight meet?" I ask trying to seem interested.

She smiles. "I'm not sure I can get used to hearing someone call him Knight."

"Sorry, I mean Ace."

"We met in high school. He was the popular football player. I was the prom queen, cheerleader type. We fell in love and started a company together. Next thing you know we are married and running a million dollar company together."

"That's incredible."

"It was a fairy tale come true."

"I'm sorry it didn't work out."

She pauses, and I have to move my handhold higher to get even with her again. That's when I see the tears staining her cheeks.

"I'm sorry. You two seemed perfect for each other. But sometimes, things don't work out."

Abri shakes her head and releases her hold on the rock, which completely freaks me out. Even though we are connected to ropes, I'm still petrified at any moment we are going to slam into the rocks below.

She climbs higher, not speaking to me, and I do my best to keep up, although at a slower pace. Finally, she stops again and looks at me, her eyes almost dry.

"I know I'm the ex, and you and Ace are keeping things professional, but I feel now that we are friends, I should tell you the truth. That way you can make your own decisions about Ace. I don't want you to fall for him like all the rest of his assistants and end up hurt."

I suck in a breath, not sure if I want to hear what she says. And I'm definitely sure we aren't friends.

"We were in love. We had passion. We were everything to each other. But then..."

"Abri? What happened?"

"We were too passionate about everything. The love turned to constant fighting."

I nod, understanding.

"The bickering turned to physical fighting. Ace has a temper, and he…"

More tears fall, and I need to know what happened. I need to know how he hurt her. I need to know the truth.

"Abri? Please tell me."

"He hit me. Hard across the face. And then…" Her voice trembles. "Then, he hit me until I passed out."

I gasp. I know it's not what she needs, but I can't help myself. It doesn't fit what I know about Knight. But then maybe the Knight I know and the Ace she knows aren't the same people.

I want to say I'm sorry, but my words would be empty, meaningless.

"I'm sorry," she says. "I need to go."

"What?"

She quickly descends. I stare in awe at how quickly she moved down the side of the cliff. She detaches herself from the rope and runs to her car. Both men chase after her, most likely worried and wanting to hit on her.

Shit, both men!

I look down at high up I am. I'm gripping the wall tightly. And I can't repel down like her; I have no one belaying me. I have to climb down. My legs are suddenly jello, and my hands are sweating as I try to grip the rock. I'm high enough up I'm sure if I fell I would die or at the very least break several bones.

My entire body is shaking now. I need help.

"Abri! Help!"

Nothing.

"Help! Someone, please help!"

The wind blows, and I grip the rock tighter. *That bitch.* The longer I'm up here, the more I replay the conversation in my head. Some of it might be true, all of it even. But the way she spoke, waited until we had reached the top before climbing down makes me believe she deliberately trapped me up here.

I shake my head. *Now I'm just paranoid. I can do this. I'm not that high up.*

But I try to move my foot lower, and it slips.

Shit. I can't do this. I'm going to die.

"Mila?"

I close my eyes and take a deep breath. *Knight.*

"My knight in shining armor, coming to save me again," I say nervously.

"I can leave if you prefer."

"No! I need your help."

I swear I hear him chuckle, but I don't look down to know for sure.

"I need you to let go, Mila."

"What? I'm not letting go. I'll die if I let go."

Now I know he's laughing, but it's an anxious laugh.

"Look down."

I hesitantly do and see him holding the rope.

"I got you. You aren't going to die."

"I can't let go."

"I can come up, but then no one will be belaying you. You're safer if I'm here, supporting you."

I take a deep breath. *He's right.*

"Trust me; I've got you."

His words again. *Dammit.*

I slowly let go and grab the rope as he carefully lowers me down. When I almost reach the ground, he cradles me in his arms as I start bawling.

"Shh, you're okay. I've got you. I won't let you go."

It doesn't stop my bawling.

"How did you know where to find me?"

He wipes my eyes as my tears begin to slow. "There is a reason most of my assistants quit. Abri is a bitch. You especially threaten her, so I knew she'd up her game."

"I could have died. You saved me. You're always saving me."

"No, if it weren't for me she wouldn't have pulled this crap in the first place."

"Oh my god, Mila. I didn't realize you were still up on the mountain. I'm so glad you are okay," Abri says running up behind us.

Knight's body stills, holding me tighter against him like he's a shield between Abri and me.

"Just leave, Abri."

"I need to apologize. I was just a wreck after I told her how we broke up. I thought Blake tied the rope up before he left. You were perfectly safe."

"Go, Abri."

"I need to talk to you first, Ace. We need to talk about our meeting tomorrow and—"

I can't listen to her talk one more second.

I know Knight doesn't want anything fake to happen between us. He doesn't want me to make Abri jealous, but there is nothing fake about what I do.

I grab Knight's neck and kiss him firmly on the lips, letting my tongue slip into his mouth. He tastes my desperation and terror and pulls me further in showing me how horrified he was in return at seeing me on top of a rock and unable to get down. Our hands tangle in each other's clothes, and I know this isn't going to end here. Once we get home, this is going a lot further. Neither of us will be able to stop.

Abri said passion turned to love and then hate. Our hate turned to fear and desperation.

I don't know if Knight did all of those horrible things to Abri or not. I know if I asked him, he would tell me the truth. But I can't ask. Not now. I need to find out my own truth. Ace may have treated Abri like shit, but Knight is my savior. I just hope my knight doesn't turn back into the asshole I thought he was this whole time.

12

KNIGHT

Mila's kiss knocked all of the air out of me. It took me completely off guard. It suffocated me and set me free at the same time.

I didn't think I would ever taste her again. I thought that ship had sailed after the way I treated her. I thought her hate for me was stronger than any desire she felt.

I've never been happier to be proven wrong.

"If we didn't have an audience, I would fuck you against the rocks right here," I whisper against her ear.

She blushes and bites her lip. "I have no objections."

Now I'm biting my lip, trying to hold back from fucking her into oblivion, while Abri and her boy toys watch. As much as I want to fuck Mila, I'm torn. Because I want to kill Abri just as much.

I tried to downplay how unsafe it was for Mila. Abri claimed Blake tied the rope off when he abandoned Mila, but the rope wasn't tied up. It was dangling freely in the air as Mila clutched to the face of a steep rock over a hundred feet up.

One wrong move and Mila would have fallen. To her death, most likely. Abri could have killed Mila.

I don't know if what Abri did was intentional or not, but I want to hurt Abri all the same for what she did to Mila.

I've never been so terrified. I've looked death in the face before. I've been helpless before, but this was different. Mila could have died because of me. That guilt would have never left me, and the pain of losing a woman I wanted, but who was never really mine, would have gutted me.

My body trembles, holding onto Mila, as the tears begin burning my eyes.

Mila wraps her arms tighter around my neck, and I grip her closer to my body.

"It's okay. You saved me," she whispers, but her voice is shaky.

"I'm never letting you go again."

I see the tears in her eyes again. I was strong before when she cried, but I can't be strong again. The reality of the situation has sunk in.

"Ace, I need you to talk to me," Abri pleads, trying to grab my shoulder to turn my attention to her instead of Mila.

"Fuck off, Abri," I say, carrying Mila toward my motorcycle.

I set Mila down gently on the back of my motorcycle and hand her a helmet. When she puts it on, I ensure it's fastened securely. Then I kiss the tears on her cheek, even as my own tears stream down my face.

"Take me home, Knight."

I feel a knot in my stomach and an ache in my throat as she says *home*. My place is her home. She has nothing else. No apartment, no dorm room. Only a rusted out Subaru to return to because of me.

I need to fix that, along with everything else I've fucked up in her life, but for now, I need to make her mine.

I climb on in front of her, and she wraps her hands tightly around my waist without protest. Then we are gone. I drive just fast enough to get us home quickly, but not enough to scare her. That's the last thing I want.

We ride in silence, only the wind and sound of engines purring around us to keep us company. It doesn't matter that we can't speak. Our bodies say enough.

We are broken.

We are hurting.

Only the other person can heal us.

I pull in front of my building, not caring there isn't a parking spot. I don't wait for the valet to take my motorcycle. They will get it or they won't. I have more than enough money to buy hundreds of motorcycles if I want. I don't care if this one gets stolen.

All I care about is getting Mila, naked and writhing underneath me in my bed. I take her hand, a gesture that a couple of nights ago would have scared her off, but tonight is more than welcome.

I don't know what has been going on in her head on the thirty-minute drive from the mountains to my building. I don't know if she wants me. I don't know if she wants to take a hot bath and be left alone. But I'm not sure I can leave her alone if that's what she needs. It will take everything inside of me to leave her for even a moment.

It's not about sex, although I'm desperate to be inside her. Feel her wet walls clenching around me as I make her come. Knowing that the pleasure I'm giving her helps ease the pain she's feeling. I need her close by. I need to know she's still breathing, her heart still beating. I need to protect her at all costs.

We enter the elevator with another couple. I grip her hand tighter, needing my lips on her, but afraid to scare her away. Neither of us has spoken since we got on the motorcycle.

Our eyes meet, and I see the desire mixed with the fear. I

wish I could take away the fear, but I'm afraid it's going to stay with her a lot longer than the desire ever will.

Mila moves her body in front of me, she grabs both of my arms and drapes them over her shoulders. I pull her body flush against mine as she leans into my body. It's the most intimate thing we've done, and she's sat half naked on my lap and kissed my stomach. But this moment is different. She's letting me in even though she knows I can hurt her.

And I no longer want to hurt her.

The only way to not hurt her is to leave. Get out of her life. Because if I stay, she's doomed.

I'm a selfish bastard though; I can't leave.

The couple gets off, and Mila pushes her ass against my swollen cock.

"Mila," I warn. She's lighting a fire, and I won't be able to stop if she goes much further.

The elevator doors open on my floor.

"I need you, Knight. Don't hold back."

"You sure? Your smart mouth won't be able to save you once we start."

She takes my hand lifting it to her mouth and kisses the palm of my hand sweetly like the innocent girl she is. Then, she has my pointer finger in her mouth, sucking viciously, swirling her tongue over the tip.

"I'm sure."

Fuck.

I grab her hips at the same time she jumps, wrapping her thin legs around me. She's a stick. I don't know how she was able to hold onto the rock as long as she did.

I slam her body against the door of my apartment and curse as I try to dig my keys out of my pocket as her lips suck on my neck. I regret not taking up the building manager's offer to install a keyless entry for me. The key finally grants us entry before I do something stupid, like fuck her against my door.

We burst inside in a tangle of arms, legs, and nerves. I've never been so nervous and so excited at the same time.

Mila pushes my suit jacket off my shoulders before she starts on my tie, as I kiss every part of her body my lips can reach without putting her down. Her lips, cheeks, neck, and ears. I get acquainted with every part of her skin. When I kiss her neck in Abri's favorite spot making Mila purr, I don't think about Abri like I thought I might. The sounds Mila makes are more angelic than anything I've ever heard.

Mila's raspy sounds. The purring, the moaning, the growling makes my already hard cock tighten with each sound. I think I could come from her voice alone.

Mila gets my tie off and starts working on the buttons on my shirt, quickly getting frustrated by how hard it is to get the shirt off.

"Slow down, pretty girl. We've got all night."

"All night isn't enough," she whispers back.

And I know it's the truth. I can fuck her all night long. Over and over and over. It won't be enough. Not enough to heal us. Not enough to rid ourselves of the desire in our core. Simply, not enough.

But it has to be. This has to be a one-time thing. I can't ruin her.

Neither of us speaks the truth though. We both know that this *is* a one-time thing. That's why she's so desperate. That's why there is sadness in her eyes.

So I give in to her. I race upstairs to my bedroom and toss her on the bed.

"You're never going to forget this night, sweetheart."

She grins at my nickname.

"Neither are you, asshole."

I lick my lips as I rip my shirt open, not caring about the expensive buttons that will need replacing. The look on her face makes it worth it.

"It's good to know you still hate me."

I kick off my shoes and remove my pants and underwear, freeing my cock that points in her direction, leading me into a dream I never thought I'd have, knowing, in the end, it will turn into a nightmare when I have to leave her.

Her eyes sear through my body. My arms and chest, covered in tattoos, over my abs, to my straining cock.

"Yep, definitely hate you."

It's a lie. She doesn't hate me, that's the problem.

She grips the covers on my bed like she's trying to hold herself back, but it makes her look innocent. So, so innocent. An angel that isn't capable of wrong.

And I'm the devil that soon will be taking her wings.

I slowly move to the bed as her legs move wide, inviting me in. But not wide enough to fit my frame. So I push her legs open further as I kiss every inch of flesh I can find. I remove her shoes slowly along with her socks until I'm kissing her feet, then calf, then inner thigh.

She writhes against me, both wanting me to kiss her in the most intimate of places and not ready for it yet.

I grin before jumping over her shorts and moving to her stomach. I push her shirt up as I kiss her concave stomach. Even with three good meals a day, she is still too skinny. I need to feed her more. She deserves to have everything she needs and more.

Even though I can see her ribs, she's still beautiful. More than beautiful. There needs to be a new word to describe how gorgeous she is. It's not just her body that has me entranced. It's her mouth, the words that leave it. It's her mind, the way she already understands my company on her second day. It's the way she pushes me to be better.

She raises her arms, and I lift her shirt over her head.

"When was the last time?" I say.

I return to kissing her stomach slowly as I inch my way up to her bra. It takes everything in me not to flip her over and fuck her roughly in my bed. But it's not what either of us needs.

"Um..." she moans as I kiss her.

I lift her bra off her body and then twirl my tongue slowly over her nipple.

"How long?" I demand.

"Over a year. Five if you're counting the last time I was in a relationship. Or the last time..."

"The last time?"

I gently bite down on her nipple making her cry out.

When I stop, she answers. "The last time a man has made me come. But even then..."

"It wasn't fucking amazing," I finish her sentence.

"No, I doubt you are capable of better, but usually I prefer my B.O.B. to what any man is capable of doing. Men are selfish."

She's not wrong. Most men are selfish. I'm selfish, but not when it comes to pleasing her. I'll put any battery operated boyfriend to shame.

"You sure about that?"

"Yes," she squeaks out.

I hook my thumb under her shorts and panties and jerk them down. Instantly reversing our positions, I grab her hips and roll her on top of me.

She gasps, but I haven't even started yet. I pull her hips forward until her glorious pussy is staring me in my face.

Her eyes are wide as she stares down at me, unsure of what do to.

"Just enjoy this, sweetheart. Enjoy the ride."

I move to kiss her and stop short when I see the tattoos on her hips, covered by her panties before. They aren't tattoos to honor a lost family member. They aren't words of encouragement or something sweet like I would have expected from my innocent girl. No, the tattoos are of fire. She's on fire, burning. She's dangerous, possibly more than I am to her. But it won't stop me from diving in.

I pull her on top of my face, as my tongue carefully swirls around the lips between her legs. I take my time, learning her body. Figuring out how her body responds to my touch. Which places are more sensitive, and which can handle a sharper attack.

My tongue darts inside of her, feeling how tight and wet she is.

Her eyes close at the intrusion. Her hands grip my head though, telling me to never stop.

"Jesus," she mutters.

"Jesus has nothing on me."

And she hasn't even begun to feel pleasure yet.

I slip a finger in her cunt, then a second. Slowly torturing her with my fingers as I find her G-spot deep inside.

My tongue finds the spot that I know is the key to making her scream my name. And then I'm relentless. My tongue dances faster and faster against her clit. Her thighs tighten around my head, begging me to keep going and to stop at the same time. I keep going, loving the mix of sweet and salty that is pouring off her onto my mouth.

I lap it all up. Needing more. Needing to milk her entirely of all her pleasure. I'm selfish in that I want this to be the best she's ever had. I don't want any other man ever to have a chance to compare to what I'm doing to her body. I want it all.

"Knight," she cries out. "Fuck, Knight."

I feel her clenching, her coming over my face. Her voice, singing my name. I'll never get enough of seeing her like this. Completely at my mercy. And completely *mine*.

She rocks her hips back gently as she comes down from her high until she's resting against my chest.

"Thank you," she breathes.

I smirk. "Don't thank me yet, that was nothing compared to what I have in store for you."

I roll us over again, placing her beneath me while I do everything I can to hold back from thrusting inside of her without getting protection first.

"Knight?" her voice is sweet, raspy, and needy.

"Yes, baby?"

I reach over to the nightstand and find my stash of condoms. I pull one out and sheath myself, hoping to God she isn't about to say she's changed her mind and doesn't want me to fuck her.

She closes her eyes and then opens them, like the time closed was needed to give her the strength to say her next words. "How long?"

I move all of my attention back to her. I hate seeing her this vulnerable. Her eyes, so full with fear of what my answer will be. Knowing I could break her with my answer.

I tuck her hair behind her ear, and stroke it slowly, my eyes and body trying to be as vulnerable in return to her. Because of all the things I've told her. All the honesty I've given her, she needs to know, this is the most honest I've ever been.

"More than a year."

She exhales like that was the answer she needed. It is also completely the truth.

"Even longer if you only count the last time I was in love and felt anything real."

She touches her fingers gently to my lips. "This is real. I may hate you, and you may despise me, but what we are feeling now is real. It may not be love, but it's something more. A passion and connection we will never experience again."

I lower my lips to hers. Kissing her carefully and passion-ately. "It's more than anything I've ever experienced."

And it's the truth. I've experienced love, passion, pain. But whatever this is, it's greater than all of it.

It's pleasure, and safety, and need, and love, and pain, and passion, and hate, and honesty. It's everything combined. It's what Mila and I are together. A connection that can't be tied to a time or place. A link I haven't been able to escape since the first time I saw her.

We both open our eyes at the same time, and I push inside her both gently and all at once. I fill her, just as quickly as she filled my heart. I can't escape Mila Burns, ever.

Her mouth opens wide in a cry of pain as I push her open. I kiss her, my tongue whisking her away to a place of pleasure as her body adjusts to my size inside her.

Our fingers intertwine together as I slowly pull all the way out of her, before slamming into her again. Her back arches as she pulls me inside her deeper. I could get lost in the depth of her. Mila has so many layers, and I've barely explored the surface. But it's now that I realize she will let me in all the way, even though she knows she will get burned. We both will.

"Come on me, pretty girl."

She does, and I follow suit.

I collapse on top of her, but I'm nowhere near finished with her.

I pull us both off the bed and carry Mila to the bathroom, into the shower. I turn the water on that chills us at first before slowly turning to heat.

I spin her around, so her back is to my front, as I let the water stream down her front. My hand hooks around her stomach and down to her most sensitive bud, playing with her slowly and torturously.

Mila started opening up to me before, but I'm afraid she may close to me now.

"What happened with Abri? What did she tell you?"

Mila leans her head back against my chest as I strum her further.

"She told me the man she married was a monster."

It's the truth. I was a monster. Mila is telling me the truth, without saying exactly what happened. I taught her that move. And I don't get to push her further. Mila is hiding the truth while being completely honest.

"What do you think of me?"

"I think my knight isn't the same person as Abri's husband."

I nod and push Abri out of my head as I make Mila come in the shower. Then in my bed two more times before I know she is spent and can't handle another.

I tuck Mila into my bed as I sit on the edge. Mila is hiding what Abri said. And if I can't learn the truth from Mila, I'm going to have to get it from Abri.

"Stay," she whispers.

It goes against everything in my body to leave her. I want to hold her against my body all night. Memorize her scent and the sounds she makes as she sleeps. I want to protect her all night long, and then let her ride me in the morning.

But the only way to truly protect her is for her to hate me. She'll hate me more if I leave her. I need to stay as far away from her as possible. Keep her as far away from Abri as possible. Before I end up hurting her like I did Abri.

13

MILA

KNIGHT IS easy to fall for. He's handsome, charming, and he saved me. *What's not to love?*

But maybe the reason my heart flutters around him is I don't really know him, and he doesn't know me. Not knowing the truth about each other's pasts makes it easy to love someone. If he knew my truth, it would be hard for him to love me. Our pasts are the key to letting each other go, but even though Knight left me alone in his bed, letting each other go right now is the last thing either one of us wants.

I saw the pain in Knight's eyes when he left me tucked in his bed. He didn't want to go. He thought he was doing the right thing. Saving me as always, this time from himself. He thought I would hate him more if he left. But I don't think hating Knight is possible anymore.

How can I hate someone that made me feel alive for the first time in years? How can I hate someone who saved me? How can I hate someone who loves me?

I can't.

Knight may not realize that he loves me, but he does. I never thought you could fall for someone so quickly, but I think we've been falling since the first moment we met weeks ago. And in some ways, I feel like the universe has been conspiring to bring us together for a lot longer than a few weeks.

I close my eyes. My body is sore. It will only be worse tomorrow. But it was more than worth it. That may be the last time Knight kisses me or touches me. The love that formed may only last one night, but I wouldn't trade it away. Even if I knew how our story would end. I would do it all over again.

Sleep, I need to sleep. Tomorrow, I will go back to reality. Tomorrow, we will see if there is enough hate to return to how we were living before or if something stronger wins. Tonight, I will dream of Knight and the future we could have together if our pasts weren't so painful.

———

No.

Stop.

No!

"Mila, shh, it's okay. I got you. I'm not going to let anyone hurt you," Knight's voice says.

Knight?

He's not here. He's not the one hurting me.

"Mila, no one is hurting you."

No one is hurting me, I repeat the words in my head.

I feel his arms wrap around me, but it takes me a while to convince myself to open my eyes. I'm not where I thought I was. I'm safe in Knight's bedroom. In his arms.

Knight strokes my hair with worry in his dark eyes. The same concern he had, holding me in his arms, after rescuing me from falling to my death.

"It was a nightmare. That's all. I won't let Abri or anyone else hurt you."

I nod. I know he won't let Abri hurt me.

"Do you trust me?"

"Yes," I whisper. I trust him, but he shouldn't trust me. I'm not even sure I can trust myself, because Abri wasn't who I was dreaming about.

"Do you need anything? Water, food, more covers?"

I stare out at the darkness. *No one is here. It's just Knight and me. I'm safe.*

"No, I'm okay."

He pulls the covers back over me, and I think he's going to leave me again. My body shakes at the thought of being alone again. My heart beats rapidly, but I try to keep from moving, so Knight won't realize how badly I need him.

"Thank you for coming. I'll be fine now. It was just a nightmare."

He lifts my chin to stare at him. I can't hide, not when he stares at me like this. "It wasn't just anything. Hearing your scream like that was one of the scariest moments of my life. I thought..."

He thought someone was hurting me now. *Does he believe Abri would break into his house and do that?*

I stroke his cheek and kiss him very lightly on the lips. "I'm okay. I promise. I used to get nightmares all the time. Today must have triggered one again. I'll watch TV or something for a little bit, and then I'll fall fast asleep again. You wore me out. I won't have a choice but to sleep. Go back to bed."

"You think I'm going to leave you again?"

I freeze. I don't know how to respond. *I did think he was leaving.*

"I'm never leaving you again."

He wraps his body around mine to make his point. Then he reaches over me to grab the remote on the nightstand. He flicks the enormous TV on and then hands the remote to me. I pick a station with puppies playing on the screen. I can't go wrong with puppies. And then I lay my head against Knight's arm. He tightens his grip around me. He's not wearing anything but his boxer briefs. His bare chest is pressed against the thin T-shirt of his I'm wearing. I need to be closer though.

As if he has the same thought, he moves the T-shirt up my body, and I pull it over my head. It's not sexual. It's the intimacy we seek. Our skin presses together. And Knight kisses my shoulder.

"Mine," he whispers.

I let his words float through me. I would give anything to be his beyond tonight. My nightmare granted us a few more moments of being together, but it won't last. When we wake up, we won't be anything but employer and employee. We will do our best to let the hate back in and guard our hearts. It's the only way either of us will remain safe.

———

"Good morning," Knight says still holding me.

"Morning," I say, smiling and blushing at how naked I am. He stares down at my breasts that are no longer covered by his silk sheets. I know what he wants. To taste them. I feel his cock at my ass, begging for entrance.

I can think of no better way to start the day then a good morning fuck.

"How did you sleep?" he asks.

"No more nightmares." *Because of you.*

He nods solemnly and presses his cock further against my ass. *Yes! Fuck me.*

An alarm blares, and Knight rolls off of me toward the alarm he must have set on his phone. I glance at it. Five in the morning. *Ugh, why does Knight have to get up so early?*

He gets up, and I know our moment together is over. *Stupid alarm.*

I move to get out of bed too, but Knight stops me. "You don't have to be into work until seven. Sleep for another hour. I set another alarm to wake you then."

"Sleep with me," I say, not keeping the double meaning out. *Fuck me and then snuggle some more. Or just fuck me until the next alarm goes off.*

"I can't. I have an early morning meeting."

He kisses me dismissively on the forehead and then goes to the bathroom. I consider just getting up and showering, but I know Knight will protest. He wants me to sleep. So I do my best to sleep.

I get into work at a quarter after seven, sore and unsatisfied after not getting morning sex.

"Work starts at seven," Knight's voice booms as I set my purse down.

I haven't seen him since he left my bed almost entirely naked. Now he's dressed in a dark suit, with a burgundy tie that matches the dress I'm wearing.

"I understand. Starbucks was slow with your coffee this morning." I hold up the coffee to him.

He stares down at it blankly. "I already got my coffee. You should have left earlier."

"What? You set my alarm! I left when you thought I should leave."

But he looks at me, and I know for sure our time is over. He's back to playing the jerk of a boss, and I'm left feeling confused and lonely. *It's for the best.*

"I'm sorry. I won't be late again."

"There is a list of things on your desk I need you to do. They are of the utmost importance. Don't bother with your usual tasks until after they are complete."

I frown and snatch the list off my desk. Try out ten different restaurants and report back which food is the best for the luncheon next week. Then stop by six different dessert places to find the best cake. Interview new laundromats, he's not happy with his current one. He wants a new bed for his guest bedroom. Pick one out for him. And he needs new patio heaters before it gets cold.

It's obvious what he's doing. Trying to keep me out of the office as much as possible. Away from Abri, and him. He's not even looking at me now. He's inspecting the floor like he's reading a story off it or something.

"If I eat at all these places today I'm going to be sick or fat," I tease.

His eyes go to my body that is far too thin. I need to eat more. He doesn't know I've been skipping lunches because I can't afford them without my paycheck or him paying for them.

I sigh. "Anything else?"

"Report to me when you are finished, I'll have a new list for you."

He disappears, and I'm left with a fake list of tasks that don't even matter. Last time he talked about the luncheon, he just wanted me to pick any restaurant that could hold the fifty people invited. He didn't care. Now I have to taste the food and select a separate dessert place.

A knock rattles me before it's opened.

"Wow," Cole says staring at me.

"What?" I snap, not able to deal with his crap.

"Whoa, I'm sorry. Didn't mean to intrude. I promise I won't kiss you. I know you aren't in the mood."

"I'm not in the mood because Knight's psycho ex-wife almost killed me yesterday." *It's only partially the truth.*

"And now I have to do these stupid errands for Knight. He's

trying to keep me out of the office so I won't kill him." I hold up the list.

Cole frowns. "I'll do some of the tasks with you, and then you and I can talk and get to know each other better. I'm hungry and could use twenty lunches today."

I laugh. "I don't think that's the best idea."

"I will not kiss you again. Well, unless you ask, but I'm pretty sure you've been kissed plenty since the last time I saw you."

"Why do you say that?"

"Because Abri has been sulking all day, Knight is more pissy than usual, and you are glowing in an outfit that matches Knight's."

I frown.

"Don't worry; you two look adorable in your matching outfits."

"I don't know how that happened. We didn't plan it, and he was awake before I left."

Cole grins. "So you were together last night then?"

"Ugh, I'm not talking to you about my love life or lack of one."

"Fine, don't talk, but I promise I'm only looking out for you and Knight."

I roll my eyes. "Yep, I'm sure that kiss was just a way to bring Knight and me together."

"It worked, didn't it?"

I huff. "What are you doing here anyway, Cole? Don't you have a strip club to run?"

"The strip club runs itself. And I'm going to be the owner of Perfect Match soon, so I need to spend more time here."

"What did you just say?"

"Um...nothing. Don't worry about it."

Is Cole planning a coup? Should I tell Knight about it? Is Cole trying to take over now that he sees Knight is weakened?

My phone buzzes and I answer it automatically.

"Yes," I snap because I know it's Knight.

"You haven't called your driver yet, don't worry, I did your job for you. He's downstairs waiting to take you to the first restaurant."

I end the call without a goodbye. I snatch the coffee meant for Knight along with my own nearly empty cup. I'm going to need both to get through this day.

———

Knight hasn't spoken to me all day. He's texted me a few more work things to do, but otherwise nothing. There was dinner waiting for me on the counter when I got back to his place, but otherwise no sign of Knight. The food smells delicious. Some homemade pasta dish Knight must have fixed before he disappeared again, but I'm too stuffed to eat anything after the day I had.

So instead of eating, I slink upstairs and into the bed. I don't even have the energy to shower or undress. I flick the TV on, ready to get lost in some drama to put me to sleep. I only make it twenty minutes into a rerun of Scandal, before the door opens.

My eyes shoot open as Knight steps into the bedroom.

"If you think I'll fuck you after how you treated me today, you're wrong."

He takes a step inside, closing the door behind him.

"I hate you," I spat.

He keeps walking.

Dammit, if he touches me, kisses me, or even speaks a word I will jump him.

He does none of those things though. He slowly removes a T-shirt and sweatpants he must have changed into after work and then climbs into the bed next to me.

"No," I say because I won't fuck him. *I can't.*

"I'm not going to hurt you. I just want to help you sleep." He doesn't say the words, but he means help him sleep too, to know I'm safe.

"Okay," I whisper. His hands go around me, and within moments he's snoring.

That's how the next two weeks go by. Knight yells at me during the day, giving me ridiculous tasks that all involve being away from the office. I dog walked for his neighbor. A neighbor he doesn't even know or care about. I did Cole's dry cleaning at a separate dry cleaner's than Knights. I got Knight's motorcycle and cars washed, even though they didn't need it, twice.

Every day I showed up, somehow in a damn matching outfit to what Knight was wearing, and he'd bark orders at me. It was our only interaction during the day, but somehow those moments meant to drive us apart brought us closer together. The words we spoke to each other were fake, the heat between us the only truth.

But the days weren't as bad as the nights. Every night we developed the same routine. Knight would cook dinner, and we'd eat together in silence. Then we would go our separate ways for a couple of hours before Knight would find his way to my bedroom to hold me all night and keep the nightmares away.

Somehow we exchanged truth for hatred and sex for keeping the nightmares away at night. I'm not sure we made a fair trade.

And in two weeks, everything could change. That's when my first paycheck is due. *Two weeks.* In two weeks, I will have enough money to move out and get my own apartment. But I'm not sure that's what I want anymore. But I have to. It's the only way to keep my sanity.

I sit down at my desk to enjoy a sandwich on my lunch

break, one of the rare times I've been in the office the last two weeks. But instead of eating, my door gets thrown open.

I growl. *I need to get a lock installed on the door ASAP.*

"Hey bestie," Abri says. "I wanted to see if you were available to have lunch with me."

Despite Knight's attempts to keep me away from Abri, she has still found me. She pretends nothing has happened between us, that we are best friends now. She's delusional.

"I'm already eating my lunch, but thanks."

"Oh, well good thing I brought my lunch today." She sits down across from me and pulls her own sandwich out of her purse.

I sigh.

"I'd rather eat alone, Abri. It's been a long week."

"We are eating alone. That's why we aren't in the cafeteria silly."

I eat my sandwich, pretending she isn't here as she speaks nonsense.

"Did you see the new secretary Knight hired? He'll be fucking her by the end of the week."

"Did you see the way Knight looked at me yesterday? He was pining bad."

"Did you hear him talking to Jessica? I think he's been fucking her."

Ignore her, I repeat. Her conversations don't even make sense. *How could Knight be attracted to so many people at the same time and be fucking them all?*

I smirk to myself. Abri doesn't know I'm the one sleeping in Knight's bed every night. Even if it's just sleeping, it doesn't matter. I'm still the only one that gets him. *At least for two more weeks.*

My phone buzzes, and I grab it to turn it off. Knight knows I won't answer on my lunch break. It's not Knight though. It's Ren, my sister.

"Hello?"

"What the fuck, Mila? You didn't tell me that you got expelled! What the fuck are you going to do?!"

"Suspended, not expelled. It wasn't my fault. And I'm enrolled for next semester, so it's really fine. I found a job in the meantime. I'm good."

"You are coming to Aspen this weekend! We need to have a long talk."

"Ren, I'm fine. Really. I work most weekends, so it will be tough for me to get off."

"Mila Kay Burns, you get your butt to my house this weekend!"

"I'll talk to my boss, Ren. But no promises."

I end the call. *Shit.* I'm sure Knight will let me go, it means I'm away from Abri for the weekend. But I don't want to spend the weekend with my sister.

"How is Ren?" Abri asks smirking at me.

"My sister is fine," I say hesitantly.

"Good, I've meant to call her again. It's been a while since we spoke. How are the kids? What are their names again? Oh yes, Bailey and Camden."

I freeze. "Wait...you know my sister?"

Abri blinks in confusion. "Of course, I do, silly. I remember you too, although it took me a while to remember you. You've changed so much. You used to have red and blue and green hair."

"Purple and blue."

"Oh right, purple and blue. You used to follow your older sister everywhere. It was very annoying."

And just like that, one truth comes flooding back. Abri and Ren were close friends in high school. I was going through a rebellious stage and didn't see my family or sister much, but who could forget Abri. The few conversations we had she would tell me how awful my hair was, and that I had horrible split ends and needed to wear a hat or wig instead of dying my hair.

Was Knight there?

I search my brain trying to bring up a memory of Knight. I find none. No, I couldn't have known Knight back then. I only knew Abri for a year at most before she graduated with my sister. And my parents would have never let them bring boys over.

I never hung out with Abri or Ren outside of the house. I was in middle school still when they were in high school. There was no way I knew Knight.

But we were so close. We could have met back then. Before life damaged us both. *Could we have been together then if our pasts hadn't ruined us?*

And how could I have forgotten, even a moment of my past?

14

———

KNIGHT

I NEED to talk to Abri, but for once, she's been avoiding me. I need to threaten her with her life if she so much as talks to Mila again. I've had Mila run ridiculous errands to keep her away from this building. Away from Abri, and if I'm honest, me.

I don't know who's more of a danger to Mila, Abri or me. But being gone keeps Mila safe.

But more than threatening Abri, I need to find out what she told Mila. I need to know how much Mila knows. So then I can figure out how to share my secret.

A loud knock pounds on my door, and I know it's Mila. There is nothing soft about her. She's fierce, independent and even though she has no business experience, if I spent a week teaching her how my company runs, I have no doubt she would take over with full energy and bring our profits up to an all-time high. Even the stupid tasks I've given her she's tackled full on with all of her strength.

She found the best restaurant in all of Denver to host our luncheon at. My motorcycle and cars have never been cleaner. My schedule has never made better use of my time. And she saved me money while finding a better dry cleaner. Not to mention the countless clients she has persuaded to use our app with a simple email or phone call. She's like a machine that doesn't stop until she's shut off.

Mila has a fire I can't find a way to extinguish. Maybe she's strong enough to survive the storm headed her way.

I don't answer. I know Mila's routine at this point, and she knows mine. She waits for exactly three-seconds for a response to her knock. One that I never give her. And then she walks in, not caring who is in my office. She's walked in on countless meetings. The women I'm meeting with, look up at her with jealousy. The men with lust.

Mila doesn't even realize she's bringing attention to herself when she does it. She's just pissed enough at me that it doesn't matter.

"Good afternoon, sweetheart."

She growls at me as she stomps into my office. I guess it's not a good afternoon.

But I can't take my eyes off her. She's wearing a light gray jacket with a hot pink shirt underneath and bright pink pumps. Her hair, which was once curled, is disheveled on top of her head instead of her usual high ponytail that stays in its perfect place throughout the day, no matter what happens.

She takes a seat across from me, crossing her legs forcefully as her arms come crashing down on the armrests of the chair. I'm surprised she didn't break the chair.

"Yes? I thought you were on your lunch break?"

She growls again.

I lean forward so I can stare down her shirt. I'm a bastard, but she doesn't give me a snide remark for being a horny prick.

"Are you going to growl at me all afternoon, or are you going to tell me why you stormed into my office, even though you said you would never shorten a lunch break for me?"

She opens her red lipstick stained lips. I've never seen her reapply lipstick throughout the day, but somehow her lips are always red. Just like her eyeshadow is always a little smudged. Not enough to make her look unprofessional, just enough to make her a real woman, instead of a pristine plastic doll like my soon to be ex-wife.

"Uh…"

I laugh at her speechlessness.

"What's wrong baby? Do I make you speechless?"

"No. Yes. Stop talking."

I cock my head and force my eyes to leave her breasts as her cheeks heat into pink circles. I love Mila when she's full of confidence, storming into my office to chew me out. But I also love her like this, disheveled, embarrassed, and speechless. She's not weaker at this moment. She's just affected. I like simply being near me can make it hard for her to breath.

"I like your outfit." I let my eyes travel up and down her jacket and skirt lazily, knowing it's going to take her a while to find her voice again.

When my eyes meet her gaze, all I see is dark fire.

"How do you always match my outfit? Every fucking day we show up in matching outfits. How? Why? You always leave before I even get out of the shower. Do you have a closet here where you change after you see what outfit I've chosen?"

I lean back in my chair as she stares at my pink tie.

"That's really what you came in here on your lunch break to ask? Why does my tie match your shirt?"

"Yes," she hisses not revealing the truth of why she's here.

I stand up, not intentionally, but because I need to be closer to her. I walk around my desk and snatch her hand off her lap. She tries to pull her hand back, and I let her.

Our eyes lock, and words flow from my mouth. "I match you because even though you hate me. Even though I push you away. Even though I bark orders at you and treat you like a slave instead of a woman more capable than any other employee in my office, of not only being my assistant but running my company. Even though I can't have you. Even though you will never be mine. Even though you deserve so much more. I need to feel like you are mine. I need to be connected to you. I need the world to know that I've claimed you. And matching you, wearing something similar makes me feel close to you, even when you are scowling at me and hating me."

Her mouth falls open as she processes my words. I pick her fallen hand up again and kiss her hand, then her fingers, then her palm. I try to keep my kisses chaste. I'm kissing her to bring her back to life, not to take things too far. But I can't help but pour everything into her with each kiss.

"How?" she barely whispers.

I take one of her fingers in my mouth, taking my time as I lick the length of it, knowing it's a direct connection to her core. I've just lit the flame I don't know how or want to put out.

"You're a planner, Mila Burns. You may pretend you left that part behind you when you got suspended and started working for me, but it's still there, hidden in everything you do.

"I know at night you've already planned out both of our schedules for not only the next day but the next few weeks. I know you have already planned and found two apartments you can easily afford once I start paying you in two weeks. One close to me and the office, the other close to campus in case you need distance from me. I know you already have your top three companies you will apply to when you graduate. I know you plan on paying your brother and sister back in January when I finish paying you. And I know you order all the suits in your closet in the order you plan on wearing them. All I have to do is look at what suit is next in your closet and match you."

Mila bites her lip, and I don't know if it's to scold me or be happy with me. It doesn't matter, either way; this isn't the reason she's in my office.

And the longer she's silent, the more I can't help but kiss her. So I kiss every part of her hand she will let me while the turmoil spins inside of her.

Please don't hate me anymore. I can't stand it.

"Your ability to plan everything lets you see your future. It lets you live it before it even happens. It's a skill that will let you go far in life. But it's also something that will hinder you from truly living. If everything is always planned, then you will miss out on some of the greatest moments."

Mila's eyelashes flitter up from her lap. Her eyes brighten, and her teeth slowly release her lip.

"Like getting fucked on the desk in your boss's office?"

I grin. "Yes, that's exactly what I mean."

My hands grab her neck as she pounces into my body, our lips colliding together like they are meant to be together. Like they can't function without being pressed together.

Her legs wrap around me as I stand, our lips still attached to each other's, desperate to never part again. My office is far away from most of the others on this floor other than Mila's. But I'm not taking any chances. People in my office prefer to storm inside rather than knock before entering. Cole and Abri especially don't honor boundaries.

I slam her body against the door grabbing her chin to separate us for a second so she can catch her breath, and I can find the lock on my door as quickly as possible.

"I hate being interrupted," I say against her lips.

"You seem to love my interruptions."

I growl and nip at her bare neck. "You are the only one who is allowed to interrupt me. In fact, I may make it part of your daily tasks to interrupt me more."

She bites my lip teasingly, but it draws blood.

I smack her ass in retribution, making her squeal.

"Quiet, baby or the whole office will hear you. I don't mind, but you might not enjoy the entire office knowing you are fucking your boss."

She shrugs. "I could care less who hears me. I'm not that close to anyone in the office anyway. You've made it impossible with all the stupid errands I've been running, Cole and Abri are about the only people I talk to. Cole already thinks we are fucking. And Abri..." She freezes.

I set her down on the edge of my desk, trying to understand what is going on in her head. Fear, regret, loss. Her eyes grow big then small.

Shit.

I kneel in front of her, pleading with her to listen to my truth before she freaks out.

"I've never fucked Abri in my office before."

She stills more if it's possible. "Why not? Didn't you build this company together? This was your baby? You can't tell me you two didn't fuck in the heat of an argument? Or after winning a new client?"

I sigh. "We did, but not here."

"Where?"

"A hotel room. Abri didn't want the other employees to hear us. She was more private than you realize."

She exhales, but I can tell her mind is still twirling. I kiss the inside of her thigh trying to bring her back to me. I see the chills run up and down her leg as she shivers, but my touch isn't enough. She needs more words.

"I've never fucked you in the same place as Abri."

"Your apartment?"

"I've fucked Abri in my apartment, but not the bed. The bed I bought new after Abri moved out." I can see the jealousy in her eyes, and I don't know whether to love her more for it or hate her jealous streak. Instead, I choose to understand her feelings. I would be jealous as hell if she were with another man recently. If she were married before or shared anything special with another man.

"Then I'll happily be your first," Mila teases.

"Thank God." I bury my head between her legs and dig my teeth into the thin, flimsy piece of fabric between her legs to pull her panties down. I grab her pink panties that, of course, match the rest of her outfit and stick them into my pocket.

"I'm getting those back, Knight."

I laugh before my tongue dives inside her. *Unlikely.*

She grips my head as I flick, tease and twirl over her sensitive, swollen bud. She responds to every touch like she's never been touched here before. I love that I'm the only one who has made her come from oral, but it also pisses me off that she hasn't had this pleasure before. It pisses me off that I've let two weeks go by without pulling an orgasm from deep inside her core.

The more I lick, the wetter she gets. The harder she grips my head until she can't hold on anymore and grabs the desk instead. True to her word, she doesn't give a fuck who hears us, which only makes me work harder to make her screams louder until I'm sure our entire floor, plus the ones above and below, hear her moans.

"Knight, Knight, Knight!" She screams at the top of her lungs, her body convulsing in an orgasm that rips through her body before rolling into another when I don't let up.

"I can't..."

I smirk. She thinks her body can't handle more, but I'm just getting started.

I slowly stand up, "You deserve more, better. You deserve the world, pretty girl with the smartest mouth."

She blushes in her innocent way.

I snatch her off the desk, spin her around, and push her

against my desk until her hands are gripping the desk and her legs are spread wide.

I kiss against her neck, keeping her wet and ready for me as I undo my pants, freeing my cock. Seconds pass, but it feels like hours as I find the condom in my back pocket and slip it on. And to think I almost left my condoms at home so I would behave.

I grab her hips and push inside her.

"Jesus," she cries as I fill her.

"I would fuck you all day just to hear that beautiful, raspy sound."

"I would fuck you all day because—"

She never does finish that sentence. We are both too impatient to wait until she finishes speaking. I thrust, and she gasps.

I thrust, and she pushes against me, meeting me, begging for more.

I thrust, and she purrs.

I thrust, and she screams.

I thrust, and I can't imagine my cock in any women's cunt but hers.

Shit, I'm fucked.

Her skirt is hiked high as I fuck her, but I need more skin. I push her shirt up so I can kiss every bit of her skin. I try to slow myself down. I try to make this moment last forever, but with each thrust, she tightens around me more, and I know she's about to release her orgasm, and the sounds she makes then will leave me no chance of holding on.

One more thrust inside and she comes.

I come after. And I'm not sure if I'm broken because I don't know when or if that will happen again, or because I know that neither of us can deny ourselves this any longer.

I need more, but I can't collapse on top of her on the desk. I don't imagine it would be the most comfortable position for her. So I grab her, and we fall to the floor in a puddle of limbs. We can't move. We don't clean ourselves up or cover skin that shouldn't be exposed when we go back to work. We lay on the cold, wood floor panting like animals.

"I need more," she says between pants.

I roll to my side so I can see.

"More?" I'm not sure what she means. *Does she need us to date? Does she need us to be in a relationship?*

"I need more fucking."

I grin in relief. *I can give her more of that.*

"I'll trade fucking for nighttime snuggles," she whispers.

I frown as I stroke her face; her hair is going to be even more disheveled than it was before.

"No."

She pouts.

"I mean, how about both? Fucking and snuggles to keep the nightmares away. I think we need both."

The light reappears on her face as her lips curl upward. "I think both would be great. I can fuck you and snuggle and still hate you."

I twirl the end of her hair between my thumb and fingers. "I know you can." She can hate me in her mind, but it won't stop her heart from falling for me.

"Butyouhavetodoonefavorforme," she says in a flush of words all scrunched together, barely comprehensible.

"Slow down, baby and try again."

She takes a deep breath. This is what she came here to tell me.

"I need to go to Aspen this weekend."

I sit up abruptly not expecting her to say she's leaving tomorrow. I can't stand her gone for two whole days without me.

"My sister, Ren, she...well...somehow she found out I got expelled."

"Suspended, because of me," I correct her hating how losing

her schooling makes her feel, even if it means I get to have her in my life a little longer.

She nods. "Ren wants me to come to see her in Aspen this weekend and make sure I'm okay. That she doesn't need to put me on suicide watch or something."

I swallow hard. I have to let her go. We usually work the weekends, but family is more important. She needs to show her sister how she's flourishing even without school.

"And..."

Shit, there's more. I can't handle more.

"And I don't know how I didn't make the connection before, but I know Abri. Well, I don't really know her, but I've met her a few times. Ren and Abri were friends in high school. I only saw Abri a handful of times, and we barely spoke the few times she was at my house, but anyway...it's probably not important, I just thought you should know..."

If I don't stop her, she's going to keep rambling. As much as I love listening to her talk, I have to stop her turmoil.

"I'm sorry you ever had to meet Abri. Now or in the past. She's not a nice person now. She was a better person before..." I can't finish that sentence. Abri was a good person before me. Before I turned her into the evil she is today.

Mila touches my arm, bringing me back to the reality.

"Of course you can go this weekend if that's what you want. I would love a chance to go to Aspen."

She grins. "Wait...what?"

"I'm going with you." I have to go. I might finally figure out the truth. I might find a way to get Abri out of my life. If Mila can't help me, then maybe Ren has a key to Abri's past to help me escape.

"No. Why would you want to go with me?"

"Because now that I've persuaded you to fuck me, I can't go

two days without it." *It's mostly the truth, while still hiding my damn secret.*

Mila tries to hide her smile, but she can't. "You sure? My family is going to think we are dating."

I kiss her nose. "Does it matter if they think we are together?"

"No, it doesn't." She pushes her skirt down and sits up as she runs her hand through her hair.

"Good, when are we leaving?"

"Tomorrow, after work."

"I'll drive."

She shakes her head. "No, I'm not riding on your motorcycle for three hours. I'll drive."

"I have other vehicles than my motorcycle you know."

"I know, but I want to drive. My Subaru runs just fine. You can chip in for gas."

I grin like an idiot. "Fine."

She pulls her hair up into a ponytail, tying it off and getting rid of the most obvious evidence that we just fucked, although she's going to smell like me the rest of the day. Her body is going to glow and blush any time anyone speaks to her when they remind her of me. And when she speaks, everyone in the office will know it was her who I fucked, because no one could mistake her voice for anyone's but her's.

"I should get back to work."

"Yes, you should. Your boss won't like that you took an extra long lunch."

She raises an eyebrow. "He won't? I thought he would demand I take extra long lunches in the future."

I stand, tucking myself back into my pants and walking over to her. I kiss her firmly, ending our teasing game.

"Get to work before your smart mouth gets you into more trouble."

"Stop giving me ridiculous tasks to keep me away from you. I'm not getting your car washed again, or going to any more restaurants. I gained three pounds this week. I made sure to eat four meals a day. And I promise to lock my door, so Abri doesn't barge in."

I kiss her again quickly. "Good, now get your cute ass out of here before I fuck you again and lose all of my clients."

She rolls her eyes. "Yes, sir."

I shake my head as my cock comes to life again. "Of course, now you call me, sir."

She unlocks the door as she bats her eyelashes at me. We both grin like idiots until Mila disappears to do whatever stupid tasks I listed for her to do today.

I wait about three seconds before I decide I should run after her and keep her locked in my office all day. But when I chase after her, she isn't in her office.

Dammit, why did all of her tasks have to involve her leaving the office?

I change course and head to the bathroom to try to clean myself up so I might be able to get work done without smelling like her. I walk into the bathroom and head to the sink to wash her scent off my hands.

The door opens, and I don't acknowledge whoever enters.

"I can't believe you fucked her while still married to me," Abri says.

My face hardens along with my heart. I'm pissed at Abri, but I've needed to talk to her for the last two weeks. I'm not going to scare her off so quickly.

"Don't even, Abri. I know you've been fucking half the office and half the celebrities, athletes, and politicians in this town while we were still living together."

She smiles as she approaches me. "I'm still the best lay of your life."

"No, Abri, you aren't."

Her eyes narrow. "You'll get bored with your new assistant, just like you get bored with all women, then you'll come crawling back to me, begging me to take you back."

"No, I won't."

Abri places her hands under the water where I'm washing my hands as she brushes against mine and then splashes me with water.

"Oops, did I get you?"

I can't deal with this. "I'm going to be gone this weekend; you'll have to ensure the company still runs this weekend." Abri is ruthless when it comes to her revenge against me, but she won't destroy the company. She feels the same way I do about it. She'll sacrifice everything to ensure it's running smoothly.

She shakes her hands roughly, not caring she is splashing me with water. "What a coincidence, I happen to be leaving town as well. I guess you'll have to put your friend Cole in charge while we are both in Aspen."

I grab her shoulders and push her hard against the wall, harder than I probably should. "What are you doing in Aspen?"

"I'm going to visit an old friend, Ren Burns. I haven't spoken to her since I ran off with you after we graduated high school."

Fuck.

"Like hell you are."

She shrugs. "You can't control me as much as you wish you could, Ace."

I growl, even her using my first name pisses me off. I've never been Ace to anyone but her.

"What did you tell Mila? Why did you almost kill her?"

"Don't be dramatic. I didn't almost kill her. Just scared her a little. I wanted her to know she should stay far away from us. But isn't that what you are doing, sending her on endless, useless errands?"

I don't answer.

"What did you tell Mila?"

"The truth." Her eyes flicker down to where my hands are forcefully gripping her arms against the wall. "You are a dangerous man, and she deserves better."

I release her, and she walks to the door.

"We all do," she finishes.

15

___

MILA

WE ARE SUPPOSED to leave for Aspen in fifteen minutes, as soon as Knight finishes his last meeting for the day. My stomach is in knots thinking about it. I don't want to go. I'd rather have a painful bikini wax. I'd rather do more of Knight's stupid errands. I'd rather listen to Abri pretend to be friends with me than face my family.

I've finished all my work today and more. I didn't do any of Knight's stupid errands. Instead, I spent my time maximizing his schedule to ensure he could get the most work done, answering emails, and writing my thoughts out about which markets they should target next.

And now, I'm stalling as I stare at the door, both wanting Knight to come through the door, and begging him not to at the same time. We both packed last night, after another fuck in his bed. I drove my car here this morning instead of having Gallagher drive me. All that is standing between Aspen and me is Knight's meeting and a three-hour car ride.

I blast the radio on from my laptop. I don't have the money to pay for Apple Music or Spotify. And I like listening to the commercials and the silly games the hosts play.

"Tonight is going to be a gorgeous night in Colorado. A perfect night to see a concert at Red Rocks. Tickets are still available for..."

Knight has never been to a concert. Here's my chance to fix that.

I pull up the Red Rocks site and grab Knight's credit card I use to run all his errands. I've been tempted before to use his credit card to get back at him. Use it to rent an apartment. Buy a new car. Or even something simple like buying myself lunch. But I never have.

I decisively click the touchpad on my computer. *Tonight that changes.*

My door creaks open, and I turn down the radio station.

"You ready to go, beautiful?"

I smile at the nickname from Knight's lips.

I nod, closing my laptop and grabbing my purse.

I walk out of the office with Knight close behind me but not touching me. He nods at his employees in their cubicles on the way to the elevator. Everyone's eyes are on us. Even though I've worked here for two weeks, I hardly know any of their names. I haven't had time to connect when Knight has been sending me on wild goose chases. They all know what happened yesterday in Knight's office. They all look at me with wide eyes and whispered comments. It will take a lot to win any of them over as real friends.

I expect my cheeks to flame when I realize that everyone knows I fucked our boss. I expect not to be able to meet their gaze. But it makes me hold my head higher because Knight isn't really my boss. Well, not in the same way as he is to everyone else. Me working here is just a way to pass the time until he asks me for a favor I don't want to give. And I'm afraid that time is growing near. He made it clear it wouldn't come until closer to December, but nothing about our relationship goes slowly.

We step into the elevator, and I expect Knight's hands to be all over me. He doesn't jump me. Our fingers brush together, and my breath catches as I gaze at him out of the corner of my eye. He's in a dark blue suit with a grey tie. He matches me, even though I purposefully picked an out of order outfit. Somehow we are in sync, even though the rest of the world thinks we should be apart.

The elevator doors open in the parking lot below the building, and Knight motions for me to step out. I do, and he follows me toward my car. I climb into the driver seat as he climbs in the passenger seat. I should have spent the day cleaning my car. It smells like fast food and old books. The fabric seats are faded and covered in dust and hair. Knight looks out of place in my car until he takes my hand and squeezes tightly.

"You sure you don't want my driver to drive? We could have a lot more fun that way."

"No," I say smiling.

His phone buzzes, and he frowns at the number. "I don't have to take this."

"Answer." I already know it's Peter from his last meeting calling to take Knight's offer. The clients always call when the meeting is over, jumping at a chance to work with Knight.

He holds my hand tighter as he answers the phone.

I push everything out as I drive with one hand on the wheel and one hand holding Knight's. *Tomorrow is going to suck, but tonight is going to be fucking amazing.*

Knight ends his call after thirty minutes. "Um...Mila, do you need directions to Aspen? I've only gone a couple of times, but I don't think this is the way."

I smile. "It's not the way to Aspen."

"Are you trying to kidnap me?"

"Something like that." I turn onto the side road that climbs up the mountain.

"I don't think now is the time to go hiking again, either."

"We aren't hiking."

"Then what are we doing?"

"We are going to your first concert."

"Who's playing?" he asks grinning far too wide.

"Does it matter?"

He laughs. "You don't know. You bought tickets for a concert, and you don't even know who's playing."

I wince. "Actually, you bought tickets for our concert. I don't have any money, remember?"

He frowns and pulls out his wallet. He starts pulling hundred dollar bills out, counting them quickly, he hands the wad to me.

"Your advance."

I blink rapidly as I take the money. "I earned it?"

"More than earned it."

I put the money in my purse as we both step out of the car. People have parked on either side of us and are walking toward the concerts in jeans and T-shirts.

I pause suddenly.

"What's wrong sweetheart?"

I frown. "We can't go in like this." I glance at his expensive suit and my skirt, jacket, and heels.

"Then, what do you suggest?"

"You packed a T-shirt and jeans, right?"

He laughs, and we head to the trunk. After five minutes of digging through our bags, we finally find something suitable to wear.

Knight removes his jacket, as I help him with his tie. We both stare at each other silently, as I slowly undo the buttons. He shrugs out of his shirt and places the items into the trunk.

"You should, uh, climb in the back seat to change," I say.

His eyes stay on me as his lips curl up. I try to keep my eyes on his face instead of his tantalizing muscles. He sits back into the car, grabs my hand and pulls me inside as well.

I giggle uncontrollably as he pulls me on top of him in the backseat. The door shuts behind me, trapping us inside.

"Knight, we can't! People will see," I squeal in a high pitched voice as he kisses down my neck to my breasts.

"We can't what? Change?"

My eyes roll back in my head as he kisses above my breast again. I would fuck him in front of the entire world and feel no embarrassment. I just want him. All of him. Even the parts he won't let me have because he's afraid I'll hate him for real.

I take control, kissing down his chest stopping when I reach the V that disappears into his pants where a bulge is waiting to be freed.

He slips my jacket off, and slowly unbuttons my shirt, as he pulls me up to his face and buries his head between my breasts, carefully keeping me covered while he kisses me.

"Yes," I moan as he twirls my nipple in his mouth.

"Fuck, we should have taken my car. We could have done so much more."

I nod in agreement, but then his fingers are under my skirt, pushing aside my panties, and then finding the wetness that has already soaked them. He moves the juices around my clit as he punishes my nipple for not agreeing to take his car.

I try to reach down between my legs to give him pleasure too, but he swats my hand away.

"If you pull me out, I won't be able to stop until I'm inside your beautiful cunt and I can't, not here. You're mine, and I won't let anyone else see how amazing you are."

I fist my hands in his hair to keep myself from grabbing his cock.

He slips one, two, three fingers inside me as I gasp and pant, riding his fingers as if they were his cock.

More, more, more.

He does. His tongue laps faster around my nipple, teasing me with his teeth as he nips at me, and his fingers move faster in my pussy. I'm sure his fingers and pants are drenched in my cum, but it doesn't make him stop.

Just as I'm about to scream his name, his mouth comes down on mine, and I scream his name into his lips.

I've never felt more alive than when I'm with him. I've never felt more taken care of or more free to be me.

This is just about sex. There is no us. This isn't a relationship.

Knight gives me an I-just-rocked-your-world smile when I finally come down off my high.

"What was that for?" I ask.

"I couldn't resist. And you needed to get out of these clothes anyway." He leans forward nipping at my ear. "Although I would suggest changing your panties as well, these are soaked."

I laugh, and then we both change into jeans. I pair a gray tank top with mine, and he wears a gray T-shirt.

"Always matching," I laugh as he takes my hand.

"Always connected."

We walk into the venue, hand in hand. I buy the beer with the new money I got paid with, despite Knight's protests. And then we find our seats in the middle.

"Wow," he says when he gets the view of the city below, twinkling in the dark night.

"It's perfect, isn't it?"

Knight moves me in front of his body and wraps his arms around me, pulling me tightly to him. "Now it is."

We hold each other as the music plays, drinking beer, and pretending we know the lyrics to the music even though we don't.

It feels like a date, and I constantly have to remind myself that it's not.

"Tell me something I don't know," I whisper into his ear.

He doesn't miss a beat as if he was anticipating my question. "I never met Ren. I know you want to ask, but I've never met her. Abri never introduced me to her friends. She didn't like me hanging out with other girls. I guess she thought I would find someone better."

I cock my head so that I can look him in the eye. More truths from my bad boy with the dark eyes. It also means if he didn't meet Ren, he never met me. I don't know if I'm happy we never met, and therefore don't have to feel bad about forgetting him, or sad we don't get to have some epic love story that transcends time.

"Your turn, pretty girl."

"Cole told me he wants to take over the company. I think he's planning some sort of overthrow."

Knight laughs and kisses my lips softly. "Don't worry about Cole. He's a good man; he'd never hurt either of us."

"The kiss wasn't hurting us?"

Knight shrugs. "Cole thought if he kissed you it would piss me off enough to claim you. It worked."

I nod. He's probably right.

"Now, tell me something real, not about Cole."

"I've never been fucked in a bathroom at a concert."

Knight laughs. "Now that I can make happen."

It was late before we decided to leave the concert and head to Aspen. And now it's almost three in the morning as we arrive outside my sister's house. A house that used to belong to my parents.

The drive was peaceful and tranquil. We didn't talk much, occasionally sharing a random fact about ourselves. Other times we would listen to music. And sometimes we wouldn't say anything at all.

Knight didn't complain about me driving. He let me take control. Something I haven't felt in a long time.

Knight is currently fighting sleep in the passenger's seat. He usually wakes up in two hours and isn't used to being awake this late.

"Knight, we are here. Time to wake up."

"I wasn't asleep," he mumbles.

I kiss his lips. "I know."

I park the car in the driveway of what most people would call a mansion. My sister just calls it home.

We both climb out, and Knight grabs my duffel bag, along with his spinner bag, and we march toward the garage. I enter the code to open the garage.

"The guest bedroom is on the second floor. Third door on the right. We have to be quiet, so we don't wake Ren or the kids." The guest room used to be my room. It holds too many memories. Most of which I'd rather run away from.

Knight nods and follows me inside. I texted Ren earlier that I would get in late and just use the code. I lied and said Knight's meeting ran late, and I had to stay. I didn't tell her Knight was coming. I didn't want to upset her further until I knew for sure he was coming.

Knight curses in a whisper as he stubs his toe on the corner of a kitchen counter.

I hold back a laugh until the lights come on.

"Ren, you're awake," I say as my sister stands in her robe in the kitchen.

"Of course, I'm awake. I couldn't sleep until you got here. I wasn't sure if I was going to have to rescue you if you got lost or stuck in a ditch somewhere."

I walk over and hug her. "Sorry you were worried," I say even though I know her worry has more to do with not wanting me to be in the news than her fear.

"And who are you?" Ren asks Knight.

Shit. I'm not prepared for this. It was the one subject Knight and I didn't bring up on the car ride over.

"I'm Ace Knight, but you can call me Knight."

Knight extends his hand to Ren, and she takes it hesitantly.

"I'm her boyfriend."

I freeze. I want to stop this. Tell Ren he isn't my boyfriend, he's my boss, but Ren is smiling brightly like I finally did something right. Ren looks to me like she has a million questions, but I'm not staying awake to answer any of them.

"It's been a long night. We should get to sleep."

"Of course, you guys can sleep in the guest bedroom. Third door on the right." She doesn't even call it my bedroom, even though it is.

Knight smiles and carries the bags up the stairs with Ren and me following. I tell Ren goodnight and then head into our bedroom.

"I thought we weren't pretending," I say.

"We aren't."

"Then what was that crap about you being my boyfriend? You could have just said friend or boss or something."

Knight smirks. "Because I wanted to go with the truth. You're mine, Mila, which makes me your boyfriend."

16

KNIGHT

Boyfriend. *Why did I say that?*

I can't be a boyfriend. For one, I'm still technically married, though separated. And two, I just can't. My heart can't love again. I can't be the man Mila deserves.

But when I look at Mila leaning against the door of the bedroom, completely broken herself, I know I want to be her boyfriend more than anything.

I'm willing to try again. Willing to risk it all for her. I just have to convince her and my heart of it.

Mila looks down at her feet instead of at me. She's nervous. It's clear from the way she twists the end of her hair. The way she shifts her weight back and forth on her feet. But there is a smile there, buried beneath the worry.

I don't know how to do this. I don't know how to be the boyfriend she wants and needs. All I know is I can't be apart from her.

I should say those words to her, but I can't find my voice.

Instead, I find myself looking around the room. This isn't a guest room. This is Mila's room. Or at least, it was. But this room isn't like the Mila I know now. The Mila who occupied this room was a free spirit. Posters of various bands I've never heard of line the walls. Sketches of tattoos she never got are mixed between the posters. There is a lava lamp in the corner and glow-in-the-dark stars on the ceiling. A pile of CDs is piled high in the corner, and a desk sits under the window still covered in textbooks and papers as if she were still studying in high school.

My eyes keep scanning the room of her youth, but I find no pictures of her family. Only one of her and a guy that looks to be in college, while she seems to be about fifteen. Her hair is blue and purple. Her makeup is dark and heavy. And her outfit looks like she is about to run away with the band. The guy next to her is covered in tattoos with long dark hair. He looks like me if I hadn't met Abri.

My eyes scan to her bed that can't be more than full-sized and is covered in a dark comforter with red throw pillows.

I laugh. "I think you are going to have to sleep on top of me because there is no way we are both going to fit side by side."

She looks at me. *Finally.*

I can't read her expression though. I don't understand her lack of smile, her breathless expression, or her stillness.

Finally, she says "This is me. I'm not innocent. I'm not a planner. I'm not sweet. I prefer dark over light. I prefer heavy metal over pop. I prefer tattoos over bare skin. I prefer wild over easy.

"I'm not your sweetheart. I'm not your baby. I'm not your pretty girl. I'm a wild flame who never wanted to be tamed. But I followed orders. I changed. I became what everyone wanted me to be. The girl who finds a normal life. Graduates college and settles down with a man who can take care of me. It's not what I wanted, but I'm not sure I can go back to this." Mila holds her hand up motioning to the items in her room.

"I can't be the untouchable girl again with the bad boy boyfriend. And yet, I can't go back to being the nurse who waits for her knight to come save her. I don't know who or what I am anymore."

Tears threaten her eyes. She's trying to give me an out. A way to take back my words about being her boyfriend.

Instead, her words make me want her more. I walk to her, even though I want to run. I pull her into a deep hug as she releases the tears.

"I want all versions of you, Mila. I want the smart mouth version who calls me out on all of my bullshit. I want the sweet, innocent version who wants to be a nurse to take care of people. I want the wild version who's a free spirit and prefers tattoos to getting her nails done. I want all of you, Mila. The good, the bad. Your future, your past. It doesn't matter. I want you."

She blinks, and the tears slowly disappear.

"I can't date a bad boy again. No matter how badly I want to."

I kiss the wetness on her cheek. "Good thing I'm not a bad boy then. That version of me died years ago, just like this version of you. The version you prefer to keep hidden."

She smiles. "You are a bad boy, but you are also kind, and strong, and fierce, and loyal, and stubborn, and mine."

Her lips crash into mine, knocking me backward as she slings her arms around me. This kiss is different than our previous kisses. Sure our tongues push into each other's mouths, exploring with such a passion our lips can barely stay together from the force of the kiss. And yes, our hands grip each other exploring each other's bodies through our clothes. And of course, Mila moans and whimpers while I growl into the kiss.

But none of those things are what make this kiss different. This kiss connects us in a way that will be painful to break. She agrees to date me with this kiss. Agrees to be mine. She gives herself to me, and I give myself to her. Whatever happens from here on out is either going to be the most wonderful thing either of us has experienced, or it's going to wreck us. There is no in between.

"We are really doing this?" Mila asks between kisses.

"Well, we were doing this, but then you stopped to ask me a question."

She laughs and hits me playfully on the chest, knocking me back onto her bed.

She releases her hair from her high ponytail, letting her locks frame her face. "Yes, we are definitely doing this," I growl.

She licks her lips, then grabs the hem of her shirt and lifts, revealing her black bra. Then she slowly undoes her jeans like she's trying to strip for me again. I'm mesmerized with her body. With everything she does. I have to be hers. I've been hers since she climbed on my back after she injured herself on that hike. But I'm not sure she's been mine until this moment.

It feels like she has a vice grip on my heart, and if she squeezes too hard, she's going to obliterate me.

"Strip," she commands looking at me with flirty eyes. She stands confidently in front of me in nothing but her underwear and bra. Another reason I'm falling. No matter which version of herself she is, she's confident.

I quickly rid myself of my shirt, jeans, and underwear until I'm naked on her bed with a condom I pulled out of my jeans pocket lying next to me.

She eyes the condom but doesn't take it initially. Instead, she slowly climbs up the bed between my legs as she eyes my rock hard cock.

When she reaches me, she kisses the tip far too sweetly.

I groan. This is going to be torture if we continue moving this slowly.

She smirks as she lazily rolls her tongue around my shaft, barely touching me at all, but driving me insane all the same.

"That's not fair; I never tortured you."

She laughs. "You've tortured me every day I've worked for you."

I frown.

She grips my cock firmly in her hand as she wraps her mouth around the tip. *Damn, I about come with just her touch.*

She smiles like she knows the power she has over me. She's always had it over my body, but now she has it over my heart too. That scares me far more than what she is capable of doing to my body.

She pumps her hand up and down my shaft with her mouth moving in unison. My eyes roll back in my head as pleasure fills every crevice in my body. I never want this to end, and yet, I want more.

This isn't enough. Not for tonight.

I grab her hand, forcing her to stop, and pull her face toward mine to kiss her.

"Let me finish."

"No."

"I owe you after what you did for me in the car."

I chuckle, shaking my head. "This isn't about owing me anything. What I did was as much for me as it was for you. You don't owe me anything. Ever. Remember that. But right now, I'd really like to fuck my girlfriend for the first time."

She smiles and grabs the condom. She rips it open with her teeth and pushes it over my shaft. I rip her panties off and unhook her bra until she is fully exposed to me. I grab her hips and pull her on top of me, but I let her make the final movement on top of my cock.

She does, sliding over my cock with ease and desire I've never felt from her before.

"I want you so badly, Knight."

Her body slides up and down on top of me, making it hard for me to speak as her breasts bounce in front of me.

"You have me. All of me."

Our lips collide again as she rides me like she's been doing it her entire life. Faster and faster she moves until I'm lost in her. Her red lips, marking me. Her breasts bouncing for me with her nipples erect for me to torture. Her pussy clenching as she slides up and down my length. Everything she does makes my decision more concrete.

This is what love should always feel like. *This.* Passion, courage, strength, desire, want, need, lust. But I've seen the other side of love. The dark side that is all pain, jealousy, horror, and heartbreak. If love was always this, no one would ever break up.

"I want this to last forever," I whisper seconds before I know she's going to release. My words aren't a proposal or a promise. They aren't even a declaration of love. But it is the truth. A wish I know is impossible to come true.

"Then take this moment with you forever, Knight, and it will," she whispers back softly before digging her nails into my back and kissing me like it's a competition.

We both climb higher and higher trying to hold out from coming so this moment can last longer. On any other night we would fuck numerous times, but not tonight. We are too exhausted to go another round. It's after three in the morning. This is our only shot tonight.

I bite her lip. She nibbles on my ear.

I growl, and she moans louder.

"Come, Knight," she commands, finally knowing if one of us doesn't stop this it will literally continue forever because neither of us wants to stop.

"Not without you." My thumb presses over her clit rubbing as I buck into her harder. Pulling an orgasm from her as I find my own.

She falls on top of me and falls asleep almost instantly. I smile, loving her on top of me with my cock still inside her. I hold her in my arms and no matter if my arms fall asleep, my muscles ache, or my body begs me to roll over I won't. I'll hold her all night. Because for the first time, I have someone worth holding onto.

———

Last night was the greatest and worst night I've had in a long time. Great because Mila is amazing. I've never felt so connected to anyone. And worst because Mila has never had so many nightmares in one night. I would wake her up and try to calm her down. Remind her that I'm here. That she's safe. But as soon as she fell asleep again, she would have another nightmare.

True to my promise, I held her all night long. Through every terror but nothing I did helped her. It was as if this house brought her back to her worst place. And not even I am strong enough to bring her out of it. *I need to tell her the truth.*

"Coffee will help," Mila says still curled up in my arms.

I nod.

Both of us are going to struggle to make it through today. Both of us lie in bed for a while longer until we hear Ren's voice yelling. Until we hear kids feet running, and we know if we don't get out of bed soon, it's going to be worse.

Mila climbs out of my arms and walks over to her duffel bag. She pulls out a sundress. I'm surprised she's wearing a dress when she prefers jeans anytime she's not working.

"I should probably shower first."

She shakes her head. "We don't have time."

"What?"

"My sister will start yelling at us to get out of bed in about five minutes. It's already after eight. That's sleeping in, in her view."

I frown, understanding why Mila doesn't get along with her family a little more now.

I pull out a pair of jeans and a T-shirt that matches the blue in Mila's dress. We need to be a united front to make it through today.

Mila bites her lip looking at the clothes I'm holding.

"What's wrong?"

"Did you bring anything nicer? A suit or khakis or a shirt with a collar?"

"No, I thought this weekend would be casual."

"Did you bring a long sleeved shirt?"

"No? Why would I? It's eighty degrees outside."

She frowns. "Sorry, it's stupid. My family isn't a big fan of tattoos, but you know what. It's fine. They need to see the real you. We aren't going to hide."

I grab the nape of her neck and kiss her trying to take her worries away.

"Mila!" Ren's voice rings through the house.

We both exhale and finish getting dressed quickly before heading downstairs for the trap awaiting us.

"Good morning," Mila says to her sister who is standing in the kitchen with a cup of coffee in her hand and a scowl on her face. She's dressed like we are going to a luncheon. In a curve-hugging dress, nicer than Mila's. Her hair is curled, and her makeup is full on. I don't know what Ren's plans are for today, but I feel very underdressed.

"More like good afternoon," Ren snaps.

Mila ignores her and walks to the coffee pot. I sneak behind her as she hands me a coffee. I whisper in Mila's ear, "Protect me."

Mila giggles.

Ren snaps her eyes at us like she just caught us making out in her car or something.

"I'm going to give Knight a tour of the house. Then we can talk," Mila says.

Ren narrows her eyes at us in a glare I'm sure is meant to persuade us to stay and talk now.

But Mila doesn't back down. She takes my hand and pulls me out of the impressive kitchen that despite its large size, felt tiny because of her sister's stare.

"Don't worry about my sister. She's a bitch to everyone," Mila says.

I hook my arm in hers. "I see why you avoided driving here as long as possible yesterday."

She nods.

"I'll try to come up with a good excuse for us to leave early. An emergency like my app crashed. Or my dog is missing."

"You don't have a dog."

"I could have a dog."

Mila laughs. "Thanks, but I don't think it will work. It's only two days. We can last that long."

I raise an eyebrow in fear.

She laughs again. "We can."

I don't think we can, but I let Mila lead me through her mansion of a house. It's beautiful. I don't understand how someone who came from so much money couldn't afford college or a place to stay.

"My parents were broke when they died. Us kids just didn't realize it. My brother Henry and Ren found a way to save the house. And now Ren can easily afford the mortgage on this place," Mila answers my unspoken question.

"How do you feel coming back here?"

"Like I don't belong here. All my demons come back when I'm here."

I pull her close to me. "Let me help you escape them by creating new memories here."

She nods and continues the tour, leading into the children's playroom.

"This is Bailey and Camden," Mila says as two kids come running toward me. "This is Knight."

"Cool name," Bailey says.

I smile, at least the kids are cool. "Thanks."

"Can you teach us to play chess? You can be the Knight!" Camden says.

"Sure," I say. I don't have a clue about chess, but I don't think I get to be the knight. I'm positive that's not how the game works.

I look over at Mila who mouths *I'm going to talk to Ren.*

I nod even though inside I'm yelling *Fuck, fuck, fuck.*

I don't want her anywhere near Ren. I want her with me, *always.*

I start making up rules for chess, trying to stay focused on the kids, instead of on the voices carrying from the other room. But each word I hear pisses me off more.

"Mila, how do you get kicked out of college in your last semester? I'm not letting you live here rent free."

"Mila, he's married to Abri. Abri is one of my closest friends. How could you do this to her? You're a home wrecker! A slut! A whore! Can't you see you are headed down the same path as before?"

I can't take it.

I move the knight forward on the chess board, and Camden captures it.

"Oh no! I lose." I mock getting stabbed and defeated. "I'll be right back. I need to ask your mother a question. Keep playing."

I get up off the carpeted floor and head to the kitchen where Ren is yelling at Mila, and Mila is frozen.

Shit.

I walk over to Mila, ignoring Ren's fierce stares and put my arm around her. "Mila isn't a home wrecker and she sure as hell isn't a slut or a whore. I was divorcing Abri long before Mila came into my life."

Ren shakes her head, ignoring me.

"How could you? After what happened with Nasser?" Ren asks staring at Mila.

I have no idea who Nasser is.

"That was five years ago. I've changed since then. Knight isn't Nasser."

Ren eyes me up and down. "He looks exactly like him except older."

She's talking about the boy in the picture. The same one I thought I looked like.

"How could you do this to Abri? She was our friend."

"No, she was *your* friend. I barely knew her. And I didn't even remember her until she reminded me of that fact."

"That's crazy; you have a perfect memory!"

Mila's sobbing now, but her voice is stronger than ever. "I have a perfect memory *now*; I don't remember anything from before. It's all a blur up until that night."

Ren shakes her head, and I pull Mila tighter, backing her up without saying anything. Just letting her know I'm here for her.

"And you!" Ren turns her attention on me. *Good, it's me she should be focused on.* "How could you do this to Abri? You loved Abri. I saw it the night our parents died."

It's like a ghost returned at that moment. A past none of us realized we were hiding from each other. The one thing none of us have spoken about because we weren't ready to share. It's also the one thing that can set me free.

Mila steps out, away from my grasp. "Wait? You were there?"

"I can explain."

"No, you told me you've never met Ren."

"I haven't."

Mila looks to Ren who clearly disagrees with my statement.

"I never spoke to Ren. I might have seen her at the hospital when I was there to support Abri who was supporting Ren in her loss, but I never spoke to Ren, and I don't remember her. Trust me, Ren is someone I would remember."

"Did you meet me?" Mila asks. All of her fury now focused on me instead of her sister.

I can't lie. I promised I would never lie. She never asked me before, which is the only reason I didn't have to tell her.

"Yes."

Mila's eyes drop in disappointment.

"Let me explain."

Mila's eyes slowly drift back to mine with wide eyes.

I don't wait for her to give me permission to explain, I just start talking.

"We talked for only a moment. And I didn't realize I had met you before until—"

The doorbell rings, stopping my thoughts.

Ren's kids start yelling.

The world doesn't stop just because I want it to.

"I need to make sure the kids haven't killed each other. Answer the door, Mila. It's probably Henry. I told him to get his ass here as soon as I realized who Knight was. He's no knight. He's Ace the asshole."

Ren leaves Mila and me alone in the kitchen.

I try again. "I didn't realize I had met you until—"

Mila ignores me and walks to the front door. She opens it, and I expect to see her brother. Instead, Abri is standing in the doorway looking smug and gorgeous in a black dress.

I didn't realize I had met Mila until I kissed her in the hospital.

Mila turns with a glare in her eye. "I'll leave you and your *wife* to talk."

Shit, now I'm fucked.

17

MILA

I LOCK myself in my childhood bedroom. I'm not speaking to Knight or Ren or anyone until I remember. If I'm going to have a chance to recall it, this is the best place to try. *Where the darkness started.*

I need to remember that night in order to have a shot at figuring out how I feel about Knight.

I sit cross-legged on the center of my bed. A bed Knight became my whole world in. And today, he became my nightmare.

I push Knight out of my head as I close my eyes. Tears have been staining my cheeks since I realized Knight knew me before. He knew me five years ago, and although he never lied, he refused to tell me the truth.

I wipe the tears on the back of my hand, keeping my eyes closed. *Remember I plead with myself, please remember.*

"NO!" I scream. My screams mean nothing though. My voice isn't loud enough to stop it from happening.

"Nasser, please," I beg for him. But it doesn't stop.

I see the bright lights shining at me, almost blinding me. I'm flying. Or falling. I can't tell the difference.

I scream, or maybe it's someone else. Or maybe it's both.

Beeping from the machine next to me as I'm lying completely broken. Pain is consuming me. Pulling me into a dark hole, I'll never be able to escape.

"This is your fault, Mila. All of this is your fault. I will never be able to forgive you," Ren's voice says over and over.

I open my eyes as I shake on the bed. No memories of Knight flooded my head. I don't remember Abri visiting me. I don't remember anything except the pain of what happened, and the guilt of what I caused.

I could ask Ren to remind me of all the details. Or as many as she remembers, but her story would be confounded with her own pain.

Knight.

He's the only one who can tell me the truth. What he remembers. How we met. Nothing else from that dark day matters, just how Knight and I met.

Once I know his truth, then I can decide what my next move is. If we can still date after this. If I can still work for him. If we can have any relationship at all.

Maybe we can start over with full honesty.

I can't remember my past, but maybe he can.

I go to the door, surprised Knight or Ren isn't already on the other side waiting for me, but the house is eerily silent.

I walk downstairs and find a note on the counter from Ren.

Took the kids to go pick up Henry from the airport. We will all talk when we get back. And you will fix this before it becomes a bigger problem.

—Ren

I leave the note on the counter and search for Knight and Abri. Hopefully, he kicked her out so Knight and I can talk. I search the living room, office, and kitchen but don't find Knight anywhere. I've been in my bedroom for over half an hour. Abri should be gone.

But as I walk toward the front door where I left Knight, I know she isn't. They are yelling, and Knight has Abri pinned against the wall.

I gasp when I see her through the window beside the door.

I walk closer because I need to know the truth. Even if this is the only way, I'll get it.

I should run away. That's what the voice in my head says. *Run away. Keep your heart from more pain.*

But I can't move.

I watch their lips move. I watch the anger explode. And then I hear the words that break me.

"You killed our baby," Abri screams as tears roll down her face. I wait for Knight to deny it. I wait for him to yell, scream, argue. It doesn't happen. Instead, he pulls her to him, and he hugs her as she grows limp in his arms.

I stumble backward. I hit the glass end table behind me, and we both shatter to the floor.

"Mila Burns! Can you do..."

I don't listen to Ren yelling. It doesn't matter what she says.

I can't be in a relationship with Knight.

I can't date him.

I can't work for him.

I can't be friends with him.

I have horrible judgment in men. I always pick the bad boys. The ones that hurt me.

I thought Knight would tell me his story, and we could find a way to heal together.

But Knight doesn't get to talk to me.

He doesn't get to apologize.

I'm pulling back my soul, but I'm afraid I've already given away my heart. I'm afraid I gave it to him five years ago.

18

———

KNIGHT

I DIDN'T GET to talk to Mila. I was never let back into the house. Eventually, Henry came out and yelled at me to leave after throwing my suitcase on the front porch.

I tried calling Mila. Texting. I tried stopping by the house, but she never answered me.

So instead, I rented a car and have been sitting in it down the block from her sister's house. Waiting. It's only been a few hours since I was kicked out of the house, but I know Mila won't last long in that house.

I spot Mila's beat up Subaru barreling down the road. She doesn't notice me; she's too focused on leaving. I don't blame her. She wasn't kidding when she said her family didn't know her or appreciate her.

And I became the asshole she always thought I was right before her eyes. I don't know what Mila's siblings told her. Or what Abri might have said. Or what nightmare Mila has come up with in her head. I deserve all of her wrath.

I start my rental car and zoom after her. I watch her the entire time back. I make a note to fix the bump on the back of her car where she backed over my motorcycle. But mostly, I just watch her drive away from me and hope, despite the tears I assume are continuously falling from her eyes as she drives, that she will give me a chance to explain.

I'm surprised yet happy to see her park her car in front of my apartment building. I take my time following her inside. If she knows I've been following her the entire time she might run off.

I open the door to my apartment cautiously, as if a lion might attack if I open it too quickly.

"Mila?" I say as I step into the bedroom.

She slowly steps out of the closet.

I suck in a breath when I see her. She's wearing one of my T-shirts along with a pair of jeans. Her face is puffy but her eyes determined.

"I'm sorry," I say, knowing those are the first words that need to leave my mouth.

She holds up a hand, stopping me from moving or speaking.

"I'm leaving."

I close my eyes to keep my pain in. "Mila, please. Can we talk first? Give me a chance to explain why I didn't tell you we've met before. Then you can decide what you want to do."

"No, I don't want to talk. I've talked enough. I've heard enough. I quit, and whatever it is we are doing, dating or fuck-ing, we are done."

She steps back into the closet, and I can't help but fight for her. I would do anything for her.

I stop at the closet's edge as I watch her throw her clothes into her duffel bag.

"Stay, please. I'll sleep in the guest bedroom."

She continues packing.

"I'll sleep at Cole's place."

She starts throwing shoes into the bag.

"Let me pay for a new place for you to stay."

Her head snaps to me. "So you can keep tabs on me and know where I am?"

"No, I'll give you the cash. I just want to make sure you're safe."

"I'll be fine."

She picks up her duffel bag, slings it over her shoulder, and storms out of the closet to the bathroom.

She starts tossing various other toiletries into the bag. Hairbrush, straightener, toothbrush. But then she stops and faces me.

"I can't remember."

My eyes widen. "I know. You have a perfect memory of everything else. You remember phone numbers, statistics, names, and spreadsheets. I know you would have remembered me, no matter how short of a time we met. I know you can't remember." *Even though I wish you would. Or maybe I wish she could forget.*

Her eyes pierce mine, and I stop talking. I don't get to talk. Only her.

"I only remember bits and pieces in my nightmares. Never the full story. I only know what the newspapers wrote about that night and what my family told me. I know I fucked up then, but I'm not going to repeat my mistake by falling for another asshole."

I nod, understanding but wishing I could help her fill in the gaps. The problem is I have gaps too. Not because I forgot, I could never forget her, but because I wasn't there. And she never told me what happened. All I know is I'm the one that fucked up, not her.

"I can't remember," she repeats. "It's like my brain shut everything off before that night. And my perfect memory now is a coping mechanism to flood out the memories from before. If I'm preoccupied with remembering my present, then I don't have enough space left to remember my past."

Mila looks at me like she wants me to talk, but when I open my mouth, she shakes her head and moves past me. I follow her as she heads downstairs to the kitchen. She walks to the fridge pulling out a bottle of water and drinks it like it's her life savior. The only thing keeping her alive. Finally, she stares at me.

"I heard you and Abri."

I swallow hard, the lump in my throat growing large as her words penetrate through me.

"Abri told me you beat her."

I close my eyes, wishing there was something I could say to make her realize the words Abri said weren't true. But I don't deserve to get to defend myself.

"She said you killed your baby."

I close my eyes. There is nothing I can say to refute those words or make my own pain lessen enough to be able to talk.

"Goodbye, Knight."

Mila walks to the door, but I can't let her leave. Despite the pain I feel every time I think of losing my child, I can't let that pain overwhelm me and cause me to lose another person I love.

"Wait," I run to the door and put a hand on it, stopping her from leaving.

"No words I say will be enough to make you change your mind about Abri and me, but I can tell you one truth. I didn't realize who you were until I kissed you in the hospital and from that moment on, I realized you could help me. I was selfish. I wanted your help to take down Abri. I created a plan to sell the company to Cole to ensure she got nothing. But I thought you could help me take more from Abri because you had a connection to her when you were younger through Ren. I'm so sorry for using you. I never wanted to hurt you. I thought I could help you."

I suck in a breath.

"But I don't care about any of that anymore. I don't care

about hurting Abri. I don't care about my company. I don't care if I go completely bankrupt. All I care about is you. I lo—"

"Stop."

"Mila please, let me finish."

"No. Most women could give you a second chance, but I can't. Not with my past. I can't afford to give out second chances."

I'm frozen watching her leave. I consider chasing after her and forcing her to hear my words. I consider locking her in my bedroom to know she's safe.

I do neither. I've made too many decisions about her life without her input. I cost her her career. I forced her to live with me. To work with me. And brought up a past she clearly needs to keep hidden. Whatever happened that night, it's worse than I thought.

I need to let Mila Burns go. I need to give Abri whatever she wants to ensure she stays away from Mila. Then I need to get drunk and forget the last five years ever happened.

I don't know how long I stand in the entryway staring at the door. Five minutes, an hour, or ten hours. But eventually, I realize I should have gone with the option that involved forcing her to stay. Because I realize too late where she's most likely sleeping tonight. In a cheap motel room or her car. I gave her a couple grand, but that's all the money she has. She doesn't have another job, although I will gladly give her the money I promised her if she will take it. But even the couple grand I gave her she won't spend out of principle.

She'll sleep in her damn car.

I jerk my phone out of my pocket and dial Lana's number. She's the only friend Mila has that she keeps in contact with.

"Hello? Who's this?" Lana answers.

"Lana, this is Ace Knight. I'm Mila's um..."

"I know who you are. And no, she's not here. She's not allowed on campus because of you."

"I know, and I'm sorry. I fucked up. I want to make things right, but I can't do that if I don't find her."

Pause.

"Her favorite place to sleep in her car was on Walnut Street, by the Old 17th Avenue Bridge."

"Thank you, Lana."

I drive to the spot Lana gave me, but I don't find Mila. I drive to the office and question everyone I can, but she's not there. I get desperate and call Abri, but she doesn't answer me.

Cole.

I dial his number.

"Hello," Cole answers.

"Is she there?"

Cole swallows.

"Fucking, answer me, Cole. Is Mila staying with you?"

"Yes."

"I'll be right there."

"No, Knight. You won't."

"You're not fucking my girlfriend."

Cole sighs. "Go to sleep, Knight. Give Mila some space."

"No, I need to be there for her. She can't sleep without me."

"She's sleeping just fine. I'll watch out for her though, and make sure she doesn't get any nightmares."

"Cole! You fucking bastard."

Silence. He ended the call.

I slam my phone down. Cole's my friend. He won't hurt Mila, but Mila might try to use him to hurt me. To make sure things end permanently between us because she knows I can never forgive her if she sleeps with my best friend. And she can't forgive me for keeping the truth from her.

I'm fucked no matter what happens.

19

MILA

I open my eyes slowly like I've been asleep all night. I don't think I slept more than five minutes at a time without a nightmare impeding my sleep. I've been lying in Cole's bed for the last hour awake, but unable to convince myself to get out of bed or even open my eyes.

I swing my legs over to the side of the bed to force myself up, taking a break from trying to sleep.

"Umf."

I retract my legs as I hit a lump on the floor. I turn on the lamp on the nightstand and look down to see Cole lying on the floor.

"Morning," he says rolling over.

I tuck my legs underneath me as I sit on the edge of his bed.

"You shouldn't have slept on the floor."

He cracks his neck as he sits up. "You were having nightmares. I didn't want to leave you alone."

"You could have slept in the bed with me."

Cole shakes his head as he laughs off my statement. "No, I couldn't. Not if I wanted to keep breathing after Knight found out."

"He wouldn't find out."

"Knight is my best friend. I would never betray him. Even if he deserves it."

Cole stands up.

"You're a good man. I'm sorry I ever thought differently."

Cole shrugs. "Don't worry; I can be as much of an ass as Knight is."

I smile.

"Breakfast?"

"Sure, what do you have?"

He frowns. "I think I have cereal, although I don't think I have any milk."

"Do you have coffee?"

"Yes, that I have."

"That's all I need."

Cole smiles and starts walking toward the kitchen in his low riding sweatpants and T-shirt. I wait until he leaves to climb out of bed. I'm still wearing Knight's T-shirt. I don't know why I put it on in the first place other than I needed to feel close to him. I needed to smell him. I needed to know we still share a connection despite how much I hate him.

I'm wearing shorts underneath his T-shirt, but they aren't visible since his shirt fits more like a dress than a shirt on me.

I walk into the kitchen, and Cole only stares at my bare legs once before he sets a cup of coffee in front of me. He also pours me a bowl of Cinnamon Crunch cereal.

"Knight would kill me if he found out I didn't feed you."

I sigh and pop a couple of pieces of the sweet cereal into my mouth. I should have snuck into Lana's dorm room. Then I wouldn't have had to talk about Knight.

"You're staying here until you can afford your own place. I'm not arguing about it. And if you think Knight is bad, I'm worse when it comes to being a controlling prick. If I find you sleeping on the streets, I will drag your ass back here and lock you up in my bedroom."

I smile. I don't plan on sleeping on the streets again. I only did that once during the summer between freshman and sophomore year. My scholarship didn't cover summer dorm rooms unless I was taking summer classes. I was stupid and thought I could find a job and a cheap place to live easily. I was wrong on both accounts.

"Don't worry, I'll find a job soon, and you won't have to worry about making sure you have breakfast for me."

"Work for me," Cole says, his bright eyes suddenly serious.

"Really? You would do that for me?"

"Of course, you're Knight's girl. I would do anything for you."

I shake my head. "I'm not Knight's anything."

"Fine, but regardless of what happened, he loves you."

I'm not sure he does. Not after I saw him with Abri. I think he might still love her.

"How about being my assistant? I know you are qualified for the job."

I groan. "Really? Can't I waitress or bartend or something?"

He opens his mouth, and I can already tell what's going to fall out of it. Knight would kill me if he found you waitressing in the skimpy outfits and getting ogled by men.

"Fine, I'll be your assistant."

Cole grins.

"When should I start?"

"I could use some help when I go into work in an hour or so." He wiggles his eyebrows as he says it.

It's Sunday. I know he doesn't work on Sundays. He's just trying to distract me. But I'll take it.

"Give me two hours. I want to go for a run and then shower."

"Deal," he says.

I get up and head to Cole's bedroom, which has now become

mine. I tried to use one of his spare bedrooms, but he wouldn't let me. He said his bed was the best and it had the only functioning shower.

I walk to the bathroom to change into something I can run in and brush my teeth, but I forgot my toothpaste and can't find any in his cabinets. I walk back out to the kitchen.

"Cole, where is your toothpaste?" I freeze. Knight is standing in the kitchen next to Cole. *Traitor*, I mouth to Cole who shrugs and slinks away, leaving Knight and me alone.

Knight's eyes take all of me in greedily, unlike when Cole looked at me. He doesn't hide his lust when he stares at my bare legs. He doesn't pretend he isn't looking. His eyes burn into my skin with a passion I can't escape.

Finally, Knight's eyes trail back to the room I just left: Cole's bedroom.

He exhales deeply with a grimace as if his words are going to fight back and hurt him. "You fucked Cole." His words aren't a question. He doesn't say them accusatorially. He says them sadly like his words are fact.

I cross my arms across my chest. "I don't think that's really any of your business. We are broken up."

He nods, dropping his head. He doesn't look like he slept much either. I figured he would be hungover, but I'm not sure he is. At least, he doesn't smell like alcohol or vomit.

He's wearing another gray T-shirt, matching the one I'm wearing. *Always matching.*

He reaches into his back pocket and pulls out a check. He holds it out to me. I stare at it skimming it quickly. It's made out to me for $250,000.

I shake my head. "I don't want your money, Knight."

"I'm the one who fucked up and caused you to want to end our contract. You should get paid for your time."

"No, we never signed an official contract. And like I said, I don't want your money. I found a new job."

"Oh." He slips the check back into his pocket before pulling out another piece of paper and holds it out to me.

"You're enrolled for next semester. The school also wrote you an apology for your suspension after realizing I was the one at fault."

I take the piece of paper confirming my enrollment for next semester. I'll take it because I deserve to be able to finish school. It was his fault I'm not currently finishing my last couple of months.

He grabs the nape of his neck as he stares at me with sad eyes. He looks completely broken and helpless.

"Is that all?" I ask.

"No, it's nowhere near all. I know I fucked up in an unforgivable way. I broke your trust in me. But know I'll wait forever for you. For you to come back to work or be my friend, or my girlfriend. I'll take whatever I can get. Even if it means we can only be pen pals. I don't care. I just need you in my life."

I close my eyes because his words sting. Nothing he does should be able to hurt me. He shouldn't be able to pierce through my armor, but he does. It's why I can't be in his life.

"I won't replace Abri. It's clear you aren't over her. You comforted her. Held her like you were still together. You still have pictures of her scattered throughout your apartment. You had me do her job. I'm not Abri. And I never will be."

Knight's mouth falls, and I think it might hit the floor and shatter, much like my own heart. He carefully chooses his next words.

"I hugged Abri because I'm the only person in her life who understands what it's like to lose a baby. The pain is indescribable. I keep the pictures to remind me of the pain I caused us both. And

I had you be my assistant because it was the only way I could think to have you in my life. I don't love Abri. Not anymore. I could never love Abri again. We've been through too much. Abri will confirm that for you. She hates me as much as I used to love her."

I nod, but it doesn't change anything. He doesn't love Abri, but I can't love him.

"I'm not ready to talk about losing Gideon yet. I wish I could. It might be the only thing that can bring you back to me."

Gideon. The baby had a name. And it breaks my heart. Even if I could forgive him, I'm not sure I want to be in his life. I will have to carry his heartbreak along with my own. I'm not strong enough to handle that burden.

"I'm not sure anything you say will help me to forgive you."

He stills like I just slid a sword through his chest. A low groan pours through him like he can't stand to continue breathing.

And I can't help but ease a tiny bit of his pain. "I didn't fuck Cole."

His eyes widen as a tiny part of him comes back to life.

"You think I would put your shirt back on if I fucked Cole?"

Hope. I just gave Knight a tiny drop of hope. And now I regret it because there is no hope.

I turn and walk back to Cole's bedroom leaving Knight alone in the kitchen.

I want to know Knight's story, despite how it could hurt me. It's clear he blames himself for the death of Gideon. And knowing the truth could hurt me more than knowing he hid it from me.

But can I blame him for the death of his baby when I'm the reason my parents are dead?

20

KNIGHT

I TRY *to open the door, but it won't budge. I'm trapped in this cage of metal, rubber, and glass. I kick the door, but nothing happens.*

I look over at Cole who is coughing profusely, trying to rid his lungs of the smoke burning its way through his body. We don't have much time left. Cole tries to push his door open, but his attempts are weak.

It's up to me.

I kick harder and harder, but it's not helping. I have to focus on the glass; it's the only way. I start kicking the glass and then use my elbow to try and penetrate it.

The smoke is filling the car now. I can't escape it. I can't breathe. We are going to die.

I need something sharp. My foot is doing nothing to the window. I feel around but don't remember anything sharp I keep in the car.

My head falls back against the headrest. I'm exhausted. I need a break. But there is no time for breaks.

The headrest falls down from the weight of my head. The headrest!

I turn around and yank as hard as I can against the headrest. It breaks free, and I see the two sharp metal prongs that usually hold the headrest into the back of the seat. I start slamming the ends of the headrest into the window.

Crack.

The glass begins to break.

Fucking yes!

I hit the glass over and over with the headrest. Each time I hit the glass, more cracks form. Until it shatters.

"Cole!" I shout, prepared to pull him through the window.

He doesn't stir.

Shit.

He needs out, now.

I hook my arms under his armpits and pull with everything I have, coughing every second as I suck in smoke along with a tiny bit of oxygen.

I climb through the window, pulling Cole with me. His body thuds against the asphalt as I yank him out of the car. I wince, watching the blood spill from his head where it hit the street. But he's safe now. He's free. I hear the ambulances. We are going to live.

"You can't save everyone. You saved Cole. You saved yourself. But you can't save Mila. She's mine."

Abri's words wake me up. *Fuck, it was just a nightmare, but it felt so real.* Probably because the first part was true. The car accident, the smoke. But I've never heard Abri threaten Mila's life, but now that I've dreamt it, I know she will. It's her next move to hurt me.

If I do nothing, then Mila is as good as dead. Abri half attempted to hurt her before while they were rock climbing. She will try worse. She will ruin Mila or kill her. She knows how much Mila means to me. She will do anything to hurt me.

It's four in the morning. I should wait a few more hours and make sure this is how I'll feel in a few hours. But saving Mila can't wait.

I pick up my phone and dial Abri's number. She answers on the second ring. "Yes, Ace?"

"I'm ready to sign the divorce papers."

I can feel her smiling on the other end of the line. "And what makes you think I'm ready to sign?"

"Because I'm giving you everything you want."

———

It takes a week to get the paperwork figured out and a time where everyone can meet. I thought waiting a week would be hard, but I know Mila is as safe as she can be with Cole. And I took the week to begin to adjust to my new found freedom. I don't know why I didn't do this in the first place. Making sure Abri paid for her crimes isn't worth it.

So I did everything I love. I hiked, I rock climbed, I rode my motorcycle too fast. I drank, I smoked, I ate fried food. I slept in late and went to bed even later. I should have felt more alive than I have in years. But I didn't.

Instead, I feel a calmness because I'm a hundred percent sure I'm doing the right thing.

My lawyer told me to wear a suit and tie to the meeting, but in about thirty minutes, I won't own any suits anymore, so it felt wrong to wear one now. Instead, I'm wearing a black T-shirt with dark jeans. I'm in mourning. Not at the loss of anything other than Mila.

I walk into the building and my lawyer, Doug Lundy, sits on a bench waiting for me. He's dressed in a blue suit. He eyes my clothes but doesn't comment. *Good, you fucking work for me. You don't get to dictate what I wear or what I do.*

"You sure about this? We can get you a much better deal. That's why you hired my firm," Lundy says.

"I'm sure. I was an idiot for not doing this months ago."

Lundy sighs.

"Don't worry, Lundy. I made sure the agreement calls for you getting paid well for your work."

"I'm not worried about getting paid. I've been a divorce lawyer for a long time. I've won several cases and lost others. But I've never felt more like justice isn't prevailing than in this case. You deserve better, Knight."

I shrug. "It doesn't matter what I deserve." *I'm protecting someone who deserves the world, and all I gave her were a bunch of half-truths.*

Lundy opens the door, and we step inside the mediation room. Abri and her team of three lawyers are already sitting on one side of the long table. She's wearing a suit. She's all business.

Lundy and I take a seat opposite them.

"I didn't think you would show," Abri says.

"I'd rather get divorced than be rich."

She smiles. "Good."

Lundy pulls the papers out of his briefcase and lays them on the table. "I know everyone involved has had time to review the settlement, but let's review all the terms and ensure everyone still understands and agrees. If there are any objections, we can discuss them and decide if we can reach an agreement today."

I already know we will easily reach an agreement today.

"First item, Abri will—"

"Please call me Mrs. Knight, as that is my name," Abri says.

Lundy looks to me, and I nod. Abri probably won't even change her last name after we get divorced. She will keep my name just to piss me off for all of eternity. But I won't let her know that now. She's won enough. I won't give her any more than what is already stated in the document.

"Mrs. Knight will get the apartment and all of its contents," Lundy says.

Everyone nods.

"Mrs. Knight will retain all of the vehicles acquired during the marriage with the exception of Mr. Knight's motorcycle, which was acquired after the two separated."

More nods.

"Mrs. Knight will receive all of the money the couple acquired throughout the almost five-year marriage."

My eyes burn into Abri. I am giving her my money. She may have earned half of it, but half isn't enough for her. She's greedy, and I couldn't care less about the money.

Lundy sucks in a breath before he states the last line of the agreement. He looks at me one last time to ensure I haven't changed my mind. I haven't. I could give her everything but this one thing and Abri would still be pissed. She would still try to hurt Mila. I won't let that happen.

I nod my head for him to continue.

"Mr. Knight will turn over complete and full ownership of his company Perfect Match. He will give her all of his stock and board membership roles, including any rights to make any decision about the company's future endeavors."

Abri's smile turns into a devilish grin. She thinks I will back out. She thinks I will object to her getting my company. The one thing I cared about almost as much as I did Abri when we were married.

I love Perfect Match. I loved starting something and building it to an incredible place. But I don't love having it used as a bargaining chip. I don't love that no matter how much I love the company, it will always be tainted with thoughts of Abri.

"Do all parties agree to the terms written out?" Lundy asks.

Abri's lawyers lean in to whisper in her ear.

"We agree to the terms if Ace does," Abri says.

Lundy leans over and whispers. "It's not too late to change your mind. You don't have to give her the company."

"I do."

"Since you are giving up everything, which isn't required under the law, I also advise you to add a clause where she can't take you to court or file criminal complaints from the time during your marriage. It's clear she wants to make you pay for the separation, and I could see her taking additional steps to ensure you pay. And at that time, you won't have any money left to fight her with," Lundy whispers.

I stare into Abri's bright eyes. "Thank you for your advice, but I'm ready to sign the divorce papers as is."

Lundy reluctantly hands me a pen as he slides the papers to me. I sign my name, more sure about this decision than I was on the day I married Abri. That day I was so certain. Today, I know what certainty feels like.

I slide the papers to Abri who signs them as fast as I did.

"Congratulations, we will file the papers today, and you will be legally divorced."

I stand and walk out before I have time for anyone else to say anything else.

Cole is standing in the hallway when I exit. I should have known he would find out about the divorce today.

"You divorced yet?"

"Yes."

"Good, I never liked that bitch."

I raise an eyebrow. "I thought you cared about her? I thought you thought I was treating her unfairly? I thought you thought she was my perfect match?"

Cole shakes his head. "I was trying to be a good friend. She always gave me a bad vibe. So what did she get?"

"Everything."

Cole gasps. "You fucking idiot. She shouldn't have gotten anything."

"You're right. I guess she didn't get everything. I'm able to walk away with my heart and body still intact."

"She did something to the car, didn't she?"

"I think so. I think she did something to the breaks, which is why I couldn't stop the car."

"And you let her get away with it! You let her take everything!"

"Yes, to protect Mila."

Cole stops screaming. "You're still an idiot, but I would have done the same thing."

I'm glad Mila has him. He's been a good friend to me over the years. But it kills me she will talk to him and not me right now.

"Are you afraid she will do anything now? To hurt Mila or you?"

"No, I'm not afraid if she does because I didn't do anything wrong. At least not to her. The truth would come out. But she won't. She thinks I have proof she tried to kill us."

"Do you?"

I shrug. "I'm not sure." Mila was the only one who could have evidence Abri tried to hurt me. But Mila hates me. She wouldn't do anything to help me, and I wouldn't want her to. Because helping me involves remembering a past that is darker than I realized. And above everything, I don't want to hurt Mila.

21

MILA

My stomach growls as I step into Cole's downtown apartment. It's not as nice as Knight's, but it's still larger than anything I will ever be able to afford. I'm tired, but not because working as Cole's assistant is exhausting. Being his assistant is the easiest job in the world. His club runs almost flawlessly. Everyone knows their job and does it without question.

Cole gives me a few tasks he needs help with each day. I answer a small number of emails and then follow Cole around and help him. Which mostly means I get to listen to Cole talk about Knight.

I now know too many random facts and stories about Knight. I know Knight let Cole sleep on his couch when Cole was broke. I know Knight gave Cole the initial investment to start his club. I've heard the story about how Knight got his first tattoo of a rubber ducky on a dare when he was fifteen. He has since covered it with a dragon tattoo.

I've heard too many stories of when Cole and Knight would fight over girls and how Knight would always win. And I know Knight once saved Cole's life when they were sixteen. Cole was drunk at a party and fell into the pool. He was knocked unconscious, and nobody around the pool attempted to help. Knight jumped in and saved him, then kicked everyone's asses for not helping.

"We should order pizza tonight. I'm starving," I say to Cole.

"I can cook."

I frown. "No, you can't."

"Fine, then you cook."

I laugh. "I can't cook. I've never had a kitchen of my own before. I have no idea how to cook."

"I can cook," Knight says, sending chills down my spine. I turn and face him for the first time in a week.

"That would be great." Cole walks over and hugs his friend.

I don't respond. I just walk into my bedroom. Well, Cole's bedroom I now sleep in. Cole has made himself a cot on the floor so he can be there for me when I have nightmares.

I slam the door behind me as I enter.

The door opens a second later. "Knight, I don't have time to deal with you—"

"It's just me," Cole says.

I turn. "What is Knight doing here? I thought you were on my side? I thought you said Knight was in the wrong?"

"He was."

"Then what is he doing here?"

"He's moving in until he finds a new job."

"What?"

"He divorced Abri and gave her everything."

I gasp. I don't know what I was expecting, but this isn't it.

Shit. I need to move out. I can't live here with him being here.

"You're not leaving, Mila. You promised me you wouldn't leave until you found someplace safe to go."

"I'll sneak into Lana's dorm. I can stay with her."

"No, you can't."

I pout. "I'll think of something."

"Until then, you are staying here."

"Fine," I growl.

Cole's smile is faint on his lips. "I have one more story I need to tell you. I know you are tired of my stories about Knight, but I promise after this one, you can get his stories directly from him."

I roll my eyes and sit on the edge of the bed. Waiting for another Knight-is-amazing story.

"Knight is an asshole."

My ears perk up at his words. Maybe this is a we-hate-Knight story.

"He was an asshole to my girlfriends. He never thought any of them were good enough. He teased me constantly when we were kids. He's punched me in the face at least six times. He's gotten drunk too many times where I had to come save his ass. He wasn't a perfect boyfriend or husband to Abri. Even though he loved her, he kept up his guard too much. But no matter what we've been through, Knight has always been there for me."

I nod. "Are you done?"

"No, that wasn't the story. I want to tell you about the car accident."

"The one that caused you both to end up in the hospital?"

He nods. "I didn't know the truth about what happened until recently. It was a sunny day. But somehow, our car ended up crashing into the median on the highway at almost eighty miles an hour. It was the scariest moment of my life. Although, I'm not sure if it even makes the top five most terrifying moments for Knight.

"Somehow, we both stayed in the car when we crashed. I guess the airbags did their job. But the car caught on fire. Smoke filled the car, and I was too beat up to be able to get out."

Cole takes a second to compose himself before continuing.

"Knight wouldn't give up on getting us out. He broke the window, but by then, I was passed out and dead weight. Knight should have climbed out and saved himself. He could have died, the smoke was that bad, but instead of saving himself he made sure he got me free."

I feel a tear at his words, but I won't let his story affect me.

"Afterwards, I was thankful he saved my life, but also suspicious of what caused the accident. I couldn't come up with anything that would have caused it. I thought maybe he had been drinking, but I hadn't noticed."

I blink, not understanding.

"Abri caused the accident. She messed with the breaks."

I gasp.

Cole walks up to me and strokes my hair. "Don't hate Knight for trying to keep you out of his messed up life. Don't hate him for keeping secrets. It's the only way he knows how to protect the people he loves."

I nod, drinking in his words.

"Knight gave Abri everything to protect you. She got his money, his apartment, his company, his life. He was ready to fight for what she did to him. To us. But he wasn't willing to risk you."

Cole leaves, and I cry until there is nothing left but sobs. *What do I do now?*

My stomach rumbles, reminding me of how hungry I am. I splash water on my face in the ensuite's sink, so I no longer look like I'm crying, and then I walk to the kitchen.

"You're just in time. Knight fixed enchiladas," Cole says.

I smile at Knight who gives me a knowing look. "It was the closest thing I could come up with to tacos without pissing you off by actually making your favorite food. But don't complain if it's bad. Cole has no food in this place."

"Hey," Cole says throwing a chip at Knight.

We fix our plates, and I take a bite. *Damn, it's delicious.* Cole and I both moan as we eat.

"What have you been feeding her, Cole? You both look like you've lost weight since I last saw you," Knight says.

Cole frowns. "Um...mainly macaroni and cheese. It's the only thing either of us can make without burning the house down."

"You were the one who burned the pizza, not me."

"And you caught our last package of macaroni on fire because you forgot to add water, genius," Cole teases.

I smile. I would love living with them if it was just like this all the time. No drama, just us teasing each other.

We all eat, listening to Cole trying to make jokes to ease the tension. Except I don't feel a lot of tension with Knight around. He seems happier than I've ever seen him. No, maybe happy isn't the right word. He seems content. Ease and calm I wouldn't have expected to see from someone who just lost everything.

Cole's phone buzzes. "I need to take this. Don't kill each other." Cole gets up and heads out through the front door.

"Don't expect Cole to come back until later tonight. He's still betting on us getting back together," Knight says.

I nod. I guessed the same.

We begin gathering the dishes, and Knight washes them while I dry. We are about halfway through before Knight starts talking.

"Abri was the perfect girlfriend. She was smart, funny, beautiful. She understood me. That although I dressed like a bad boy and got into constant trouble, there was more to me underneath. She believed in me when I couldn't."

"We don't have to do this." *I don't think I can hear him talk about Abri.*

Knight doesn't stop though. "We ran away together after high school. Like I told you, we eloped and started a company together. I was the CEO, and her title was officially assistant, but she was my partner in every way. Three plus years later, the company was worth millions. We had it all. We were young, happy, and successful. But then I got Abri pregnant."

Knight's voice catches, and he stops washing the dishes and turns to me. His eyes are already burning with tears.

"It wasn't planned. The condom broke. I thought she was on birth control, so I didn't mention it to her. I didn't want her to worry. But she was pregnant, and it was the best news I ever heard. Even Abri who was skeptical at first, she thought we were too young, was ecstatic."

Knight swallows hard as he convinces his lips to keep moving and tell the rest of his story.

"The first couple of months went by quickly. We found out the baby was a boy, and we started buying everything. Decorating a room in the apartment. We went all out. But then the fights started. The worry set in. I felt Abri was working too much, and she didn't want to give up her dreams for our baby. I told her I would take time off when the baby was born. We'd hire help. It would be fine."

His tears fall hard and fast, but I can't comfort him. I can't make them stop, not until he finishes the story.

"Then, one night, the fighting got worse. I don't even remember the words we were fighting about. Abri fell. I didn't touch her. I tried to catch her, but I couldn't. I raced her to the hospital. She gave birth a few hours later to Gideon. They said stress and anxiety caused her to go into labor early. It was far too early. The doctors couldn't save him. He died in my arms as he attempted to take his first breaths."

Tears are flooding our eyes now. "It's not your fault."

"It is. I got her pregnant even though she wasn't ready. And I fought with her when all she wanted was help. Abri was perfect before I ruined her. She wasn't the same after she lost the baby. Neither of us was."

I want to comfort him. I want to make the pain go away, but

it's impossible. No words will help. No touch will soothe. This is his pain to bare.

"I should have stopped it before it came to this. You gave me a chance to stop it, and I didn't listen."

"Huh?"

Knight wipes his tears and then brushes mine away with his thumb. "Can I hold your hand?" His breathing is erratic, his chest rising and falling too quickly.

He's asking permission to hold my hand. I want to hold his hand. It's the first step toward forgiveness if I hold his hand. *Am I ready for that?*

I stare down at his hand, and before I realize what I'm doing, I reach out and take it.

He exhales at my touch like he wasn't whole until I touched him.

He gently pulls on my hand, leading me out to the patio where a small loveseat sits. He motions for me to sit and I do, pulling him next to me. I've never wanted to be closer to someone as I do right now.

He tries to pull his hand away, but I hold it firmly. His eyes widen, and his pupils dilate. But his breathing calms at the gesture.

I open my mouth, but no words come out. I need him to finish talking. I need him to tell me how I tie into all of this.

"Abri and I were close to graduating high school. It was a Thursday night, and I picked Abri up from her house. We were going to go to a movie, but we never made it past my car. We parked in the parking lot of the movie theater and made out in the back of my old Crown Vic.

"It was an ordinary night. We were making out, and whenever we came up for air, we talked about skipping college and running away. Traveling the world and starting our own life together."

His eyes meet mine again as he traces the lines on my palm with this thumb.

"Then Abri got a phone call. Her mother would sometimes call and demand she come home early, but it wasn't her mother. It was Ren."

I suck in a breath, both from his words and the way his fingers feel on my palm.

"Ren said it was an emergency. She needed Abri to come to the hospital.

"I'd never met any of Abri's friends before. She was afraid if I did, I would like them better than her. She was the jealous type back then."

"Still is," I mumble.

Knight pauses before continuing. "We got to the hospital, and it was chaos. Nurses and doctors were running around frantically. Ren and Henry were there with tears and fear in their eyes. Their bodies frozen with shock.

"Abri tried to comfort Ren. And soon I was lost to the shadows. No one even remembered I was in the waiting room. No one talked to me or looked at me. Everyone was too occupied with trying to save the three lives that stood on the edge between life and death."

"My parents," I whisper.

He touches my chin. "And you."

I nod, needing more.

"I needed an escape. I had never faced death before. And it felt wrong to take part in someone else's worst moment when they had no clue who I was. So I made some excuse about getting them coffee, and then I slunk away. I walked down the hallway aimlessly just trying to find a place to cry like a baby in the corner.

"I found what I thought was an empty room. No nurses were hovering around it, and when I knocked no one answered. So I opened the door and pushed inside, but the room wasn't empty."

"I was there…"

———

"Please, Nicole, I'm not ready to face Henry or Ren yet. Please, just tell them I'm still unconscious, and I can't have any visitors yet. At least until I find out how my parents are doing," I say.

Nicole looks at me with sad eyes. "Rest Mila, don't worry about your siblings. Just try to rest. We will give you an update as soon as there is one."

"Thank you," I whisper as she leaves.

My body is riddled with pain. My head is on the brink of explosion. My chest feels too tight. But my core and legs hurt the most.

I feel tears, boiling up inside me, but I won't let them out. I won't cry for myself. I won't cry until I know the outcome of my parents' surgeries.

The door opens before I even have a chance to close my eyes. And a man walks in. He's tall, muscular, and sad. A few tattoos are scattered along his arms and the way his chiseled jaw moves and his five o'clock shadow seems to grow as the seconds pass seem to indicate that he is a few years older than me.

I grab the covers harshly and pull them up to my chest.

"Did Nasser send you?" I ask nervously.

The man's eyes flicker to me slowly as if he didn't realize I was here. "Who is Nasser?"

I shake my head. "It doesn't matter."

"I'm sorry I should go."

"No, stay. I could use the company."

"Don't you have family waiting for you?"

I nod. "I do. I'm sure my family is in the waiting room frantic to talk to me."

He stares at me longer, then says, "You're Mila Burns."

I nod.

"I'm Ace Knight. I should talk to your brother and sister and let them know you are awake. They are worried sick."

"No, please don't. I can't face them yet."

He frowns. "Why?"

"Because this was all my fault."

His frown deepens until he's red with fury. "I don't know what happened, but I can assure you, it's not your fault."

"That's kind of you to say, but you don't know the whole story."

He sits down in a chair next to my bed. "Tell me what happened then."

"How about you tell me about your night instead? I need something to distract me." I wince as I move and my cracked ribs sting.

He takes my hand almost instinctively, comforting me as I deal with the pain.

"My story isn't very interesting."

"Just tell me. I could be dying for all you know. You could fulfill my final request."

He laughs and strokes my face lovingly. "It would take a lot to kill a spirit like you. You've been hurt, but you aren't going to die. I won't let you."

"My knight in shining armor will save me?"

He laughs again. "Yes, I'll save you."

"Good, now tell me a story, Knight."

He smiles again. At least I can make his sadness go away, even if there is nothing that can erase my own. Even if my parents survive, I will live with the guilt forever. The pain is too much to survive.

"Ok, my pretty girl. This tale is a happy tale. It starts with a princess, who didn't realize she was a princess, and a knight."

I smile, liking him too much. To some he might seem like a bad boy, but not to me. I've met a real bad boy. The kind who hurts you to your core. Knight is just playing one with his tattoos and mischievous grin.

Knight is the kind of man I could fall for if I got rid of my purple and blue hair, risqué clothes, and heavy metal music. And most importantly, if I started behaving and playing by the rules. I think I've finally realized why I will always follow a plan. I'll never risk my life, or anyone else's again.

"This princess was locked away in a castle, surrounded with white walls," he glances around at the walls around us.

"Every day she laid in bed alone, waiting for a prince to come and save her. And every day she was disappointed that none came."

I bite my lip. "Go on."

"But then after waiting for years, a knight came. This was no ordinary knight. He was tall, dark, and handsome of course, but he was better than the other knights, for he had the strength to defeat the evil dragon guarding the castle gate.

"He knew not of the prize that awaited him when he defeated the dragon, but he hoped the greatest treasure would befall him if he bested the beast. So after an arduous, vicious fight, the knight risked his life for a chance to see the beauty beyond the white castle door.

"And when he entered, he found a princess so beautiful, so smart, so sexy that he fell at her feet, unworthy of such perfection.

"In his fall, he injured his heart, and it shattered into tiny pieces. So torn was he that he knew he could never stand again.

"But the princess was strong. Even stronger than he, she found all of the tiny pieces of his heart and quickly put it back together. She saved him, as he had saved her. And then they lived happily ever after."

His grin is contagious.

"Lame," I half moan, half tease.

He laughs. "Sorry, I'm not the best storyteller when put on the spot."

"And you're taken."

He nods.

I sigh. If only he were truly my knight.

"Who's the lucky girl?"

His eyes don't meet mine anymore. "Abri. Her name is Abri; she's friends with your sister."

I gasp. I knew Abri had a boyfriend, but I didn't listen when she talked about him. I hardly listened to anything Abri said.

"Break up with her."

He laughs, thinking I'm joking and teasing like we have been all night.

"I'm serious. Break up with her."

He frowns. "I'm planning on marrying her."

"No."

The memories all come back. Flooding me with the entire night. But I can't keep reliving them. I can't go any further.

"Mila?"

Knight. My thoughts come back to the present.

I realize now why he hired me. Why he wanted me in his life. He wants me to tell him why I told him to break up with Abri that night. Was it just a hunch or did I have a valid reason? One he could have used against her in the divorce filings?

I can't help him now. It's too late. But it won't stop the memories from coming back. I need it to replay more in my head, but right now, I need Knight more.

"I forgive you for not telling me," I whisper.

Knight inhales like he's taking in every word of my forgiveness. Then he kisses the palm of my hand.

"I thought I needed you to tell me why I shouldn't have married Abri, but I'd rather you not have any more pain. I love you, Mila. I would have loved you that night if my heart wasn't already taken. But when I found you again on the mountain, I fell harder than I've ever fallen. I used you and don't deserve your forgiveness. After Abri, I didn't think I could love again.

That I could trust someone again. But you changed that. And regardless of what you want next, know I will love you forever pretty girl."

Knight destroyed my heart, and I don't know if I have enough left to love him with. Just like his story that night, he shattered my heart into tiny pieces, and it will take both of us to find all of the shards.

But I want to try again with Knight. Because he is the best and one of the worst things that ever happened to me. He's had my heart since that night in the hospital. I tried to save him then, but he wouldn't let me. He couldn't see the danger coming. But maybe I can save him now.

22

KNIGHT

I TOLD Mila I love her.

I never thought I would be able to say those words again. After what happened, I didn't think she would ever forgive me. Staying with Cole was never about getting Mila back. Sure, I thought maybe I'd get her to talk to me, eventually. But the words started spilling out of me. Words I've been holding back from everyone, even Cole. And Mila listened.

I thought she would run away or storm out. I thought it would take months of begging and pleading to get her to even sit at the same table as me. But that's what makes Mila so special. She's able to look past people's flaws to find the beauty within. It's a blessing and a curse. Because it makes her vulnerable. Bad people can take advantage of her forgiveness. She will let people in who don't deserve to be let in.

If I wish for one thing in the world, it would be to protect her. That's all I want.

But I'm getting more than the ability to protect her. I'm getting a second chance.

She forgives me. She remembers. I don't want her to dive too far into that dark place. If she does, I'm not sure she'll find her way back out. And I'm selfish; I want her all to myself.

I'm still holding her hand, but I don't dare do more. I won't push my luck. I want her completely. I want to feel a connection again I haven't felt since we were in Aspen, but I don't deserve it. Tonight, I'll take her forgiveness and pray we can be more at some point.

Mila's breathing is fast like she's just ran a marathon and is about to pass out.

"Mila? Are you okay? Do you need water or something?"

She shakes her head, but she doesn't look at me or say anything. She hasn't spoken since I told her I love her.

"You don't need to say I love you back. You don't need to say anything back; I just needed you to know."

Her long eyelashes flicker up as her gaze focuses on me. She pulls her hand away, and I reluctantly let my hands fall to my lap. She's pulling away from me, and I have to let her go.

But then her small body turns to face me. Her hands tremble in her lap.

"Mila, please tell me what's wrong. If you are remembering something bad, please let me in. Let me help you."

She takes a deep breath in and out, and I sit on my hands to keep from touching her. Don't push her away. She will come to you when she's ready. For now, simply sit until she asks for help.

If she passes out from not breathing enough, I'm never going to stop touching her to make her better.

Her hand reaches out toward my hair. She gently takes a few strands between her fingers, pulling gently, as if she's remembering my much longer hair before. Her fingers slip down to the side of my face. I want to close my eyes at how intense it feels for her to be touching me again, but I don't. I don't want to miss a thing with Mila. Because I'll never know when it will be the last time she touches me like this.

Her eyes pierce through my pupils into my soul as she strokes my cheek. What she sees, I don't know. But I implore my heart to show her the love I feel for her is true.

I always thought Abri was the one for me. Perfect in every way, but my heart lied to me. Mila is who I love. I thought I would do anything for Abri. I would have died protecting Abri. But I'll do more for Mila. I will let her go to keep her safe. And the difference between Abri and Mila is Abri would ask me to take a bullet for her; Mila never would.

Her gaze and hands drop over my black T-shirt. To my biceps, then forearms covered in tattoos.

She smiles when she finds a dragon on my forearm.

"This used to be a rubber ducky?" she asks.

I laugh. "What has Cole been telling you?"

"Everything."

I don't doubt it. He's been trying to get Mila and me together since the first moment I told him about her. If I had told him about Mila all those years ago, he would have persuaded me to date her then.

She traces her fingers over the outline of the dragon. "They did a good job covering it up. I can't see the rubber ducky anymore."

I swallow the lump in my throat. "I got the dragon to remind me of you. Of the story I told you that night. I realized after I left you are no princess. You are more of a dragon."

She nods.

"I don't need a knight to save me."

"I know, but maybe I need a dragon to protect me," I whisper.

Her hands hold onto either side of my face. She holds my head steady as she lowers herself until our lips are inches apart. "I'm sorry for forgetting you. If I had remembered, I would have saved you earlier."

"Save me now."

She closes the gap and our lips touch so gently I have to keep my eyes open to ensure we are, in fact, kissing. And then we are really kissing. Her lips crash down roughly, kissing me in one long kiss trapping me beneath her.

I give her everything with this kiss. I tell her how sorry I am as I slip my tongue into her mouth.

She forgives me with a sob and moan as I nip at her bottom lip.

Her hands tangle in my hair as I kiss away her tears and continue down to her neck.

We both apologize profusely.

For everything.

For forgetting.

For remembering.

For not telling the truth.

For hiding.

For hurting.

"Touch me, Knight. Hold me, kiss me, fuck me."

I realize I'm still sitting on my hands, not sure if any of this is true.

But at her words, I grab her desperately, sliding my hand beneath her black jacket. A jacket that matches my dark shirt.

"We've always been connected, even when we were miles apart. Even when we didn't remember. Or tried to hide from our past. Even if our connection isn't healthy," she whispers.

Her words are true. I doubt we wore the same outfit every day for the past five years. But I know there wasn't a day that went by I didn't think back to her. When I didn't think of my pretty girl and what she was doing. It wasn't love. At the time, I gave my whole heart to Abri. It was a connection to a woman I thought would never be mine.

"Fuck me," she says again.

I take her mouth with mine and kiss her with everything I can give her.

She moans and grinds her body on top of mine. I know if I let her, she'd fuck me right here and come from the grinding she's doing alone. One week is too long for us to go without being with each other when our connection is so passionate.

"I'm not going to fuck you on this tiny couch," I growl into her lips.

I lift her up and carry her back into Cole's apartment. *Bed, I need to get to a bed.*

But Mila starts unbuttoning her jacket and I know I won't make it to her bed. I need to see her breasts. Need to kiss and torture them. Now.

I set her down on the edge of the kitchen counter and quickly help her rid herself of the jacket and black tank top she was wearing beneath it. I see the black sparkly bra drawing me in with promises of what lies beneath its pretty lace and sparkles.

I'm not patient enough to find the clasp on her back, so I push the bra up until her breasts fall out for me.

She gasps as I lean down to taste her nipple, hard and begging for me.

Her body falls back against the counter as I lick the hard point. Her body shivers against the cold air and my heated touch. I move quickly to her other nipple, needing both at the same time and cursing that I only have one mouth. My hand does its best to give her other nipple attention while my tongue is focused on the other.

Her legs tighten around my waist and I know her wetness is pooling between her legs. Everything about her makes me want her more. Her whimpers, how she arches her back, how she begs me for more while wanting this to last forever.

Suddenly, she grabs the hem of my shirt and pulls herself

back up. She grabs fistfuls of my shirt and yanks it off. Her eyes dilate as she drinks my body in. I see the drops of drool as she stares at my tattoos. Her lips start kissing me places, and I can't focus on what I want to do to her body anymore.

She kisses each muscle, each spot of skin, each tattoo claiming it all as hers. She hesitates when she gets to my heart where the words Abri are written. I need to change that. It's not fair to either woman, but then Mila drops her lips to kiss over the words and my heart.

"Mine," she purrs.

I suck in a long, hard breath. "Yours forever."

She smiles, and I lift her off the counter, regaining my focus on getting her to a bed as fast as possible.

She kisses me hard on my lips, and I close my eyes as I carry her, getting lost in the desperation and love pouring out of her. I stumble, and we fall onto the couch in the living room.

She giggles as I fall on top of her. She grabs my jeans as her eyes suddenly grow heavy.

"Off," she moans into my lips as she pulls at my jeans.

I'm desperate for her. I would do anything for her. But getting out of my jeans while still holding her is an impossible task, and I can't decide which is more important. Getting out of my jeans or kissing and holding Mila.

She laughs. And finally pushes me off her body. I reluctantly stand up, and she follows after. She starts kissing me roughly, sucking on my bottom lip while I work on my jeans.

It's never taken me so long to undress, but I've also never enjoyed undressing more than I do with her lips pressed against mine.

When I'm finally naked, I grab her hips, and we stumble back toward the bedroom. I work on finding the zipper to her skirt, but I can't find it. It doesn't matter. I slip my hand up her skirt and pull her panties down as we stumble onto the bed.

My head moves between her legs, kissing every sweet part of her. Her sensitive bud, her lips, and then I dive inside her, filling her with my tongue.

"Knight," she moans as he grabs my hair roughly, pulling me from her pussy.

I pout, but she tosses a condom at me.

I grin. *How could I have forgotten to bring a condom when I came over to Cole's apartment? Good thing Cole has his own stash here.*

I rip the condom open, slip it on and pause, waiting to push inside her. *What the hell is wrong with me? Just fuck her.*

But I can't. I need more than fucking. If this is all she wants, I'll kill myself when I pull out and know it's the last time. *Man, I've turned into a pussy.*

Her eyes brighten as she reads my mind. "I want more too."

I kiss her tenderly and then pull away.

"But I swear, if you don't fuck me now, Knight, I'm going to kick your ass."

I grin and slide into her slick entrance. She moans and curses as I fill her. Her body readjusts to me after going without me for days.

"Damn, I've missed this," I moan.

"Not as much as I have," she purrs back.

I grab her hips and slam harder. Her body writhes beneath me, angling her body to let me reach deeper than I've ever been inside her.

She doesn't tell me she loves me with words. She doesn't tell me she wants to start our relationship again. But I can feel it with her body. She needs me as much as she needs air to breathe.

So I fuck her, harder, faster, longer. I watch as her face turns from pleasure to bliss. Her mouth goes from panting to screaming. Her body goes from sensitive to exploding.

We come together, now in sync. And I hope we never lose this connection again.

We aren't a perfect couple. We are broken and tragic. Our lives have always intertwined, but we were never headed toward a happily ever after together. But now might be that time.

I pull out of her, lie down next to her in the bed, and pull Mila to me as her eyes begin to drift close. Neither of us has slept much since we've been apart. And as much as I want to fuck her again and again, I want to protect her while she sleeps more.

The door opens, and light floods in as Cole stumbles in, presumably to sleep on the cot he made for himself on the floor. He spots me, stops, and smirks.

"You know that's my bed right?"

I nod.

"Ugh, fine, it's your bed now. You owe me a new bed, Knight."

I stroke Mila's face. *I'll buy him whatever fucking bed he wants. I have Mila back.*

Cole leans down and picks up his blanket and pillow off the floor. "I'll go sleep on the couch. Glad I'm not on nightmare duty anymore. She sleeps better with you than me."

I growl at Cole, and he laughs before leaving us alone. It's been years since I didn't know what my future held when I closed my eyes at night. But I welcome it. My greatest adventures always came when I didn't know what was coming next.

23

MILA

I love Knight. I've always loved Knight. One of the reasons my mind forgot that horrible night was to forget about him choosing her over me. I tried to stop him. I tried to warn him. But he was loyal to a woman he loved, even if she didn't love him back.

I glance at Knight who is holding me close to him in Cole's bed. Knight thinks he saved me from Abri. He thinks losing Gideon was what caused her to deteriorate. To hate him. He's wrong. We aren't safe. I remember everything. I won't let her ruin us. Even if we deserve it.

I ease myself off the bed, cautiously, so I don't wake Knight. He doesn't move. I don't think he's slept since Aspen.

I quickly put a pair of jeans and a T-shirt on and leave before I change my mind. It's six in the morning. Knight is usually awake by now. The only thing keeping him asleep is his exhaustion.

I tiptoe toward the front door, smiling when I see our discarded clothes strung about the apartment.

"What are you doing?" Cole asks, sitting up on the couch.

I stop and smile, pretending nothing is wrong. "What are you doing sleeping on the couch? You have a spare bedroom."

"The spare bedroom shares a wall with my bedroom. I didn't want to listen to the two of you all night."

"Sorry if we kept you awake. And for stealing your bed."

"Don't worry; it's your bed now."

"I'm just going to run and get breakfast for us. Do you want something?"

He stands and walks to me. "I want to know what you are doing sneaking out at six in the morning."

"I'm getting breakfast. I can't cook so this is the only way for me to do something nice for Knight."

"You and I have become good friends, Mila. I know you pretty well. And you are a horrible liar. What's going on? Are you and Knight broken up again?"

"No."

Cole studies me a moment and then grabs my arm. "You are going to Abri."

"If I don't go, we will all die. Knight thinks he fixed the problem. He just doesn't realize what she threatened me with before. She's not done. She may have all of his money, but it's not enough. If you don't let me go, we die."

My words may be a little harsh, but it's the truth. Abri will do anything to survive, to get revenge.

Cole releases my arm and steps aside. I run to my car and begin driving as fast as I can toward Knight's old apartment that Abri now owns. It's a long shot that she is there, but it's my only hope of finding her quickly. Even though Cole let me go, I have no doubt he will wake Knight, and they will be right behind me.

The elevator ride up to the apartment is quick. Faster than I remember. I try to think of the words I'm going to say to fix this, but I'm not sure I can. I just know I need to confront Abri.

I fidget with my phone as the elevator opens, and I walk to

the front door. I still have a spare key Knight gave me, and I doubt she has changed the locks on the door quickly. I knock once, and when no one answers, I use the key to get inside.

"You know, I could shoot you for breaking and entering," Abri says, standing in the entryway.

"So shoot me then, it's what you want. To hurt Knight and punish me for the pain we've caused you."

She narrows. "Since when do you know anything I want?"

"Since I remember that night."

Abri studies me a moment and then turns toward the kitchen. I follow her and watch as she pours us each a glass of whiskey.

I take mine, thankful we might be able to have this conversation woman to woman. Or we will get drunk and turn this into a cat fight.

"Why are you here, Mila?"

I take a sip of the whiskey for encouragement. Abri is in a robe, and it's clear she's not wearing much underneath it.

"Because I want to apologize."

She raises an eyebrow as she laughs. "You want to apologize?"

"Yes." This is my only chance to protect Knight.

"I hurt you that night. I knew you and Knight were together. I knew you were in love and I hurt you anyway, and I want to say I'm sorry."

"Your apology is five years too late."

"I know, and I'm sorry for that as well."

She drinks all of her whiskey. "It doesn't matter. I don't accept your apology."

Shit.

"What do you want then, Abri?"

She paces back and forth as if no one has ever asked this question. "I want to be happy. I want to never worry about feeding myself again. I want to be with someone who loves me back. And I want you and Knight to pay for what you did."

I wince at her last words.

"You were a princess, Mila. While I was trailer park trash. You had everything while I had nothing. I fought even to find enough food to live. I shivered in my bed at night because we didn't have any heat while you had everything. Why did you have to take my boyfriend too?"

"I didn't take him. And I wasn't a princess. It was all an illusion. My parents were broke. I've slept on the streets. I've done unspeakable things for food. I understand. You're a survivor, just like me. You would do anything to survive."

"I did anything to survive."

I nod.

"I don't blame you for dating Knight. He was set to make a lot of money. You saw your chance, and you took it," I say.

"I was happy. I had choices. I could divorce him and take half, or find a way to fall in love and live happily ever after."

I still. "I get it. But you can still be happy now. You have the money. You don't need to hurt us anymore. We've suffered enough."

She laughs. "I've suffered for five years. I will suffer more from the memory of losing my baby. You haven't known suffering."

I catch my breath. *This was a mistake. I won't convince her to change her mind.*

"Five years ago, when Knight stumbled into my room, I fell for him, but he didn't fall for me. I kissed him, but he didn't kiss me back. I begged him to stay, but he chose you. He loved you. You could have been happy."

Her sob catches in her throat, and I realize the pain she carries. From seeing me with Knight. From losing her baby. From losing Knight's love.

I walk over to her and hug her. She cries into my chest.

"I'm sorry. I'm so sorry," I say.

Finally, she pulls away, wiping her tears. The moment is gone, and anger fills her eyes.

"You should still pay."

"We did. You have everything. Money, the apartment, the company."

"And you have *him*."

I suck in a breath. "You never loved him, only the idea of him."

She slaps me, and I deserve it, but it's the truth.

"I remember hearing you and Ren talk about Knight. You weren't in love. You said he was a way out of your trailer park life. You planned on getting a divorce. You even said if it looked like you wouldn't get enough money in the divorce, you'd kill him and get the insurance money."

Abri stills at my words.

"Is my memory wrong?"

"No."

"Did you try to kill Knight in a car accident?"

"Yes."

"Did he ever hurt you? Beat you?" I suck in my breath, waiting for her honest answer. I love Knight; I might be blind to his faults.

"No. I lied to try and keep him away from you."

I exhale all of my pain in that moment.

"That kiss destroyed me. Even though I never loved Knight, it hurt. Not as much as losing Gideon, but I can't forgive you for it either."

I nod, and then I see the flash of metal.

I hold my hands up cautiously. "Abri, relax. We are just talking."

"Abri, what are you doing?" Knight asks from the hallway.

His hands are up as well, showing caution. But his eyes are all fear.

"You both hurt me so much. And yet, I was the one punished. I lost my baby," Abri cries again.

Shit. What did I do? This isn't going to end well.

"You will find happiness again. You have money now. You have a company you love. You can adopt a baby or find a sperm bank and have your own. You don't need a man to be happy. Or you can find a man and fall desperately in love. You can have anything you want, Abri. I want you to be happy. I just don't want to spend my life wondering if you will come after us," I say.

Abri raises the gun, and I turn to Knight. We both freeze, unsure what is going to happen. *I love you*, I mouth to him.

I love you too, he mouths back.

It probably isn't the smartest thing to do in front of Abri. It makes her pain worse and gives her more reason to shoot us, but if this is my last moment on this earth, I want to leave it loving Knight.

I turn back, and instead of the gun pointed at my head, Abri holds out the gun for me to take. I do, hesitantly.

She looks at me. "I won't come after you. I won't think of you again after today. I'm starting a new life. This is my surrender. Be happy. Just know that Ace isn't a saint."

"Thank you. We won't press charges. We won't take our evidence to the police unless you force us to, but know if either of us ends up hurt, this entire conversation will be played in front of a court."

"It won't come to that," Abri says.

I nod and watch as she walks to Knight. "I'm keeping everything. You still deserve to suffer some for what you did, you asshole."

"You deserve to be happy, Abri. For what it's worth, I loved you and would have loved you forever if I could. And I'll love our time together because it gave me a brief moment with our son." Knight pulls Abri into a tight hug, and they both cry into each other's shoulders.

I walk out of the apartment giving them a moment alone together. I take the gun and put it in my back pocket. I've never held a gun before and will never hold one again. Hopefully, Knight or Cole knows how to get rid of it.

I take my phone out of my pocket and stop the recording. I'll keep the evidence, but I don't think I will really need it.

Knight comes out of the apartment a few minutes later. "Thank you," he says.

"For what?"

"For forcing us to talk and saving my life."

His lips crash down on mine.

"I love you, Knight."

"I love you, pretty girl. Let's go back to Cole's place."

I smile. "We can, but first, I need to tell you what happened that night. The whole story. Abri is on her way to healing. Now I need a chance to heal."

24

MILA

Five Years Ago

"You are grounded, and that's final," my father's voice booms through the whole living room.

My mom sits idly by on the couch, not bothering to give any input. I know she hates my boyfriend as well. But she won't even bother to talk to me. She hates him and thinks I'm already a lost cause. Her efforts would be wasted, she thinks, so why bother?

But my father, he's too stubborn to ever give up. He wants to control me. What color my hair is, what I eat, when I sleep, where I go to school, and what I do. Even who I date.

"What am I grounded for? I didn't do anything wrong?"

"Your hair is the color of the sky, your clothes are ridiculous, and as I've already said, you aren't going anywhere with that boy!"

I glare at him. He's stubborn, but so am I. I won't give up so easily.

"Fine, I'll just stay locked away in my room forever."

I storm upstairs, not bothering to listen to anything else. I slam my door shut, and sit on my bed with my phone, prepared to text my boyfriend, Nasser, that I won't be able to meet him.

The wind gusts and the screen over my window shudders against the sill. I stare at it for only a second before I make up my mind. I'm leaving. I can't stand to stay in this house another second. I'll drink my frustration away tonight, and tomorrow I will make a plan to leave town for good. I can graduate from high school early, get a job, and then decide if I want to go to college. I don't care if I have money. I'll be free.

I tiptoe over to the window. My room is on the second floor, but it overlooks the covered deck. I push the screen off and watch it blow away with the wind. I text Nasser.

Me: Meet me at the end of my block in five minutes.

And then I climb out, sliding onto the roof. My body glides to the edge. *It's not that far; I can make it.*

I let go, and my body falls to the grass below with a loud thud. I look back at the house, expecting someone to have heard me, but no one comes out.

I start running down the street to meet Nasser even though my heart is begging me to stop. I don't want to stop. I want to move faster. I want to escape the nightmare that is my home.

If I were to return now, I would get my ass kicked. I would be grounded for real. I would know a whole new level of punishment.

Nasser is the lesser of two evils. He may not be my ticket out of this town, but he is my ticket to freedom tonight.

Nasser's car is parked at the end of my block. I spot his Camry two houses away. This block isn't the nicest in Aspen, but it's nice. Too nice for his old Toyota.

I climb in the passenger seat, and we drive off before I have a chance to say anything. Nasser doesn't ask me any questions about my family, and I don't offer up what happened.

He plays his loud music and drives. That's what I like about him; he gives me space. Doesn't pressure me to be anything the way my family does. We've only been dating two weeks now, and I don't see a future. But I like that I can be free when I'm with him.

Nasser pulls into the driveway of the house he shares with his three other roommates. It's a large house, but it hasn't been updated since the fifties and could use some work. But I'm not here to critique the decorations.

Nasser doesn't open my door. He just turns the car off and gets out. I follow him at a leisurely pace. By the time I'm gone, he's already disappeared into the basement.

I head downstairs where the music is blasting. I find Nasser with his roommates and their friends drinking and passing around a joint.

I walk over to the bar and grab a beer before joining them. When the joint hits my lips, I'm in heaven. Finally, I can let go.

Hours go by as we listen to music, drink, and smoke our worries away. No one asks me to be anything but who I am. I don't have to change my hair color or remove my tattoos or pretend I want to go to law school. I'm just me.

I lean against Nasser's chest as he strokes my hair.

"Let's go for a walk. I want to show you my favorite part of the house," he whispers against my hair.

I smile and nod as he takes my hand and leads me to the door of the basement. We haven't had sex yet, and tonight won't be that night. I'm too drunk to think properly. But I'm fine with some heavy making out and sleeping in his bed while he gropes me all night.

He slides the glass door open, and we slip out into the night.

"You look beautiful tonight."

I blush at his compliment. "Thank you."

He leads me to a gazebo. "Dance with me."

I giggle as he wraps me in his arms and we dance to a silent melody. My head starts spinning from the movement, and if I'm not careful, all the alcohol I've drunk will come back up.

"I need to sit down," I mutter.

"How about lie down?"

"What?"

Before I can respond, Nasser is lying me down on the couch in the gazebo. *Yes, I need to lie down.* My head already feels better.

But then Nasser is on top of me, kissing me harshly.

"Slow...down," I mutter between kisses.

He doesn't slow down. Instead, his hands slide up beneath my skirt.

"No, I too drunk."

"Shh, you won't remember this."

He pulls my panties down before I can stop him. My body tries to push him off, but the alcohol and drugs make it feel like I'm fighting in a fog. I can move, but slowly. I can think, but only one step at a time.

"No," I say again as his fingers slip inside me.

"You want me."

I try to say no again, but my words don't leave my mouth. I'm paralyzed now as I hear him undoing his zipper. *He's going to rape me.*

You deserve it, my dad's voice says in my head.

You were asking for it, my mom says.

If you would have just listened to us, Ren says.

If you dressed in jeans instead of a short skirt, Henry says.

No.

No.

NO.

The word never leaves my mouth again. I feel his slimy cock against my entrance. I don't want this. I need him to stop.

But I'm frozen. I can't move.

You're a fighter, a new voice says. *You can fight this.*

I can fight him. I won't let him win.

His lips come down hard on me, and I bite as hard as I can.

"Fucking Christ," he cries out as blood spills from his mouth.

I push him off of me with everything I have, and then I run toward his house.

Suddenly, I've never been so sober as I run. My skirt is ripped, my panties gone, but nothing will stop me.

I run up the steps to the deck leading into the kitchen. The doors to the walkout basement are closer, but I don't trust his friends.

I get the back door open, and I slip into the house, but I'm not safe. I need to be safe.

His car keys lay on the stand by the door. I grab them and run out into the night again, as much as it scares me to be out in the dark. I don't pause to see if he's following me. I run straight to his car, jump in, and start it all in one movement.

Then I'm backing out of the driveway. I just need to drive a few blocks away, then I can call for help. Then, I will be safe.

I've been drinking; I should stop. But when I reach into my pocket, I realize I don't have my phone. I can't stop. I need to find someplace safe. I need to find a police station.

So I keep driving. My heart beats erratically, and my foot hits the gas harder.

I close my eyes to keep the tears back, and when I open them, I see lights coming straight at me. I try to swerve, but it's too late. The light hits the car, and I'm jolted back into the cold night.

Pain. My entire body aches as I shiver in the cold. I feel lights on me and hear sirens in the background, but I don't know what's happening. And then I see her. My mother is lying on the cold concrete next to me.

"Mom?"

She doesn't respond.

I sit up, but the second I do, the world spins out of control around me. I blink, but the world doesn't stop spinning.

I see another car. My parents' car with the front smashed in. My father sits in the driver's seat with blood pouring down his face.

What did I do?

I close my eyes and open them again. When I take in my surroundings again, I'm in the back of an ambulance. *How did that happen?*

"She's conscious again," a man over me says.

"Where does it hurt?" he asks.

"Everywhere."

"Do you remember what happened?"

The images of Nasser trying to force himself on me flash through my head. But I can't make the words leave my mouth.

"Driving drunk," comes out instead.

The man nods.

And I can't keep my eyes open anymore. I have to close them.

When I open them again, I'm in a room. It's white and cold. A woman is standing over me.

"Try to rest. You have a lot of injuries."

"My parents?"

"They are in surgery. We will update you with their condition soon."

My parents are in surgery because of me. Because I drove drunk.

It was to escape, the voice says.

What if I hadn't escaped? What if I had let him rape me? Then my parents wouldn't be dying in a surgery room.

I close my eyes again, and the guilt comes, but I don't see images of my parents' lifeless bodies. Instead, I see the look in Nasser's eyes. The aggression as he takes what he wants from me.

I escaped, and because of that, my parents might die.

I open my eyes to escape the nightmare.

"You're awake. Your parents are still in surgery. But your siblings are here. They will want to see you. I'll go get them," Nicole, according to her name tag visible on her chest.

The tattooed older boy at the end of my hospital bed insists on marrying Abri to my total dismay.

I spot Abri coming around the corner. He can't marry her. She'll destroy him. She's only looking for a rich man. She will take all of his money in a divorce, or kill him if his life insurance policy is worth enough. She will do anything to survive. Those were the words she spoke.

Anything to survive.

I understand now. After what Nasser did, I will do anything to take away the pain I feel.

I won't let Knight feel a similar pain.

I yank on his hand until he falls forward toward my bed and then I kiss him. As soon as our lips touch, I'm lost. I don't know if it's the drugs I'm on or him, but I've never felt so desperate. I want him. His lips are soft and perfect. And when I push my tongue into his mouth, he moans softly before he realizes what's happening.

He pulls away with a stunned look.

My eyes drift behind him to Abri, who looks like she's going to punch someone or throw up.

Knight turns to her. "I love you, Abri. She took me by surprise. I think she thinks I'm someone else. She's on a lot of painkillers."

Abri looks at me, and a gracious smile covers her face as she turns back to Knight. They walk toward each other, meeting in the middle. He kisses her with a passion I wish he would kiss me with. Their kiss kicks my kiss' ass.

Their kiss is between two people who love each other.

Maybe I was wrong. Maybe Abri truly loves Knight if she's willing to look past a mistake like this so easily.

They are a perfect couple. They have what I want.

And my life is in shambles. My family will blame me for tonight, and they will be right.

I need to tell someone about Nasser.

I need to tell Knight what I know so he can make the best decision about Abri.

I need to...turn all the pain off.

I close my eyes and shut off the world.

I shut off Nasser. I shut out my parents' corpses. I shut out Ren, Henry, and Abri. And I force Knight's kiss from my lips. This night didn't happen. I will not remember.

———

Present

"That night was my fault," I whisper.

"No, it was Nasser's fault. You never pressed charges against him?"

I shake my head. "Until recently, I didn't even remember the details of what happened. Only the newspaper clippings and stories my siblings told me."

Knight kisses my cheek as we sit in my car. "You shouldn't have kissed me that night."

I look at him with sadness. "You shouldn't have kissed me and gotten me fired, either."

"I thought you would remember you tried to save me with a kiss."

I smile. "I couldn't remember you without remembering the pain."

He kisses my lips again gently.

"Both of those kisses were so perfect, yet so destructive," I whisper against his lips.

We kiss again.

"If I had felt anything less than love for Abri, I would have been mesmerized with you after that kiss."

"And if I hadn't lost my scholarship and ability to finish school after your kiss, I would have fallen for you then."

Another kiss unites us, each of us promising we will let nothing come between us.

"How could I forget you?" I whisper.

"Because you had to survive the pain and guilt. It wasn't your fault."

I nod. It will take me a while for the guilt of what happened to vanish completely. And the pain of everything I lost that night will only ease with time. But in the meantime, we have each other.

We get out of the car in Cole's parking lot.

"You realize neither of us has any money or a job now," Knight says.

"Speak for yourself, I have two hundred dollars in my bank account, and a job as Cole's assistant."

Knight laughs. "That's more than I have."

I pull him to me. "I would live on the streets with you if it means I get to have you."

He smirks. "I don't think I would survive sleeping on the ground. I'm a bit of a germaphobe."

I laugh. "You're right. You wouldn't survive."

"I guess we will be living with Cole then."

"You get to be the one to tell him."

He kisses me. "I think you should tell him. He'll punch me in the face. He owes me a few punches."

I smile. "Fine, I'll tell him."

We kiss again, and I know we won't be able to stop kissing for the rest of the night.

"Our relationship won't exactly be perfect then, will it?"

"Perfect is overrated."

I smile. "Kiss me and make me forget."

I fell in love with Knight with one kiss, and with one kiss I brought him from the brink of despair.

"No, I'll kiss you, so you never have to forget again."

25

EPILOGUE

KNIGHT

"Hey, Knight?" Mila shouts from the couch of our living room.

Why she's shouting, I don't know. I'm cooking in the kitchen three feet away from her. The apartment we occupy is tiny. Less than five hundred square feet. But it's ours.

"Yes, baby?" I stir the marinara sauce.

"How accurate were the results at Perfect Match?"

I raise an eyebrow as I glance her way. "You would know better than me."

"You had a hundred percent guarantee. And when you matched couples, you had less than five percent report incompatibility after they started dating."

"Then I guess we were pretty good."

She frowns.

"What's wrong?"

"I just filled out both of our profiles, and it says we are incompatible. That we shouldn't be together. Do you think Abri knows it was me filling out the questionnaires and rigged it just to mess with us?"

I laugh and turn off the burners before walking over to Mila

253

on the couch. I stand behind her, rubbing her shoulders gently that have tensed from reading the results.

"We are incompatible, huh?" I ask, ignoring the part about Abri. Neither of us brings her up often, but last time I checked, she had grown the company by ten percent and was dating a finance guy from Manhattan. She seems to be doing just fine.

"Yes," she groans.

I lean down and kiss the top of her head, then trail my kisses down to her ear.

"What do you think now? Are we still incompatible?"

She nods. "Yes."

"Hmm." I move my lips to her neck, sucking her sweet skin.

She moans.

"What about now?"

"Still incompatible."

The top of her scrubs gives me a fantastic view of her chest. I let my hand gently glide down her chest until I squeeze her breasts, letting my thumb trace over her nipple.

"And now?"

"Mmmhhh, still incomp—"

My lips land on her mouth as I tilt her head to me. Her tongue sweeps into my mouth and then I'm gone. I forget about making dinner. It will have to wait. I can feel her desperation and mild heartbreak, and I won't ever let her feel that way again.

I climb over the couch, so I don't have to end the kiss and kneel in front of her feet. With one last kiss, I pull her pants and underwear down, burying my face between her legs.

"Yes!" she cries at my touch.

"Yes, we are compatible?"

She pants. "Ahh, almost."

I laugh and then drape her legs over my shoulders as I go to work on making her feel like mine. I should have had her the second she got off her twenty-four-hour shift.

My tongue licks, finding her clit with ease as I trace circles just the way she likes. I slip a finger into her tight cunt, and within moments, I feel her clenching around me.

"What about now?" I smile against her leg before kissing her inner thigh.

"I think we are perfect for each other."

"Good, now get dressed before dinner gets cold."

She pouts.

I laugh. "I'll fuck you more after dinner."

"Or you could fuck me while eating dinner."

My eyes darken. "Dammit, I love you."

———

Two hours later we are fucked, our tummies full, and we've showered and changed.

"Where are we going?"

"To one of my favorite places."

She climbs onto the back of my motorcycle without any more questions. Today is the anniversary of her parents' deaths. The anniversary of when we first met. Most of the day she's been distracted with work, but now she's mine.

I drive quickly away from our tiny apartment to our destination, loving how her hands feel wrapped around my waist. I could spend the whole night driving, but then I wouldn't know what is going through her head. I wouldn't be able to see if she's having nightmares or dozing peacefully behind me. And I can't stand not being able to save her from any pain if I can.

So I pull up in front of the tattoo parlor, and Mila takes my hand as we get out.

"We are getting tattoos?" she asks.

"Yes, I thought what perfect way to mark you as mine?"

"I love that idea."

"That is if you can afford it, my sugar momma."

She laughs. "I'm not your sugar momma."

"You make all the money saving people's lives at the ER. You pay all our bills. That's the definition of a sugar momma."

She rolls her eyes. "You just got investors to invest over five million dollars in your latest app idea. I don't think I will be paying for anything for long."

I kiss her hard. "I won't see any of the money in my pocket for years. In the meantime, I'm in your debt."

She kisses me back before running into the parlor.

I chase after her.

"What tattoo do you want to get?" Mila asks as she looks at various designs in the office.

"I want your name, here," I say, pointing to ring finger of my left hand.

She gasps.

"What tattoo do you want?" I ask.

"A dragon."

I raise an eyebrow. "Really? Where? I think that tattoo will take more than one night."

She laughs. "Kidding. I want your name here." She points to her own ring finger.

We've talked several times about it. Marriage may or may not be in our futures. It's not something that is important to either of us right now. But I want her to know she's mine, and I'm hers. This is the way to show it.

We both take a seat in chairs next to each other as the artists begin needling the ink into our skin.

I've already gotten one tattoo since I met Mila. A cracked heart around Abri's name. Mila wouldn't let me erase her or mark over her, but she agreed to let me have a broken heart.

Mila's phone buzzes and I glance over just catching Ren's name as Mila silences her phone. Mila is meeting her siblings tomorrow for brunch. Things haven't completely healed between them yet, but they are all working on mending their relationships with a lot of therapy sessions and brunch meetings. Something about how none of them can yell if they are eating brunch.

"What's going through your head, pretty girl? What's your plan for the rest of our lives?"

She smiles as she thinks for a moment. "I don't have one. I had a plan for a perfect life to replace my horrible life, but I found you instead."

I laugh at her jab against me.

"You sure you don't have our entire life planned out yet?"

She smirks. "I guess you'll have to wait and see."

The End

Thank you so much for reading *Finding Perfect*! If you want to receive updates on when the next book is coming and get a **FREE** book, sign up here: ellamiles.com/freebooks

Continue reading to get a sneak peek of Pretend I'm Yours, another contemporary standalone romance I think you will love!

PRETEND I'M YOURS

CHAPTER ONE — LARKYN

"I can't do this," I say, as Serena and I walk toward the front door of Sebastian's party.

Serena cuts her eyes to me. "You can totally do this."

I'm a twenty-two-year-old virgin. Tonight that changes.

I spent all afternoon scrolling through the ridiculously small number of men on my phone. Danny, Alan, Gavin, and Pat. None of them are great options to accomplish the deed. Danny is too short. Alan is too nice, and I think has a girlfriend. Gavin is hung up on Serena, and I don't want to sleep with him so that he can make Serena jealous. And Pat is not an option for so many reasons. But I need to find someone. Hence, why I'm attempting to get into the most exclusive party of the year. To find Mr. Perfect. I will not graduate from college next month still a virgin.

Who am I kidding? I once thought it mattered who the guy was. I wanted the ideal guy, to be in love. I wanted flowers and a sunset, followed by wine, candles, and a man who adored me and wanted my first time to be special. After four years of dating and no guy coming close to the picture I painted in my head, I'm desperate.

I want sex.

Maybe my first time won't be fantastic, but then I can experience a second or third time. And eventually, I'll meet a guy to give me the toe-curling moment I only dream about now.

I stumble again in my heels, and Serena takes my hand and rests it on her arm. "Well, you can as long as you don't fall flat on your face first." She chuckles. "Although, if you fell and showed the bouncer you aren't wearing any underwear, we wouldn't have any trouble getting in either. So, it doesn't matter what you do."

I glare at her. "Well, that wouldn't work because I'm wearing underwear. And I would like the school to not think of me as a laughing stock."

"Who cares if they do? We graduate in less than a month, and you won't have to see any of these people ever again."

I take a deep breath, letting the air fill my lungs before slowly exhaling. Serena's right. I can do this.

We strut, arm in arm, up the long driveway to the door. We get behind a group of loud girls chatting excitedly. I recognize them. They are in a sorority, and no doubt were invited. They are all in short, expensive dresses that accentuate their bodies and show how much money they are from. They don't flirt their way in. They are invited in.

We are next, and my stomach is doing flips. My legs are shaky, and not just because of the heels my feet aren't used to being shoved in. My heart is fluttering a million miles a minute in my chest. I should have taken a shot with Serena before we came.

"Name?" the tall man asks.

"Serena Toomer and Larkyn Day."

He scans his list, not bothering to glance at us. Our plan isn't going to work.

"Your names aren't listed," he says.

"Let's go," I whisper to Serena.

She ignores me, looking past the bouncer, who won't be seduced since he won't stop staring at his clipboard.

"Sebastian!" she shouts.

My eyes widen in fear. "What are you doing?" I hiss.

"Getting you in so you can get laid."

Sebastian turns in our direction and grins at us goofily. He doesn't know either of us, but Serena smiles at him and his eyes drag over my low-cut dress, and suddenly he's walking our way.

"Hey!" Sebastian says, and my heart sinks. I bite my bottom lip to keep from drooling. He's hot in his dark jeans and buttoned down shirt, which is open at the top, revealing his muscular chest. All he said was 'hey,' and my body reacts like he said the most charming pickup line. I need to get laid, so I stop fawning over every guy like this.

"Hey, we aren't on the list. A mixup, I'm sure. Any possibility you can change that?" Serena asks, shoving me forward, so my body brushes against his.

I'm going to kill her for this later.

But it does the trick. Sebastian's eyes glue to the cleavage the dress makes me appear to have, and then down to my abs, defined beneath the material.

"Absolutely!" Sebastian holds out his arm to me, and I nervously take it. I cut my eyes to Serena who winks at me as Sebastian leads me into his house.

"I'm sorry you weren't on the list. I don't know how I missed a beautiful woman like you. I wish we had classes together so I could have noticed you earlier."

I bite my lip and blush. "We do take a class together. You are in my marketing class." I don't add we did a group project together last year in finance, and he has been in almost every single one of my classes starting freshman year since we are both on the same business track.

He doesn't blush or show signs of embarrassment. I wish he

would have noticed me before or realize who I am. I know his name and who he is.

"What's your name?" he asks.

"Larkyn Day."

He grins. "I love that name. I'm Sebastian King."

His smoldering blue eyes look at me, and my heart is his. I don't know how I ended on the arm of Sebastian, basically the king of the popular crowd, and I know that soon, he'll be leaving me alone to enjoy his other guests, but I'll remember this moment forever.

"Can I get you a drink?" he asks.

I nod, knowing this is when he dismisses me. I look hot, but I'm not hot enough. I'm wearing a nude colored sparkly dress, but it's not slutty enough to compare with the women skirting around us in dresses that are so short they can't wear underwear. Their dresses leave no curve on their bodies to the imagination. While I, I just hope this dress is enough to snag one decent looking guy that isn't already too drunk to fuck me.

Sebastian leads me over to one of the bars and gets me a white wine without asking what I want. He gets himself a beer. I start peering around for where Serena is so she can help me find a guy for the night.

I feel a hand on my waist and glance down to see Sebastian's hand wrapped around my waist, pulling me closer to him.

"Do you have a date for tonight?" he asks, leaning down to my ear so he can talk to me over the loud music blasting through the house. The band is out back, and we are in the front of the house so I can only imagine how loud it is out back.

"No," I say, taking a sip of my wine, so I have something to do with my hands, and I can stop blushing. The wine tastes overly sweet. I don't often drink, caring too much about staying healthy, but when I do, I rarely choose wine.

"Good, I needed someone to hang out with tonight."

Yep, now I'm blushing again like an idiot. I need to stop getting so affected by this man. I've had a crush on him since forever, but that doesn't mean anything. He's just being nice. He won't be the guy that pops my cherry. Even though I should be searching for that guy, I can't pass up an opportunity to spend some time with Sebastian first.

"You don't have a date either?" I ask, finally getting my voice back.

He looks down at me, his eyes lingering on my cleavage. "Now, I do."

My heart stops. Sebastian did not just say that. I must have misheard him. He's the most popular guy at our school. He can date any woman he wants. He's fucked most of the popular women. He doesn't want me to be his date.

But the way his hand grips my waist, as he starts leading me outside, it seems I heard him right.

Eyes. That's all I see when we walk outside, where the band is playing by the infinity pool. Everyone's eyes are on me. The guy's eyes rake over my cleavage and smirk at Sebastian approvingly. While the women alternate being glaring at me and giving Sebastian a sweet, come-here look.

I swallow, trying to get the lump in my throat to go down, but it's no use. I'm not in my element. I don't do parties. I don't hang out in crowds. I don't like attention. I prefer running down the road by myself with nothing but my playlist to keep me company.

Sebastian ignores the stares and leads me over to where a group of his friends is hanging out drinking their beer and wine around a cocktail table.

He greets them, but never takes his hand off my waist.

"And you are?" one of the women to my right asks. Her voice is much too high. And she chugs her wine in one motion, before she looks at me again, as she makes a noise in her throat that sounds like a threatening growl.

"I'm—"

"This is Larkyn. She's my date for tonight," Sebastian says, pulling me tighter into his body, so I get a whiff of his cologne. It's a strong scent, and it seems he used too much, but it doesn't matter. He's still appealing no matter how much of the stuff he uses. Especially, when he keeps calling me his date.

The woman scuffs and signals the waiter for another drink. The three men standing around the table all chuckle in unison like they know a secret I'm not in on.

Sebastian glances behind us. "Dance with me."

"Um..." I don't get a chance to say I don't dance. That I've *never* danced. He takes the last swig of his beer before taking my almost full glass of wine from my hands and sets it down on the cocktail table.

His hand moves to the small of my back as he leads me to the dance floor. My body feels hot as I gaze around at all the other people on the floor grinding their bodies together. It doesn't look like dancing. It looks like sex.

My eyes stare up at Sebastian's as he stands in front of me and starts moving to the music. While I stand frozen. I don't know how to dance to this music. He doesn't seem to notice. Instead, he grabs my hand and gently pulls me to his body. He twirls me around and grabs my hips, pulling me to his body, so my back presses against his front.

His hands guide me, as his body sways to the music, and I do the same. Our bodies glide together to the beat of the music. I don't know what to do with my hands, but I find them running over his, which glue to my hips.

I spot Serena out of the corner of my eye. She's dancing with her boyfriend. She must have snuck him in.

I smile.

Tonight is going to be a good night, even if nothing else happens. Dancing in Sebastian's arms, I can pretend I'm his. Pretend I live in a world of popular kids with fancy cars. I can pretend this is what I want. And who I am.

"You smell incredible," Sebastian says, grinding harder until I can feel the strain of his erection against my ass.

I blush. I can't take a compliment.

I want to turn and look at him, but I don't dare. My knees are already weak enough. If I turn and see his blue eyes staring at me like he wants to devour me, I'll lose my mind. I'd probably melt right here. Merely disappear into a puddle on the floor. Or worse yet, he might kiss me, and I'm afraid the act of him sweeping his tongue into my mouth might be enough for my body to orgasm. Here, in front of everyone.

He needs to stop the public displays of affection before I lose it.

He doesn't listen to my inner turmoil though. Instead, he makes it worse, by nuzzling my neck. And then, yep, I'm going to lose it, he kisses my neck, running his slick tongue across my sensitive skin.

My knees buckle, and he catches me in his arms, tightening his grip around my waist.

He chuckles. "Don't worry; I got you. I'm used to women getting a little weak around me."

My cheeks are bright red now. He's cocky, but I don't care. Usually, I would hate guys who say shit like that. But not guys who are as hot as Sebastian is. Not when he's holding me tightly against his hard body. I'm especially intrigued by the hardness, which continues to push roughly into my ass. Every time I move, it grows larger until I'm terrified, but also desperate, to feel the slick beast inside me.

Sebastian King could be my first. And that petrifies me. He could ruin me for all other men. Because it's not like he will stick around after the first night. Not when he realizes how inexperienced I am in bed.

He starts kissing my neck again, and my eyes close, enjoying his touch and trying to forget about everything else. Who cares that this won't last? I didn't set out tonight to get into a relationship. I set out to find a guy who wants to fuck me. And Sebastian King wants to fuck me.

"Want to get another drink?" he says suddenly against my neck.

I moan.

He chuckles again.

Shit, I need to stop moaning and getting weak in the knees every time he speaks, or he's going to realize I've never had a man touch me like he's groping me now.

"Drink?" he asks again, reminding me of the question.

Drink? He wants to get a drink now?

I sigh. I guess Sebastian isn't as into dancing as I am with him. Drinking means he won't have his hands all over my body as he does now. But I don't have a choice. If I say no, he might stop hanging out with me altogether.

"Sure."

I open my eyes as his hand slides down to my ass. I squeak when he pinches it, and I chance a glance.

He's smirking at me, his hands guiding me off the dance floor back to where his friends are still drinking. I glance over at them as we approach with his hand still on my ass. They are all staring, and then the woman who asked who I was before is no longer blinking her eyelashes as she glares, trying to make me disappear with her eyes.

I swallow hard and turn my glance away from them, trying to keep my confidence to continue letting Sebastian touch me like he is.

My eyes lock with a pair of dark eyes. The eyes of a man

sitting by himself. He's holding a full whiskey glass, wearing a dark suit, which makes him blend in with the darkness around him. I can't get a good look at his features, except for his eyes. Intensely would be an understatement. This man has already undressed me with his eyes, peeled off a few layers of skin, and reached my soul.

I don't know who he is or why he's staring. He glances away a second later, and I'm not even sure if he was staring at me.

I turn my attention back to the table as we stop at the edge of it.

A waiter appears the second she sees Sebastian off the dance floor and without a drink.

"Wine again or something stronger?" he asks me.

My stomach churns and my heart races.

"Stronger."

He grins, liking my answer. He speaks to the waiter, but I don't hear what he says, and a few minutes later I've taken three shots of tequila. I feel good. Amazing. And I no longer give a shit what Avril and Naomi think of me. That's what the bitches' names are, I've learned.

I've also learned drinking with Sebastian is just as enjoyable as dancing. He's spent the entire time with his arms wrapped around my body while he presses against me from behind. The only time he ever stops is when he has to speak with the waiter to get us another round of drinks.

"Hell yes!" Blake says. This is the third time I've heard him say, 'hell yes' to anything anyone suggests, so it's not surprising he says it now.

"Fuck yea. It's finally warm enough to use the pool without you women complaining it's cold," Duncan says, eyeing Naomi.

Naomi doesn't look at Duncan's hungry eyes. She's only interested in Sebastian's. I try not to let any jealousy in. But I know Naomi and Sebastian have hooked up before. And if I don't hold Sebastian's attention, he could easily decide Naomi is the better option for tonight.

Sebastian holds a shot of tequila out to me, and I grab the glass, although I'm not sure if my stomach can handle another.

I suck in a sharp breath when I feel him place the salt on my neck. I've seen several of the men do it to some of the other girls here before. But he's never done it to me.

I feel lightheaded, like I'm floating out of my body. Even though he's had his mouth on my neck several times now, this feels more intimate.

"Shots!" Duncan yells.

Then, Sebastian's mouth is on my neck, sucking, as he licks the salt off, and then we both do the shot. I shake my head, hating the taste since I forgot the salt first. I need to try this game in reverse, so I get to lick the salt of one of his body parts. But I'm not brazen enough to try it, not without his suggestion.

He grabs for a lime and expertly drops it, so it buries in my cleavage. I go to snatch it, but he spins me around and leans down, retrieving it with his teeth as his lips brush over my cleavage.

My body warms, and my thoughts shatter. That was...hot.

He sucks on the lime a minute and removes it, smirking at me as usual.

I'm frozen. I can't move. I'm pretty sure I just dreamed that, because there is no way Sebastian had his face buried between my breasts.

But I get an evil glare again from Naomi, and I know it happened.

Sebastian interlocks his hand with mine, and he tugs me toward the pool, which has been mostly empty the entire night, except for the occasional drunk guy who decides to toss a girl into the pool fully clothed. *Why do guys think that's a good idea?*

Women *hate* it. There is no way they are persuading any woman to sleep with them after that.

I glance around, looking for the pool house or someplace where people are changing clothes. I don't see one, but this house is large enough I'm sure there is one.

My eyes pop open when I see Naomi grab the hem of her dress and jerk it over her head until she's left in nothing but her black lacy thong underwear. Her dress was low cut, so she isn't wearing a bra, and she has no problem with the stares she's getting. I'm pretty sure every man in the area's erection grew at the sight of her.

Shit.

I can't strip. I'm not wearing a bra either, and there is no way any guy here is going to be impressed by my much smaller chest.

Women all around me continue stripping down to their bras and underwear, while the men remove their dress pants and jackets down to their underwear.

"Oh!" I squeal unexpectedly, when one of the guys strips until he's butt naked.

Sebastian laughs.

"Don't worry. I won't let Duncan touch you or come near you. You're mine, for tonight," Sebastian says.

I grin like an idiot. I love hearing him call me *his*.

But my grin falters the second I see Sebastian begin to strip next to me. His shirt is gone, revealing the muscles I've been feeling all night, and then his pants are gone, making his erection much more noticeable beneath his boxer briefs.

I gulp as my eyes rake over his body and become glued to his straining cock. I need to stop staring, but I can't. I want to know what that glorious erection would feel like rocking in my body. But it also terrifies me because I'm not sure my body is ready for such a massive intrusion.

"Like what you see?" he chuckles in my ear.

I force my eyes to drag up to his eyes instead of his cock. But my heart hates me a little for it.

"Sorry."

He lifts my chin up and then his lips are on mine. Exploring, tasting, devouring.

He stops and kisses me a moment later. "Don't be sorry," he says like the kiss was nothing.

Kisses mean nothing to a guy like Sebastian, but to me, kisses like that are rare. No, kisses like that never happen in my world.

I'm frozen as I watch Sebastian walk to the pool's diving board.

"Come on, baby," he says, doing a flip before diving in, in a perfect arch. His body gracefully hits the water and people cheer, holding up their hands, giving him a score of a ten for his incredible dive.

My mouth drops open, and I know I'm drooling. I snap my mouth shut, but it doesn't stop my erratic breathing.

I start taking a step forward, needing to be in Sebastian's arms. I realize I'm supposed to strip, so I hesitate at the edge of the pool while a dozen or so eyes stare up at me.

My hands tremble. I can't do this. I can't strip in front of these people. I'm not ashamed of my body, in fact, I love my body. But these people come from money. They have perfect bodies to go with their flashy dresses and expensive houses. Their parents have provided them with an incredible start to life with substantial trust funds waiting for them when they graduate to turn into billion-dollar businesses.

They are elite, while I'm ordinary. I may have abs of steel, but I don't come from money. I didn't get a boob-job like half the women in the pool to add curves. I'm flat, yet strong. And I have no intention of showing them just how ordinary I am.

Sebastian stares up at me expectedly, but even his gorgeous body isn't enough to convince me to strip naked.

Then, I see Naomi swimming toward him planning on taking advantage of my hesitation. If I don't jump in, she'll be the one in Sebastian's bed tonight. Not me.

My hand goes to my back, pulling on the zipper without thinking. The zipper slides halfway down and then stops. No matter how hard I pull the zipper, it won't budge.

Naomi swims faster, and I jerk my body, trying to get the damn zipper to go down far enough that I can rip the dress over my head. The jerking makes me lose my balance though, and before I realize what's happening, I feel the warm water consuming me as I crash into the pool.

I pop my head back up hoping people won't care, but of course, they care. Laughter, hysterical laughter is breaking out all around me. Even Sebastian is laughing at me.

Dammit.

I give up. I can't fit in with these people even for one night. Not long enough to get laid, that's for sure. I should have stuck with someone in my own league.

Sebastian swims toward me.

"Here, let me help you," he says.

"No, that's ok—"

I stop when his hands touch my back. In the few moments of embarrassment, I forgot how electrifying it feels to have his hands on my skin.

He unzips the dress and reaches for the hem, pulling the dress off my wet body. No one can see my body under the water. This might actually work out for me. Then I move and realize my stupid heels are still on.

Before I realize what's happening, Sebastian has lifted me to the edge of the pool so that he can work on removing my shoes.

Silence.

I glance around, as the stares burn into my body. No one is laughing. And the men are wide-eyed as they stare at my body. My cheeks flush and my heart races, but I soon realize they are looking at me like they ogled at Naomi. Even some of the women are gazing at me appreciatively.

"Wow," Sebastian says, as he removes my second shoe. Somehow he already removed the first one without me noticing.

My eyes fall to his, as he stares at my boobs, and then my abs, like I did his cock earlier.

"Like what you see?" I ask, boldly repeating his words.

He smirks and grabs my waist, pulling me back into the pool and to his body.

"Fuck yea. Incredible."

I smile.

"How did you get abs like this?" he asks, raking his fingers over my stomach. "I might need some tips." He winks.

I laugh. "I don't think you need help getting abs." I glance down at his eight-pack.

He shrugs. "I guess we have something in common."

He kisses my lips again without warning, while my legs wrap around his waist and my arms wrap around his neck. I've never been this naked with a man before. But I'm not sure I want to wear clothes ever again.

His kisses trail down my neck, and I shiver.

"You cold?" he asks.

I shake my head no, as I shudder again when he licks my neck.

He smirks. "We are getting out. Larkyn's cold."

I pout. "I'm not—"

His lips slam into mine again, shutting me up. I moan as his tongue brushes against mine. I kiss him back hungrily, knowing at least my kissing skills are on par. But if he wants sex or a blow job, he's going to have to take the lead, because I have no clue what I'm doing.

He finally forces me to stop kissing when I realize the others are protesting us leaving the pool.

"I'm sorry, but Larkyn's cold. I'm going to get her some clothes from upstairs to change into. You guys enjoy the pool. We will see you later." He winks at me to play along with being cold.

"Yes, I'm so cold," I say, faking trembling again to keep up the ruse.

Sebastian chuckles as he carries me up the steps of the pool. I keep my legs wrapped around his waist, and my front pressed firmly against his chest, so no one gets a view of my breasts again.

"Let's get you into some dry clothes, but first you need to get naked and have a hot shower to warm you up."

I bite my lip to keep from smiling too brightly because I know what he's not saying. He wants to fuck me. And I'm more than happy to let him.

Continue reading Pretend I'm Yours Here!

ALSO BY ELLA MILES

Pretend I'm Yours

Savage Love

Too Much

Aligned: The Complete Series

The Maybe Series

The Definitely Series

Not Sorry

Heart of a Thief

Heart of a Liar

Dirty Series

ABOUT THE AUTHOR

Ella Miles writes steamy romance with a twist. She's currently living her own happily ever after near the Rocky Mountains with her high school sweetheart husband. Her heart is also taken by her goofy four year old black lab that is scared of everything, including her own shadow.

Ella is a USA Today Bestselling author, author of the Amazon top 100 bestselling books: TOO MUCH and SAVAGE LOVE. She is also the author of the ALIGNED series, MAYBE series, DEFINITELY series, UNFORGIVABLE series, NOT SORRY, and DIRTY series.

Stalk me at:
www.ellamiles.com
ella@ellamiles.com